WHERE ARE YOU,

Caleb?

A NOVEL

CHRISTA ST. GERMAIN

Trigger Warning: This book contains references to child abuse. Reader discretion is advised.

Where are You, Caleb? is a work of fiction. Names, characters, places, and incidents are the products of the author's imagination or are used fictitiously. Any resemblance to actual events, locales, or persons, living or dead, is entirely coincidental.

Published by Little Pink Press, Beacon, NY

ISBN-13: 979-8-9906436-2-8

DEDICATION

For my four incredible children,
Lydia, Charlotte, Branden, and Asher, your love, strength,
and inspiration shape every part of my life. I could not have
solo-parented for over two decades without your undying support.

ACKNOWLEDGMENTS

I am deeply grateful to everyone who has supported me, especially my four children and my parents. Your love and encouragement have meant everything to me.

A special thank you to my mom, Ann, for reading and editing the book multiple times. Thank you for generously reading the early drafts and offering invaluable feedback to my daughter Lydia, my sister Katherine, Tom Murphy, Kathleen Kane, and Melissa Carroll. I also want to thank my dad, Bob, for his guidance on theology and historical events.

I also want to express my deep gratitude to the rest of my family and loved ones who've walked this path with me. To my sister Alison, my brother-in-law Tim, my nieces Alessandra 'Ali' and her husband Lyles, Ella, Audrey, and Reese, my nephew Patrick, Lewis Derenzis, and all my aunts, uncles, cousins, and friends—thank you for your constant support, love, and laughter. All those I have not mentioned, you are forever in my heart.

I am also grateful to Roxana Coumans, whose thoughtful editing improved the book and demonstrated her connection to its message of hope.

Finally, a profound thank you to my publisher, Keryl Pesce, of Little Pink Press. Keryl's insightful ideas, unwavering faith in this project, enduring patience, and steadfast commitment have been an immeasurable gift.

CHAPTER 1

Diane

Wrapped in a cozy blanket on my dock, I savor the crisp, early autumn air and the earthy scent of rain as I gaze over the lake's tranquil beauty. The soft, pink glow of the rising sun illuminates the landscape, casting a warm radiance across the water. I absorb the peaceful scene and feel profound gratitude for my journey's unexpected twists and turns—a path that ultimately led me to discover my true self.

I absentmindedly thumbed the necklace Caleb had given me as a little boy. The cool touch of the green gem felt comforting, a tangible link to memories I cherished. I could still hear his excited voice: "Mommy! Mommy! I have a surprise for you!" His enthusiasm was contagious as he rushed through the door.

"What is it?" I asked, my heart racing with anticipation.

"Mom, you have to wait! I have to get it ready!" His eyes sparkled with mischief, and I couldn't help but smile. Finally, after what felt like an eternity, Caleb declared, "Okay, Mom! You can open it now." I unwrapped the small package, a perfect necklace adorned with a green gem.

"I'll never take it off," I whispered, slipping it around my neck; I remembered the pure delight on Caleb's face.

"Thank you, Mommy! I'm glad you love it." His smile stretched from ear to ear, reflecting his love for that simple gift. I knew I would cherish his gift forever. At the time, I had no idea that the necklace would eventually play a key role in unraveling a mystery I would spend years trying to solve.

I grew up in the quaint village of Milford Falls, New York, surrounded by towering maple trees. The architecture was a captivating mix of stately Victorian buildings and charming family-run shops among farmlands and sprawling estates. The day I first saw Phil, he was leaning against the brick wall of the local grocery store, sunlight catching in his tousled hair. There was a disarming kindness in his expression. "Hey, you okay?" Phil's voice jolted me; I jumped, startled by his sudden words.

"Oh, you scared me! I'm just waiting for my friend," I replied casually.

Phil nodded and said, "I—uh, have a good day."

"You too!" I responded, my pulse quickening as he turned to leave.

I recall my first date with Phil; it was at the picturesque park atop the hill in Milford Falls. Little did I know the dark history that lingered there, a history that would go on to shape my life in ways I couldn't have imagined. Even now, the memory unsettles me, especially after recently discovering the truth. Phil and I climbed the steps to the park; "Can I hold your hand?"

A shy smile crossed my face as I replied, "Sure." We settled onto the swings, the gentle creaking harmonizing with the evening's stillness.

"I'd like to see you again," Phil said.

"Okay, that would be nice," I responded.

He laughed. "Just nice?"

"I had a great time," I assured him.

"Me too," Phil said, his eyes bright.

"I'm looking forward to it."

"How about a movie at the drive-in Friday?" he suggested.

"What's playing? Is there anything good?" I asked, curious.

"I don't know," he shrugged, a smile on his lips. "It doesn't matter. Just as long as I get to spend time with you." His words made me feel special, and I couldn't wait for our next date.

Our romance blossomed over the years, but after high school graduation, we ultimately parted ways. I pursued a career as a lawyer. Even though I had left the town, purpose and fulfillment seemed to pull me back. Phil remained in the village, working within the local union and laboring in a mine a few towns over. It was a matter of time before we rekindled our relationship.

As I walked down the street after grabbing lunch in town, I bumped into Phil. He was standing there—tall, handsome, and unmistakably familiar. Phil approached me, "Diane, how are you?" He pulled me into a big hug.

"I'm doing well; how about you?" I replied.

With that familiar grin, he said, "You're going out with me tonight."

I stammered, "What? I've got stuff to do."

"Nope," he insisted. "You're going out with me." I couldn't help but smile. "Okay."

We dated for a few years, eventually leading to marriage. Our wedding was on a classic September fall day in upstate New York, the landscape adorned with vibrant red, orange, and gold colors. Phil and I exchanged our vows under a radiant sun and a clear blue sky, with a church atop a hill providing the perfect backdrop for our ceremony. Phil stood over six feet tall with a rugged appearance and a scruffy beard; his faith and steadfast values were a constant source of strength for me. Overcome with eagerness, I blurted out, "I do!" prematurely, eliciting an amused smile from Phil.

When the priest finally announced, "You may kiss the bride," I nearly leaped into Phil's arms. Phil pulled me close, and with a grin on his entire face, he sealed our vows with a kiss.

Cheers erupted from our friends and family; on that blissful day, it was as if the world had melted away, leaving just the two of us. When Phil and I broke apart, laughter spilled from my lips, and I couldn't help but beam at him. "We did it!" Phil took my hand and led me to the waiting white limousine, where "Just Married" was written across the back. The car gleamed in the sunlight, and I felt a rush as we climbed in, with the thrill of what lay ahead. "Ready for our adventure?" he asked, a glint in his eye.

"Absolutely!" I replied, leaning back against the plush seats.

Our daughter, Anna, was born within a few years of marriage. Her blue eyes sparkled with curiosity and wonder. I remember holding her for the first time, a wave of love crashing over me. Phil's expression was brimming with love. "I'm so proud of you," he said. My chest swelled as he continued, "We have our blessed baby girl. I couldn't be happier. Thank you for giving me this gift, this precious child."

I was constantly exhausted and always ensured that I met Anna's needs while trying to stay afloat. The sleepless nights blended, and I often wondered if I would ever feel like myself again. I began planning Anna's first birthday party, and a flicker of my old energy returned. But lightheadedness and nausea lingered beneath the surface, threatening to dampen my spirits. It was an unwelcome presence I hadn't fully acknowledged—unaware that I was pregnant again.

The party was a whirlwind of laughter and colorful decorations. "Anna, this is your first time having chocolate cake. Dig in, get messy, and don't forget to lick all the icing!" I could hear Phil's laughter in the background, a rich sound that made me flutter, mingling with the playful squeals of our friends and family. Anna giggled, covered in frosting; I turned to watch Phil lift her into his arms, his face alight with triumph. "Look at our little cake monster!" he exclaimed, playfully bouncing her. Anna squealed in delight, and I couldn't help but laugh.

Cara arrived just eight months after Anna's birthday celebration. Weighing just five pounds, Cara was tiny but perfect, graced with the same blue eyes as her sister. Phil was a natural with the girls, his patience and tenderness shining through every interaction. I watched him cradle Cara in his arms, a gentle smile on his face. Fatherhood came with such ease and grace for him as if he had been preparing for this role all his life.

We settled into our new routine; Phil turned to me one evening, "I love you so much," he said, brushing his fingers across my cheek. "You've given me the greatest gift—the family I've always dreamed of having—two perfect daughters who look just like you."

"We did this together," I replied, my voice thick with gratitude. "I couldn't have asked for a better partner on this journey."

He smiled, his gaze shifting to the girls. "It's amazing, isn't it? Our little family, just perfect."

As Anna and Cara grew older and settled into school full-time, I had more time to focus on my career. With our financial situation stable, Phil and I felt ready to expand our family. However, the pain of past miscarriages had taken a toll. "I can't do this anymore," I cried. "I can't face another loss. My strength is gone, and I feel sad every day." Phil understood.

"I agree. It's too much for you, your body, and your mental health. I think two children are plenty." I nodded, feeling a sense of relief wash over me.

"Thank you for understanding. I have to be happy with the family we have and accept that I will never have another baby."

A few months after we decided we wouldn't have any more children, I began feeling physically exhausted. "I think I need to see a doctor," I said.

"Would you like me to go with you?" Phil asked.

"No, I just want to get some blood work done. I don't feel well," I replied. I sat in the doctor's office, waiting to hear the news of my illness.

"Diane, you're pregnant," the doctor said.

"That's impossible. Are you sure?" I responded, shocked.

"I am sure," he calmly replied.

I drove home as fast as I could. I blurted out before I could say hello, "I have a big surprise for you! We're going to have another baby; I can't wait to tell Anna and Cara!" Phil's reaction was delightful—he scooped me into his arms, twirling me around.

"I can't believe it!" he exclaimed, laughing. "I love you so much; you have made me the happiest man in the world."

"And it's a boy!" I announced. I'll never forget the look on his face; Phil's jaw dropped, and a moment of silence hung in the air as he processed the news. But then, just like that, his face broke into a smile, his infectious energy filling the room.

"I am so excited to have a son!" he said, his eyes sparkling. As I reflect on that moment now, I realize I had no idea how profoundly my son and my husband would transform my life, nor the heartache that would soon follow.

A few months later, Caleb was born—a beautiful nine-pound baby. His mesmerizing eyes were sapphire with blue encircling irises that sparkled with every color of the rainbow; I didn't know his eyes would become a key piece in the mystery I would chase for many years. While Phil adored his girls, something special seemed to sparkle in his eyes the first time he held Caleb.

Six weeks after Caleb's arrival, I returned to my work routine, juggling caring for three children alongside my professional career. I could hear Phil whispering lullabies to Caleb at night, their bond forming with each soft note. It warmed me to see how close he was with his daughters, but there was something uniquely special between him and Caleb. I checked on them one evening and heard Phil's playful voice bouncing off the hallway walls. "Come on, buddy, we must change you before you get a rash!" I chuckled, knowing how long it had been since Phil had changed diapers.

"You're getting rusty, aren't you?" I called out, half-joking.

"Rusty? I've still got it!" he replied, mock-serious. "Just you wait! I'll have this done before you even get here!" When I entered the room, he stood there, Caleb happily cooing in his arms, the diaper changed, and Phil's face was triumphant. "See? All taken care of!" he declared, and I couldn't help but laugh at the sight of them.

I had been in a constant state of bliss until life took an unexpected turn. That dreadful morning, I rushed to work without kissing Phil goodbye, leaving me uneasy as I went about my day. Dropping Caleb off at kindergarten, a wave of nervousness overcame me. Later that morning, my cell phone rang with a familiar number. Phil's secretary's voice crackled through the phone, laced with a tremor. "Diane, there's been an accident at the mine, and it's bad. I think you should get here as soon as you can." A sinking feeling settled in my chest as her words echoed in my mind, each one sending a chill through me. I couldn't shake the shock.

"Diane? Are you there? You must get here now."

Finding my voice barely a whisper, I asked, "Where is Phil?" There was a pause, and I could hear the worry in her breath.

"I'm... I'm so sorry. Please come." My mind was a whirlwind, thoughts colliding in a storm of disbelief.

"Okay," I said, unable to process anything more.

I could not tell you how I arrived at Phil's place of work that day. Everything had blurred together—the stoplights, faces, and the city's sounds fading into a distant hum. My mind was full of thoughts of Phil.

I approached the mine entrance, once nestled in a small

passageway at the mountain's base, now buried beneath rocks and debris. The familiar sight was shrouded in darkness, and the air was thick with the sounds of shifting timber. I exited my car, and my eyes scanned the scene, and then I saw him—an enormous shadow emerging from the debris.

"Phil!" I shouted, my voice breaking through the confusion. "Phil!" I yelled. His eyes met mine, filled with a mixture of relief and turmoil. Phil was on the ground before I could get to him; everything happened so fast.

Multiple men surrounded him, pushing on his chest, as the alarms blared and the sirens sounded in the distance. Panic surged through me, "Phil! Are you okay? I'm here!" I called out, longing to connect with him. Phil was trying to mumble something, his lips moving, but the words were inaudible. My pulse raced as I strained to hear him. "Phil! Just hold on!"

Phil was alive. A wave of relief washed over me, even as the tension hung thick.

The sterile, white hospital walls pressed in on me, suffocating, as the harsh reality of the news I had just received clouded my thoughts like thick, choking smog. The young doctor stood before me, his expression grave and sad, too young to bear such heavy news. "Diane," he began, "I'm sorry. We weren't able to save him. We did everything we could, but there was just too much trauma to his body and too much blood loss. I am so sorry." The words hit me like a punch to the gut, and before I could process them, I fell to my knees, a raw scream escaping my lips. "No! Phil! No!" My voice carried through the hallway, filled with anguish and disbelief.

I felt the cool floor beneath me, grounding yet so far removed from the reality I was trying to reject. The doctor's face blurred as tears streamed down my cheeks, each sob tearing through me like a wave. "Help him! He can't be gone!" I knew the truth was settling in, even as I fought against it. I shook my head as if my denial could reverse what had happened. "Please, there must be something more you can do! He was just here—he was alive!"

The doctor knelt beside me, his eyes filled with sorrow. "I'm so sorry, Diane. I wish there were more we could have done. I truly do."

My breath stopped, and I pressed my palms to my forehead to gather my thoughts, my mind full of emotion. All I could think about were the moments we'd shared—the laughter, the dreams, the plans for the future. "Phil!" I cried out as if my voice would somehow reach him, and he would return to me.

The emptiness inside me felt insurmountable, a void that dug so deep within me. I walked into Anna and Cara's school later that day, feeling the unbearable pressure to tell my children the truth about their dad. I entered the principal's office. I caught sight of their faces; their smiles instantly vanished, replaced by wide eyes brimming with fear. I decided to hold off on telling them about their dad until we got home. I led them to the couch, bracing myself for what would come. "Anna, Cara," I began, my voice trembling, "I love you very much, but I need you to know that your dad was in a work accident, and he did not survive. Your dad is gone."

The words hung in the air like a dark cloud. I couldn't tell which girl screamed first or who yelled at me, but I felt the sharpness of their emotions. "I hate you!" one shouted, the emotion raw. Their anguish hit me like a tidal wave.

"Please, I'm so sorry," I whispered, wrapping my arms around them tightly. "I love you both, and I promise we'll get through this together." But even as I comforted them, my mind raced with the next challenge—how to explain this loss to Caleb, our sweet baby who was too young to realize the depth of what had happened.

Reeling from the devastating news, I sank into a state of despair, unable to process the unthinkable. With a heavy heart and tear-streaked face, I sought to ease my children's suffering and guard them against this unimaginable reality. Confronting an uncertain future as a widow and single parent, I had to face the challenges ahead.

Over time, my children gradually readjusted to their regular routines. They returned to school, reconnected with friends, and participated in extracurricular activities, slowly regaining a sense of structure and purpose. The children's schedules were full of academic and social commitments. Though we had to navigate this new reality, we had no choice but to accept our fate.

After Phil's passing, my memories were intermittent, but certain moments remain forever imprinted in my mind. It was the day my light went out. With a week off from work, I eagerly anticipated tackling the ever-present mountain of household tasks. I can still picture that crisp autumn day, the air cool against my face as I gazed at the vibrant red and orange leaves. My mind drifted as I closed my eyes, savoring the sensation. Anna and Cara were high schoolers then, while little Caleb was just starting first grade.

Stepping inside my home, I glanced at the clock and felt a rising panic. "Come on, girls! You're going to be late!" I called out, my voice tinged with exasperation. They were always running behind, and today was no exception. "Caleb, we have to go! The bus will be here in twenty minutes!" I added, trying to keep my tone light. But Caleb, as usual, dragged his feet, taking his sweet time as he fiddled with his shirt.

"Mom, I don't feel good! I'm not going today; I want to stay home!" Caleb pouted.

"Come on, Caleb, we've got to get moving."

Anna and Cara scrambled to find their shoes; their bickering broke through the fog of my thoughts. "See, Mom! We made it on time!"

Cara's cheerful voice called out. "I love you!" she added, her enthusiasm contagious.

I couldn't help but smile. "I love you both so much."

I grabbed Caleb's arm and hurried him to the bus stop. "Come on, buddy! We have to go back to the house. You left your backpack!" I pleaded.

Caleb dug in his heels, shaking his head. "No! My friends are here! I'm not going!" he protested.

My patience was thin, and I insisted, "Caleb, come on! You're going to miss the bus!"

I convinced him to follow me, but on the way home, he mumbled angrily, "I'm not going to get to play with my friends today because of you." We rushed back to the house, and I frantically searched for his backpack as the distant rumble of the approaching bus reminded me we were running out of time. I handed him his backpack, and we ran outside just as the bus pulled up. I caught my breath and exchanged a quick hello with a neighbor, but when I turned around, Caleb had already gotten on the school bus.

The school called me several times that morning, their messages filling my voicemail with dread. When I picked up the phone to call back, the secretary's voice greeted me with a practiced calm. "Diane, I'm calling to confirm that Caleb is not in school today."

"Yes, he is. Can you please double-check?" I replied, anxiety rising in my chest.

"Sure," she said, her tone still reassuring. "Let me put you on hold." I paced the room, glancing out the window as I waited. When the secretary came back on the line, she said, "I'm sorry, Diane. Caleb is not in school today."

Silence fell heavy between us. I didn't respond, my mind racing with questions. "Where could he be? Why wasn't he there?" The confusion and worry spiraled into my thoughts, drowning out everything else.

"Diane? Are you there?" I could hear her voice faintly concerned. "Diane? Still there?" I nodded absently, even though she couldn't see me. "Was he sick? Did something happen?" My thoughts were a whirlwind, drowning out her words. "Diane?" she pressed again, her voice pulling me back to the present.

"I... I don't know?" I finally said, my voice trembling. "Where is Caleb?"

I contacted Anna and Cara at school, my heart racing, "Have you seen Caleb? Do you know where he is?" Their responses were vague, filled with uncertainty, and provided no leads. Restlessness gnawed at me.

"I'll call the local police," my fingers trembled as I dialed. After hanging up, I reached out to the parents of Caleb's friends, hoping they might have seen him. "Hi, it's Diane Hart. I'm looking for Caleb. Have you heard from him?" I asked, but my calls went unanswered. Each ringing tone felt like a dark omen, amplifying the realization that my son was missing.

Overwhelmed by panic, I felt disoriented and disconnected from reality. I heard voices around me—police officers, detectives, neighbors—but I did not hear their words. I couldn't process their questions or identify the speakers.

Despite the escalating nightmare, I knew I had to return the girls to school. "It's important to keep some sense of normalcy," I told myself, though my heart ached with uncertainty. I smiled as I packed their lunches, desperate to maintain a semblance of routine in an increasingly surreal world.

Volunteers from all over rallied to search for Caleb. I joined them, fueled by the resolve to find my son. The physical toll was overwhelming—blisters covered my feet from endless walking, my skin had turned pale, my eyes were shadowed with fatigue, and my body felt utterly drained from exhaustion. At times, I would simply collapse to the ground, tears streaming down my face in anguish. Yet, kind strangers would approach and urge me on, their voices awakening me from my despair. "Come on, Diane, you've got to get up! You've got to do this for Caleb! Without you, we can't find Caleb!" Their encouragement gave me the strength to push myself back up and continue.

The search and rescue team vowed to persevere until they found Caleb. But even after years passed, I couldn't shake the feeling of abandonment when they eventually stopped their efforts. The anger simmered within me, fueled by unresolved questions that felt like open wounds. I never gave up, compelled by the hope of bringing my son home.

One evening after Caleb went missing, two policemen stood solemnly in my kitchen, their grave expressions conveying the gravity of the situation. "Diane, we'll be searching the Hudson River today, looking for Caleb," one officer said, his steady voice betraying an undercurrent of concern.

"Please, no."

The officer continued, "It's just a formality. We need to rule out every possibility of where Caleb might be." But the words rang hollow—the river's powerful currents and frigid waters offered no chance of survival.

"Caleb has taken swim lessons, but I know he's not strong enough to withstand the river's force," I argued.

The police barraged me with questions, and I realized I was a suspect in my child's disappearance. These allegations plunged me further into a state of darkness and despair. "Did you hurt your son?" the detective asked calmly.

"No," I replied, shock washing over me, "I would never hurt my son."

"Maybe it was an accident," he continued, his gaze unwavering. "What if you gave him something, and he passed out? Are you hiding his body?"

"I would never hurt Caleb! Please, just find him!" I pleaded.

The cop leaned closer, pen poised over his notepad. "Diane, we need to rule you out. You were the last person to see Caleb. It's usually the last person who's responsible."

"I can't believe you're questioning me! I would never hurt my son!" I cried, tears welling in my eyes.

"Please," the detective urged, "we need to understand what happened. Were you and Caleb fighting that morning?"

"No, he was just a bit moody, that's all. It's normal for his age!" I explained.

"Was he unhappy the night before?" the detective pressed.

"No! We had dinner together, and then I helped with his homework!" I insisted.

"Diane," the detective interjected, "when's the last time you punished Caleb? How severe was it?"

"I discipline him, but I don't hurt him! I'm a good mother!" I protested.

"Do you hit your children, Diane? Have you ever hit Caleb? Are you angry? Do you scream a lot?" the detective continued.

"No!" I cried, "I try to stay calm! I've never laid a hand on him! Please, I had nothing to do with this!"

The media began publishing reports that portrayed me as guilty. The indictments fueled the hatred from my daughters, Anna and Cara, who would make comments like, "I knew you did this," and, "You killed my brother." It was the darkest and most agonizing period of my life. I had neither the financial resources nor the emotional strength to fight these accusations effectively. People started leaving me hateful voicemail messages, calling me a "child killer" and saying that I "deserved to die." At times, I doubted whether I would even make it through another day, but my will to find my son was the only thing that kept me going.

The police got a search warrant, discarding my family's belongings and leaving my home trashed, and Anna and Cara hated me more than before. The police still interrogated me repeatedly: "Diane, when was the last time you saw Caleb? What was he wearing? Did Caleb say anything specific that day? What color shoes did he have on? Did he have a baseball hat?"

I recited the same answers mechanically as if reading from a script. "He wore a brown hoodie, blue jeans, and white sneakers."

These details had become my last connection to Caleb, seared into my mind. However, when they finally cleared my name, the accusations had already caused too much damage. Anna and Cara had stopped speaking to me, and the townspeople I once loved now called me a "monster."

Desperate for answers, I pleaded with the officers for any information that could shed light on my son's mysterious disappearance. The officer shifted uncomfortably. "Ma'am, we're doing everything we can. Search teams are out there," he assured me.

"But how could this happen?" I demanded. "He's just a boy!"

The officer tried to reassure me, saying, "We're following all leads."

The search teams dwindled, and the chances of finding Caleb alive grew increasingly slim. I watched the bleak news reports, listening to their grim predictions, feeling a growing sense of helplessness. Determined to correct the narrative, I called every reporter I could reach, insisting they had the story wrong. "People need to be on the lookout for him!" One journalist kept asking the same questions, "Did Caleb have any friends? Was there somewhere he'd been wanting to go?"

I would repeat, "Someone kidnapped my child. Let's focus on that so we can help find him!" Most of my calls went unanswered, and I still never received the media coverage I desperately needed.

Anna's high school graduation loomed; a celebratory mile-stone overshadowed by her brother's absence. I watched her prepare; her spirit dimmed by the loss that hung over us. I wanted to celebrate her achievements, to make her feel as important as she was. "Mom, are you going to show up to my graduation? You have been absent all year," she said, her voice laced with disappointment. A pang of guilt twisted in my stomach; she was right.

"Of course, Anna," I replied, forcing a smile. "I wouldn't miss it for anything. I'm very proud of you." Anna rolled her eyes and walked away, leaving me with my promises and the reality of my absence.

The aftermath of Anna's graduation was a blur. At the time, my sole concern was being left alone with Cara, worrying that my presence would add to her deteriorating mental health. A year had passed, and I was still searching for Caleb. I wandered through fields, ditches, and waterways, oblivious to the world around me. Unaware of the circumstances, I lost more time watching Cara complete her senior year, a year behind Anna. Her graduation mirrored her sister's, but I attended in body, my mind elsewhere.

Years had passed, and flipping through the photos, I noticed Cara's collarbones jutting sharply beneath her dress, giving her a skeletal appearance. In the picture, my eyes were dark and distant, my hair unruly and gray. I barely recognized the pale, vacant face staring back at me.

Cara repeatedly urged me to stay out of her way. "Mom, don't come to the school," she said, annoyance creeping into her voice. "I don't want you there."

Hoping for a different response, I asked, "Why can't I come to the open house?"

"Mom, you've done it a hundred times. I don't want you there," she replied firmly. I could feel the distance widening between us. "And I'm not going to my graduation, so don't worry about embarrassing me."

"Cara, I wouldn't miss it for the world," I insisted.

Hurt, she snapped back, "Mom, you miss everything. Why should you care about this?" Her words lingered in my mind, reflecting the painful sentiments I had heard from Anna.

The girls progressed through college and into law school while my struggles with grief left me disconnected—their years during college and law school moved quickly. Anna called to inform me that her law school graduation was in May. Though I knew it was coming, the news caught me off guard. "Hey, Mom! How are you feeling?" she asked.

"I'm great! How are you?" I replied. But then her tone shifted, and she got serious. "Mom, you need to come to my law school graduation. You can't just skip this like you do everything else. It's important, and everyone else's parents will be there."

I took a deep breath, trying to steady my nerves. "Anna, I plan on coming. I'll stay for a few days, meet your new friends, and celebrate with you."

"I don't want you to meet my friends; just get it together and show up, please," she urged, the aggravation evident in her voice. I could tell how much this meant to her, and I knew I had to make the effort, no matter how daunting it felt.

Cara's call had a sharper, more nasty edge compared to Anna's plea the previous year. "Mom, my graduation is in May. You have to be here, no excuses. I can't bear showing up alone like I do for everything else. I feel like an orphan; I'll never speak to you again if you don't come." My daughters were holding onto a deep anger—anger at me for losing their father, for losing their brother Caleb, for being an absent parent.

I took a steadying breath, "I will be there, Cara," I said firmly.

She exhaled sharply on the other end, clearly unconvinced. "I doubt it," she replied before hanging up, leaving me to sit with her disappointment.

During those years, well-meaning friends and acquaintances would call, trying to offer comfort, as if they could genuinely understand losing both a husband and a son. They'd say things like, "You need to get out of the darkness," or "Caleb wouldn't want you to suffer," and "Maybe God needed another angel." Each time, their words would make my blood boil.

I used to argue, insisting, "That's not how God works; He doesn't just take people from us." But now, I'd simply respond with a hollow "Thank you," realizing they were more interested in saying what they thought I needed to hear than genuinely listening to my words.

I spent most days in Caleb's bed, consumed by memories. I was living off Phil's social security; I had stopped working at the law firm, and the days bled together in a haze. I hardly spoke to anyone, allowing me to withdraw deeper into isolation. My once-vibrant blonde hair had become unruly and gray, and the bright blue of my eyes had faded to a dull, lifeless shade. I felt like a ghost of my former self, adrift in a world that continued moving on without me.

Anna and Cara got settled into their legal careers and urged me to move to South Carolina. Anna called me constantly, trying to bridge the gap between us. Still upset with me, Cara joined the push but did so out of fear of losing me too, "Mom, you need to come move and be with your family. Your family isn't in Milford Falls anymore," Anna insisted.

I replied, "Anna, I'm just not ready to leave Caleb's things or the home where Dad and I built our life together."

She would respond, "Mom, move on, please." Now and then, Cara would call, and her voice would get my attention since she barely spoke to me.

A deep longing consumed me daily; I cried to God, "Where are you? I need you to answer me!" Silence hung heavy, mocking my pleas. "Why are you ignoring me?" I continued, anger boiling over. "I've begged and bargained, but still nothing. What do you want from me?" Tears streamed down my cheeks. "Step up! Show your face! Why have you abandoned us, Caleb, and me?" I yelled, "You coward, you can't just leave me here to suffer!"

After six years, Anna and Cara, now successful lawyers, convinced me to leave Milford Falls. With a heavy heart, I carefully packed Caleb's belongings, my hands trembling as I labeled each box, knowing they would be the first unpacked in my new home. I called the new homeowners, my voice quivering, and pleaded,

"Please, here's my address in South Carolina. Hold on to it in case my son, Caleb, comes home."

The kind new owners reassured me, "Of course, Diane. We'll keep your information handy." I instructed the movers to handle those particular boxes with the utmost care.

I moved into a cozy basement apartment in Anna and her husband, Ted's home. The apartment featured a private entrance and a beautifully landscaped garden patio. A gently winding cobblestone path led to the backyard, where a wrought-iron table and four plush, throw pillow-adorned chairs beckoned me to sit and relax. Lush, thriving potted plants framed the inviting seating area.

Anna approached me in the yard one day, "Mom, I want a baby, but I can't get pregnant. Even in vitro fertilization hasn't worked, and I can't keep going through multiple miscarriages."

Wanting to offer support, I gently reassured her, "I know this is incredibly difficult, but I believe you will be a mother one day. God has a plan." However, my words seemed to upset her rather than comfort her.

"Mom, why do you want to be a parent now? You were never there for me, so why would I need you now? I don't mean to be harsh, but your words aren't helping me." With both Anna and Cara, I was always wrong.

Amid Anna's turmoil, I was dealing with my own emotions. Then, one blessed day, Anna announced, "Mom, I'm pregnant!" The arrival of my newborn grandson, James, brought me profound joy, something I hadn't felt in a long time. This precious child seemed to revive my weary spirit, reminding me of life's beauty amidst the heartache. I whispered to little James, "You are a perfect gift from God." I could have sworn he returned my smile.

CHAPTER 2

Anna

I am the oldest daughter of Diane and Phil and the big sister to Cara and Caleb; I've always felt a natural sense of responsibility, much like the wavy, golden-highlighted hair that has been a part of my identity. My curious, aware blue eyes reflect the inner workings of my soul. From a young age, I gravitated toward the caretaker role, always ready to support my siblings—whether that meant helping with homework, comforting them after a tough day, or simply being there to listen. Academics have consistently been a strong suit for me.

I remember the day Caleb came home from the hospital. Eager to hold him, I begged my mom, "Please, I want to hold him!"

She cautioned, "Anna, you must be careful with the baby and support Caleb's head."

But my will to care for him overcame her concerns. "I know, Mom," I reassured her. "I'll be gentle, I promise." Unable to resist, I would sneak Caleb out of his crib, cradling him until his stirring and cries prompted my mom's rushed return.

"What happened?" she asked, her face betraying signs of

fatigue and concern.

"I think he's just hungry," I said. "He's got that look!"

Caleb's blue eyes were captivating; there was no way to put it. Little did I know his eyes would bring me closer to solving the perplexing mystery I would long pursue. I showered Caleb with love, treating him like my own child—dressing him up and constantly fussing over him. Taking him around to show him off to friends filled me with a deep sense of pride, even stirring jealousy in them. They all yearned for a baby brother like mine, and honestly, I couldn't blame them. Caleb was my world, and I treasured every moment we shared.

I had come to terms with my childhood up to a certain point, but circumstances beyond my control drastically altered the course of my life. I have always been reluctant to revisit the day my father passed away. The principal summoned me to the office early that day at school. I sat at my desk, tapping my pencil nervously against my notebook. The classroom buzzed with the usual chatter, but I couldn't shake the feeling that something was off.

Suddenly, my teacher approached me, "Anna, the principal called for you. She wants you to come to the office now." My heart sank.

"Did I do something wrong?" The teacher shook her head.

"I don't think so, Anna. She didn't specify. Just pack up your things and head down there. We'll see you tomorrow, okay?"

"Okay…" I replied, anxiety knotting in my stomach.

I saw Cara sitting in the office and asked, "What are you doing here, Cara? Did they tell you why we are here?" Cara simply shrugged.

"I don't know what's going on."

Feeling frustrated, I snapped, "Well, if you can't tell me anything, then don't talk to me for the rest of the day."

Cara said, "Fine, I couldn't care less if I ever talk to you again."

I tried to brace myself for whatever news was coming, but my thoughts spiraled into a whirlwind of dread. Rushing to my mother, I bombarded her with questions, "Mom, what's wrong? Is Caleb okay? What about Dad?"

Her composed response amplified my growing panic. Calmly, she urged, "Anna, let's go home, and we'll talk about it."

I persisted, "Mom, tell me now! I'm not getting in the car!" Eventually, she got me home; I nervously waited on the couch. When my mom revealed that my father had passed away, time seemed to freeze. Lashing out, I screamed, "I hate you! It's your fault! I'd rather him be alive than you!" To this day, the guilt of those hurtful words still haunts me. In the days that followed the loss of my father, the tears came quickly. I struggled not only with the loss of his passing but also with the realization that I would never have any more memories with my dad.

All I had were the fragments of the past, and even those seemed to slip away, fading into the distance. My patience wore thin, leaving me quick to anger and easily annoyed by my brother Caleb. He would burst into my room, his voice cheerfully calling, "Anna Banana!"

I'd snap back, "Caleb, would you shut up? Leave me alone!" and slam the door behind him.

But unfazed, he would just come back in, grinning and taunting me, "I'm back!"

I would scream again, "Caleb, get out of my room! I can't stand you!"

I had naively believed that my father's death would be the most devastating event of my adolescence, but I was mistaken. I recall that fateful day with clarity. My mother had forgotten Caleb's school bag, and I boarded a different bus, blissfully unaware of the unfolding tragedy. When I heard the devastating news, the sudden, irreplaceable absence of Caleb left me in shock. "This is all your fault!" I shouted at my mom, the words tearing from my throat.

"You should have been watching him better! You should have been a better parent! If Dad were here, Caleb would never be gone!"

Tears glistened in my mom's eyes as she replied tremblingly, "I'm so sorry. I love you very much, and I'm doing everything I can to find your brother."

I could barely hear her over the roar of my anguish. "Well, it's the police's fault then! It's everybody's fault! Nobody was taking care of him!" My despair crashed over me, and I sank to the floor, sobs wracking my body. My mom rushed to my side, wrapping her arms around me, but I pushed her away. "Leave me alone! I can't stand you! I hate you and everybody else!" My voice cracked as anger swirled within me. "Please, just let me help," I pleaded. "We have to look further!" I screamed. "Why isn't anyone doing anything? It feels like you're just giving up!"

"I promise we will find him," my mom whispered, desperate. "We have to keep the faith."

"Faith?" I scoffed, bitterness flooding my words. "Faith won't bring him back! I'm so tired of everyone failing him!" I glanced around the room, the walls closing in as my anger surged. "Just get out! I don't want to see anyone. Leave me alone!"

At that moment, I felt alone, consumed by rage. I wished I could turn back time and change everything that had led us to this point. Overcome with panic, I asked the officers, "Where is my brother? Are you looking for him? We must find him, or I will lose my whole family!"

The officers tried to reassure me, saying, "I know this is hard. We're doing everything we can to help you find your brother." But their words rang hollow, like a mere bandage on a wound that seemed impossible to heal. The regret of not being there for him and my inability to protect him weighed heavily on me. The world had shifted beneath my feet, leaving me with a hole in my heart that would forever remain.

I eavesdropped on the adult conversations, trying to grasp the gravity of Caleb's absence while obsessively seeking answers. Questions swirled around me. The cops asked, "Do you have any enemies? Has anyone been stalking you? Have you noticed anyone lurking around the house? Have the girls made any new friends? Have any new families moved in?" I listened, confused, not understanding why they asked those questions. It felt like an intrusion into our fractured lives, adding to my helplessness.

High school became a delicate balancing act as I struggled to fulfill daily obligations while dealing with my despair. Though a few understanding friends provided some comfort, they could not fully comprehend the depth of my loss. My typically keen attention faltered, and I found it increasingly difficult to recall the details of that fateful day. Waves of sorrow threatened to pull me under, and each day was a battle to stay afloat, searching for fleeting moments of calm amidst the turmoil.

The days turned to weeks and weeks to months; the harsh reality of Caleb's abduction had finally set in, leaving me with a crushing sense of responsibility. Though the specifics of that fateful day remained elusive, the blame I felt was suffocating. My life had become a constant barrage of reprimands— "Anna, pick up your clothes! Anna, do this! Anna, clean up your dishes!"— leaving me feeling perpetually wrong and inadequate. Yet when I truly needed her support, my mother was nowhere to be found. I would lash out in frustration, snapping, "Shut up, Mom! I hate you!" Looking back, I deeply regret those hurtful words.

I couldn't shake the haunting feeling that she held me accountable for everything. Eager to channel my self-loathing into something constructive, I threw myself into my studies. I poured every ounce of energy into learning, driven by the dream of becoming a lawyer and uncovering the truth to bring justice for Caleb.

Fighting back became my way of coping and finding purpose

amid my suffering. Graduating as valedictorian should have been a triumph, but the achievement felt hollow. The absence of my family, who were distant and detached, cast a dread over what should have been a momentous occasion.

The overwhelming sadness in my life overshadowed my achievements. Leaving home for college in the South marked a significant physical and emotional shift. While I grew fond of the Southern charm and hospitality, I became more introverted, a stark contrast to the outgoing person I had once been. Over time, I accepted this more reserved side of myself as my authentic self.

When I first met Ted, I walked by him; I barely acknowledged him. But then he caught my attention and introduced himself. "What are you studying?" he asked.

"Political science," I replied, my tone matter of fact.

"What's your name?" Ted continued.

"Anna. And yours?"

"Ted. Nice to meet you, Anna! Where are you from?" Ted inquired.

"New York. You?"

"Tennessee." Suddenly, he asked, "Would you like to go on a date with me sometime?"

I hesitated, "I don't know you." Yet somehow, I found myself saying, "I guess."

"Okay, great! That's all I needed to hear," he said, a grin spreading. His enthusiasm was infectious, and despite my reservations, I felt a flicker of intrigue at this unexpected connection.

Ted's face lit up with enthusiasm. "How does Friday night sound? I've been wanting to try a new Italian place downtown."

I paused, considering his offer. "Friday works for me. What time shall we meet?"

"How about 7 o'clock? I can pick you up if that works for you," Ted suggested, his eyes sparkling with glee.

"I will meet you there."

"Sounds good. I'll see you then," he replied.

Ted's persistent quirks initially annoyed me, but over time, his charming nature drew me in, and our friendship blossomed. I found comfort in his steadfast support, which provided a much-needed respite from the complexities and turmoil of my life. As a reliable companion, Ted became someone I could truly confide in. His genuine kindness and encouragement helped me navigate my challenges. Driven by Caleb's memory and a promise to uncover the truth, he was the beacon guiding me through the darkness as I pursued justice. I immersed myself in study and exercise, using these to distract me from the void left by Caleb's absence.

The next phase of my education led me back to New York, where I enrolled at Columbia Law School. To my delight, I discovered that Ted would attend the same law school. We moved into a cozy, cramped apartment in the city. Ted often joked, "When we make it big as lawyers, I'm going to buy you a mansion filled with flowers."

I'd laugh and reply, "I can't wait for that day."

Returning to the state where the events with my father and Caleb had occurred left me uneasy. "Having you by my side makes me feel grounded," I told Ted. "You help me navigate the suffering of my past." Little did we know that becoming a lawyer alongside Ted would eventually lead us to the answer to the question, "Where are you, Caleb?"

Ted's legal expertise and people skills proved invaluable in our search for answers about Caleb's whereabouts. It was as if fate had intertwined our paths for a greater purpose than we could have foreseen.

After graduating, I asked Ted, "Should we stay in New York or head down south?"

He quickly replied, "We're not staying in New York." Feeling that was the right decision, we both agreed to return to South

Carolina and start anew. However, beginning a family proved to be a daunting challenge. We endured countless cycles of in vitro fertilization and several devastating miscarriages, leaving me in complete despair. I would ask my doctor pleadingly, "Is this ever going to happen? How many babies am I going to lose? Should I just give up?"

My doctor gently reassured me, "Anna, this takes a lot of time and effort, but if you stick with it, I promise you'll have your baby." Her words provided much-needed encouragement during that difficult journey.

During those dark times, Ted would try to lift my spirits. "Anna, I love you. We don't have to do this anymore. It can just be the two of us," he said.

"Ted, I want babies! I want to be a mom! I want a family." Despite the grueling process and emotional toll, my drive never wavered. One evening, I decided to take a pregnancy test. I knew I wasn't pregnant, but I did it anyway. I looked at the test several times to ensure I read it correctly. "Ted! Ted! Hurry! I am pregnant!"

"Anna, I knew God would bless us; I am so happy." Our son James arrived like a beacon of bright light and renewal, transforming my life. Being a mother to him filled the emptiness I had carried for so long, giving me a sense of purpose.

I grasped Ted's hand in the hospital bed, "Thank you for believing in me; I know I can be quite challenging at times, even somewhat demanding."

Ted responded with a charming grin, "I love you. Thank you for all your hard work bringing James into this world." I knew I had found a true treasure in him.

"I'm starving now that I just gave birth to your son," I said playfully.

With a warm smile, Ted asked, "What would you like, my princess?"

I grinned back, "No, Ted, now I'm your queen!"

When I became pregnant again with Samuel, I couldn't wait to tell Ted. "Ted, we'll be parents again; I'm pregnant!"

Ted replied, "Wow, this is like a dream, Anna. I can't wait to meet our new baby."

Unfortunately, the pregnancy took a severe turn when I developed pre-eclampsia, forcing me to give birth to Samuel a few weeks early. Panicked, I called Ted at work, trembling, "Ted, get home—something's wrong! I'm bleeding!"

He immediately yelled back, "Call 911! I'm coming now!" I could hear the urgency in his voice as he told Cara to call for help. In that moment, fear consumed me. My hands shook, and sweat poured down my face as I fought to stay conscious, terrified of losing the baby. "Ted, help me!" I yelled, panic rising in my chest.

"I'm here," he reassured me, his voice steady. "Just rest your head on my shoulder. I'm going to take you to the car. I can beat the ambulance." His strength gave me a sliver of hope, but the moment Samuel was born, I felt like the trauma and pain had never happened. I held Samuel in my arms, and the overwhelming joy of meeting him overshadowed every moment of fear. In that instant, I knew that everything had been worth it.

Ted's eyes glistened with tears, but his grin conveyed relief. "I'm so thankful you are both okay," he said, his voice trembling. "Our family is complete now. We can't go through this again. I can't watch you put yourself through that kind of torture." He squeezed my hand, his touch a mix of love and concern.

"I agree about keeping things as they are for now. But if I change my mind and want another baby, I can make that happen."

Returning to full-time work was a significant change, and leaving my sons in my mother's care felt bittersweet. I couldn't help but notice a shift in her demeanor—the happiness she now radiated was a welcome change from the depression and anger I had grown accustomed to. Seeing her smile and engage with

Samuel and James was beautiful; it felt like a new, healing chapter for our family. I was much kinder to my mom, realizing she had done her best.

I was home more now, being that I was on maternity leave, and noticed my mom still wearing her old junky necklace with the green gem. "Mom, why do you still wear that?"

She explained, "It was a gift from Caleb, and I never take it off."

I couldn't resist pointing out, "But Caleb has been gone for years."

My mom replied, "I know, Anna, but it's important to me."

I didn't fully understand the necklace's significance then, but I would learn how that unassuming green gem would hold the key to many answers about my family's past.

One morning, I was at work when the phone rang. "Hi, this is Frank Bennet. May I speak with Anna?"

I replied, "This is Anna. How can I help you?" My mind was foggy from caring for Samuel through the night, and I found it hard to focus.

Frank's voice sounded familiar, but placing it took me a second. "It's Frank. Frank Bennett—remember me from high school?"

I blinked, surprised. "Frank! Wow, it's been a while. How have you been?" We exchanged a few pleasantries, reminiscing about old times before he got to the reason for his call.

He cleared his throat. "I know this is a bit out of the blue, but I'm a detective, and I'm calling because we've reopened your brother Caleb's investigation. We believe it's connected to a series of kidnappings along the East Coast, which occurred around the same time Caleb went missing."

My heart skipped a beat. "Wait, are you investigating Caleb's case?"

"Yes," Frank confirmed.

I felt a flood of emotions—hope mixed with frustration. "Frank, I'm at work and having trouble following. My family has had multiple leads on Caleb's case before, and nothing ever came of them."

Frank's voice softened. "I understand, Anna. But this is different. I need you and your sister, Cara, to provide DNA samples. It could be a breakthrough."

His words hung in the air. A wave of anger at the detectives who had failed Caleb rushed over me, but there was also a tiny spark of hope, one I hadn't allowed myself to feel in years.

I immediately called Cara. "Cara, do you remember Frank Bennet from high school?" There was a pause, and then Cara's voice came through, a little surprised. "Yeah, of course, I remember him. How could I forget he was always copying my schoolwork? What's he want?"

"He's reopening Caleb's case," I said quickly, my words tumbling out. "He believes it's connected to some kidnappings along the East Coast. He needs our DNA samples to help with the investigation."

Cara was silent for a moment, processing the news. "Wait, they're reopening Caleb's case? After all these years?"

I could hear the disbelief in her voice. "Yes. Frank also said that DNA could be a breakthrough. I know it's a lot, but we must do this, Cara."

There was a long pause before Cara responded. "Of course, Anna. I'll send the samples. It's just... hard to believe, you know?"

"I know," I replied quietly. "But it's something. We have to try."

"Okay, I'll get the samples to you right away," Cara conceded. "Let's keep this to ourselves for now," Cara said. "Mom's been so fragile. We can't upset her—just mentioning Caleb's name sends her off the deep end."

"I agree," I said.

Navigating conversations about Caleb felt like a delicate dance. Cara and I shared a bond over our memories of him, but we both understood that bringing him up around our mom was off-limits. The renewed investigation into Caleb's case highlighted the emotional tightrope I had to walk.

When I returned home from work that evening, my mom introduced me to her new friend. "Anna, this is Mike," she said, and I shook his hand.

"It's nice to meet you, Mike. How are you?" I greeted him.

"I'm doing well, and it's nice to see you again," he replied.

"Again?" I asked, puzzled.

"Yes, we met at bingo when you came with your son to pick up your mom," Mike explained.

"Oh, right!" I exclaimed, the memory returning.

He said, "If it weren't for you forcing her to go, we would have never met." I felt a sense of satisfaction, knowing I had played a part in their introduction.

When Mike walked away from my mom, I felt a surge of confidence. Knowing he was a retired detective, I saw this as an invaluable opportunity to gain a fresh perspective on Caleb's case. With apprehension, I approached him. "Mike," I said, "would you be willing to look into a cold case for me?"

He paused, his expression shifting to genuine interest as he considered my request. "What exactly are you looking for?" he asked.

I took a deep breath, ready to share my family's past and my desire for answers. I told Mike the story of Caleb's abduction, my voice trembling as I recounted the details. "So, Mike, are you willing to help us?" I asked sharply.

He considered my request and replied, "I guess so, but to a limited extent." Mike wanted to keep his detective work from my mom to avoid upsetting her. I appreciated his willingness to assist, even if it only was a small commitment.

Mike approached me the following week with a somber expression. "Anna, I know you asked me to look into Caleb's case, but I have some findings you may not want to hear," he said, his voice heavy with concern. I braced myself as he continued, "After speaking to the other detectives on the case, it's most likely your brother is not alive." The words struck me like a punch to the gut, sending shockwaves of despair.

The unsettling details about the other missing boys along the East Coast lingered in my mind, and the grim conclusion that anyone connected to the kidnappings was likely dead felt like knives to my chest. "Mike, you have no right to say that!" I snapped, my emotions boiling over.

"I'm so sorry, Anna," he replied gently.

"Stay out of it! Don't ever mention my brother's name again. I don't want your help!" My voice shook with anger and sorrow. Mike remained composed, repeatedly apologizing, but I could feel my world unraveling. Needing space from the devastating reality he had shared, I turned away, desperate to block out Mike's words.

That night, I had a vivid dream about Caleb. He called out to me—a rare and unsettling experience that evoked many emotions. I was comforted by Caleb's apparent happiness, which starkly contrasted with the uncertainty and despair surrounding his mysterious disappearance.

CHAPTER 3

Cara

I am Diane and Phil's middle daughter, Anna's younger sister, and Caleb's older sister. Though Anna and I share striking blonde hair and blue eyes, our personalities differ significantly. While Anna is introspective, I am emotionally intense, unapologetically assertive, and fiercely outspoken. Growing up, I cherished every moment with my dad. We had countless shared experiences that forged our bond, from working on my softball skills to exploring the great outdoors and biking nature trails.

When Caleb was born, I couldn't shake the feeling of being displaced as the middle child, sandwiched between the attention lavished on Anna as the oldest and the new focus on Caleb as the baby. I often joked that I was the original favorite child, squeezed in the middle between Anna and the new favorite, Caleb.

My dad's death has shaken me deeply; the day he died, I remember spotting Anna in the principal's office; her troubled expression told me everything I needed to know. Unease surged me as she rushed over, asking, "What's wrong? Why are we here?"

I shook my head, "I don't know, but I don't think it's good." Anna pressed further, "What could it be? Is Caleb sick or something?"

I replied, "I don't know, and I don't want to talk about it right now."

Feeling a rush of resentment, Anna shot back, "Fine." The heavy air around us hinted that whatever was about to unfold would change everything.

After my father passed away, my memories of that time became hazy. I can't recall my mother's exact words about him, but I remember the intense fury I directed at her. For months, I yelled, "I hate you," repeatedly. "I wish you were the one that died instead of Dad. He was a better parent." Looking back, I'm struck by how gracefully my mother handled my outbursts.

Rather than retaliate, she would simply murmur, "I love you, Cara," further fueling my anger.

It felt like a raging storm was consuming me, and she was the closest target. Even now, I still find it difficult to discuss my father. The grief often resurfaces, making me feel as though I did something wrong or wasn't good enough to deserve him. A part of me still believes I'm unworthy. Yet, during that dark period, my life was about to take an even worse turn.

The details of Caleb's disappearance remained a mystery, but the impact of his absence was a constant presence. I will never forget the tumultuous emotions I faced during that time. I was in continuous disrespect of my mother and her feelings. I would yell, "I hate you! You did this; it's all your fault!" Those accusatory words poured out of me daily, and I saw the fear and anguish in her face each time.

She would respond heartbroken, "I'm so sorry, Cara."

The endless nights of searching for Caleb had replaced my once vibrant social life. Friendless, I found solace in schoolwork, though maintaining acceptable grades drained me. Anger consumed me, leaving me miserable and isolated from everyone and everything. Resolute in the fact that I would keep my troubled home life hidden from the school, I dreaded the prospect of my mother's disruptive involvement. This embarrassment drove me to distance myself from my remaining friends further.

I was cruelly harsh to my mother, though I'm still unsure why. One night, I unleashed a torrent of vicious words: "I'm not searching anymore! You lost my brother; you lost your son. You find him! But God—God is going to punish you for a long time! Mom, you don't deserve anything but to go to hell. You killed my father, making him work those long hours in that mine, and now you've lost my brother. What use are you? I can't stand you! Don't ever talk to me again!" These scathing accusations poured out of me like a flood. Looking back, I still don't fully understand what drove me to be so cruel to her.

Despite my mom's immense grief of losing her husband and child, my mother navigated the challenge of raising two unruly teenagers with remarkable grace. I doubt I could have handled such a difficult situation with the same poise and resilience. "Cara, I'm so sorry you're hurting. I know you've suffered a terrible loss with the death of your dad and losing your brother. But I need you to know how much I love you, even if you don't like me right now or even hate me. Please remember that I love you. Hold on to that. I'm doing everything I can to find Caleb, and I need you to believe that deep in your heart. Please, Cara, believe me." My mom's voice was thick with sorrow.

When Anna graduated high school, a wave of terror washed over me at the thought of being left alone in that house with my mom. I pleaded, "Anna, there's no way you can leave me. I can't stay here with her by myself!"

"You have one year. You can do it and then come down south with me," Anna reassured.

"I can't! There's no way I can handle this. You can't leave

43

me!"

Anna firmly replied, "Come on, Cara. Stop. I have no choice. I'm leaving. You'll deal with it."

Hurt, I lashed out, "I hate you too!" At that point, I realized I hated Anna and everyone else. She had been the person I could count on, and now she was abandoning me to navigate the despair alone—with a depressed mother, a dead father, and a missing brother. The walls of our home felt suffocating, and I couldn't escape my rage.

When I would go to the store or for a walk, I'd catch a glimpse of someone holding a child's hand. "Excuse me. Oh, I'm sorry, I thought you were someone else." My palms would sweat, my pulse racing, as I chased after them, trying to glimpse a license plate or get a better look, only to discover it was just another boy who bore a fleeting resemblance to Caleb. It was always someone else's child—going home with their family or playing in the park, watched over by a big sister. But it never was Caleb. Reflecting on my past, I realize how pivotal Anna had been in shaping my life.

She pressed me, "What will you wear for prom?"

I shrugged, "I am not going to prom."

"We're going prom dress shopping this weekend, whether you like it or not."

"I'm not going, so I don't need a dress," I shouted back.

"Cara, you're going to prom because it's important," she insisted. Eventually, I agreed because of her perseverance.

As my high school graduation approached, I felt like I was merely drifting through the days, unnoticed by my disengaged mother. I was biding my time until I could leave the prison of my home. "I'm not planning on attending my graduation."

My mom responded firmly, "Absolutely not, Cara. We're going."

Confused, I challenged her, "Why? You don't even do anything and are never present, so why do we have to go?"

"Because it's a big celebration for you," she insisted. "It's a momentous time, and you've accomplished something positive."

"I don't care about it," I replied angrily.

My mom hardly ever raised her voice, but this time she said, "Cara, we're going. Don't start this crap now," leaving no room for argument. I reluctantly agreed, though I was still furious with her.

During my college years down south, I often called my mom, struggling to find a genuine connection despite our strained relationship. "Hey, Mom, what's up?"

"Oh, I'm fine, Cara! How are you? How's school?" she replied, her voice sounding overly cheerful.

"It's good," I said, noticing the same predictable routine we navigated when we spoke. Each call felt like an exercise in avoidance, a way to sidestep the underlying tension between us. I knew I was calling more out of obligation than genuine concern. These conversations were less about her well-being and more for my peace of mind—a way to quiet the nagging voice that insisted I should reach out. Deep down, I suspected she wouldn't notice if I stopped calling. I longed for a genuine connection, yet each exchange reinforced the distance I had created over time.

"After I finish college, I plan on attending Vanderbilt Law School. I need a fresh start in a new city," I said.

My mom listened quietly, and I could hear the resignation in her soft response, "Okay." It was as if she didn't feel she had the right to say more after being absent for so long.

I added, "Anna and Ted want me to join their law firm, but I'm ready for a change."

She paused, then said, "I agree, Cara. I pray you're well and happy." Her words sounded supportive, yet there was a robotic quality to them.

After law school, I approached Anna. "Anna, I know you and Ted want me to join the law firm, but I'm not sure I'm ready yet," I said.

"I understand, Cara. You should do what works for you," Anna replied, her tone supportive.

"Well, can I take some time to think about it for a few weeks? Then we can go from there."

"Of course, Cara," she reassured me.

That summer, after graduation, I took my time to reflect on what I truly wanted to do. "Anna, I've decided. I'd like to join the law firm, but can we do it temporarily? I want to see how it goes, and if I choose to pursue something else, I need the freedom to leave."

"Cara. I told you, whatever is easiest for you," she responded enthusiastically. And that's how I began my legal career, back with Anna and Ted, ready to see where this path would lead.

One evening, I was working late, and Anna approached me with a somber expression. "Cara, I'm not happy. Mike said that Caleb is likely...dead."

I quickly retorted, "But everyone else always says the same thing. Why would you trust him? Caleb's been missing longer than Mike's even been around. You can't believe that crap."

Anna responded, "It's like he had some inside information." Anna sighed, disappointment evident. "That's what set me off. I freaked out on him, and I'm still so angry that he felt the need to tell me Caleb was dead."

I placed a hand on her arm. "Anna, try to stay calm. I've got to go—I have work to do."

A surge of determination swept through me. I had to make a choice—it was now or never. "This may not be wise, but I'm going," I declared, my mind made up. Driving through Milford Falls's familiar streets, childhood memories flooded my mind. The town seemed frozen in time, unchanged despite the passing years. This return to a place steeped in stagnant nostalgia felt like a chance for closure.

As I approached my old childhood home, a sense of unease

crept over me. The once vibrant house now appeared eerie and forsaken, as if the fringes of the town had swallowed it whole. Knowing the house's tragic past compounded the pain of seeing the new owner let it wither away.

The chipped paint revealed the rotting boards beneath, while weeds had overrun the patio and crept through the cracks. The once-bright blue exterior had faded to a mournful shade of gray, blending into the surrounding desolation. The old play set stood neglected; the grass reduced to a withered remnant of its former lush self. Tangled, overgrown flowers and drooping hydrangea bushes amplified the air of decay and abandonment. I thought, "If I could turn back time, I would beg my father to stay home from work and never leave Caleb's side." The pressure and responsibility I placed on myself were too much to bear.

After leaving Milford Falls, I had leads about a small town in western Pennsylvania called Yellow Dog Village and decided to go there. I had reports that indicated that two men had parked a suspicious white van along the streets years ago. I walked into a local convenience store with a photo and asked the young clerk, "Have you seen a van that looks like this?

The clerk, who appeared to be no older than twenty, shook his head and replied, "Nope, not me."

Pressing further, I inquired, "Is your boss around?"

The clerk shrugged and said, "I don't even know who my boss is."

Urgency crept into my voice as I said, "This is important. Can I put this up?"

Curious, the clerk asked, "What is it?"

I explained, "It's my brother. He went missing over twenty years ago."

After a brief pause, the clerk responded, "I guess. Sorry for your loss."

Snapping back, I said, "I don't need your sympathy. He's not dead. I'm just trying to piece together where he is. I have leads that he might have been in this village."

The clerk said, "Okay, well, if I see anything, I'll let you know."

As I walked out, I muttered, "I doubt it, dude!"

I'd heard the same about Falling Creek, Virginia, so I drove there next. I got out of my car and approached an older man nearby. "Excuse me, sir," I called out. "Do you remember any strange vans that disappeared from these roads years ago?"

The man looked confused. "No, ma'am, I'm afraid I can't help you with that."

I asked, "Would you mind if I gave you my contact information? I'm also curious—were there any nuns who used to live in this area or come into town?" The nunnery was another lead I'd gotten.

"Oh yes, there was a nunnery not far from here," the man replied, his eyes lighting up. "The nuns would come into town for supplies and the occasional snack. They were a regular sight back in the day," he told me.

"Do you remember anything unusual about them or their interactions with the community?" I asked.

"Not unusual, just very kind," he said. "They always had a smile and a wave. It's been years since I've seen any of them."

Trying to organize a timeline, I continued, "Do you know if they ever had any events or gatherings?"

The man responded, his gaze drifting, "I'm afraid I don't know much more. They were kind ladies, but I can't recall any specifics," he replied.

"Thank you for your time; here is my business card if you ever hear anything. Please let me know if you remember anything about those vans or the nuns."

I walked away, and an unsettling feeling gripped me. I strolled toward the old stone bridge, hearing water crashing against the rocks. The change in the energy made me feel like Caleb's presence still lingered there despite the soothing ambiance. I couldn't shake the suspicion that he had been here at some point, lost among the shadows of my memories. Had I known my time in Falling Creek would lead me to my brother, I would have stayed longer, driven to find the nun who would provide me with the needed information. Unaware of this, I stopped my search of the town.

Defeated and exhausted, I drove straight through Virginia, the state seemingly endless. Crossing into South Carolina finally brought a sense of relief. Dragging my suitcase inside, I collapsed into bed, desperate for rest. All I craved was sleep, to let the stress fade away and emerge feeling lighter and unburdened. The fatigue left me barely stirring the next day.

Yet, in the dead of night, my phone shattered the silence with news from my mother. "Cara, Anna's gone into labor—weeks early! I can't go to the hospital because I have James. I need you to get there and be with Ted and Anna."

A wave of confusion and concern washed over me. "Mom, where is she? What happened?" I asked.

"She's at the hospital. You need to go now!" my mother's voice sounded frantic.

"Now?" I questioned, disbelief creeping in. "Is she okay?" I asked.

"She's in poor condition. Please, just go!" she pleaded.

"Okay, I'm going. I'll call you when I get there," I promised.

Arriving at the hospital, I struggled to gather my thoughts. I approached the front desk, consumed with worry for my sister. "Hi, my sister Anna Hart is in the emergency room; I must find her," I told the officer, my voice trembling.

The officer's expression was unreadable as he replied, "I'm sorry, but we can't give you much information unless you're next of kin," he told me.

"I am next of kin! I'm her sister!" I insisted.

Just then, my brother-in-law Ted rushed over. "Excuse me, sir, this is my sister-in-law. She's with me," he said to the officer, who responded, "Oh, okay. No problem. Go on in."

Ted's face was pale, his eyes filled with fear. "Anna developed dangerously high blood pressure. She had severe headaches and vomiting. Anna called me—there was blood everywhere, and then she passed out. I got here faster than the ambulance. It was terrifying. I've been waiting for news ever since," he shared.

"Where is she? How long has it been?" I asked, my heart racing.

"It feels like forever, Cara. I do not know what's going on," Ted replied, his worried voice strained.

After hours, a nurse approached Ted and said, "You can come back now."

Ted replied, "I'm bringing my sister-in-law, Cara." She nodded, and they hurried down the corridor.

As I stepped into Anna's room, the depression lifted from my mind, clearing my mind for the task ahead. "Thank God you're okay!" I exclaimed, tears welling in my eyes. "I couldn't have survived without you. I can't lose another person."

Anna looked at me, tears glistening. "Cara, come here! I'm fine. Hold your new nephew, Samuel." Immediately, my stress and sadness lifted. Samuel's bright blue eyes, full of innocence and curiosity, stared at me.

I could see Ted's beaming love shining through as he embraced Anna. I dialed my mother's number, eager to share the news that our family had welcomed a little light into our lives.

CHAPTER 4

Caleb

I am the youngest and only son; I'm constantly teased by my sisters, Anna and Cara, for being the spoiled "baby" of the family. I can easily manipulate my parents by giving them my best sad puppy-dog eyes, which they struggle to resist. "Caleb gets away with everything. I can't stand how spoiled he is," Cara would complain.

"It's not fair that he gets so much attention just for being the firstborn son," Anna would add.

My mom frequently commented on my striking blue eyes, likening them to the shimmering hue of sea glass. While her admiration is well-intentioned, it can become embarrassing. When we're out in public, she'll often interrupt conversations to exclaim, "Caleb has the most beautiful eyes!" and then demand strangers validate her assessment, asking, "Aren't his eyes just perfect?"

The resulting chorus of agreement— "Wow, he has the most amazing eyes!"—leaves me feeling self-conscious. As a big boy now, I don't particularly relish hearing I have "pretty" eyes.

I love the exhilaration of climbing trees and soaring on the swing, feeling the rush of wind. Losing myself in video games for hours provides my ultimate escape. Playing tricks and pranks is one of my favorite pastimes. I take pride in being skilled at it. Whether it's a harmless prank or a clever joke, I delight in making my sisters laugh, even if they roll their eyes. Being the youngest has perks, and I fully intend to savor every moment. Whenever Cara is on the phone, I sneak up behind her and shout, "Boo!"

Cara, aggravated by my harassment, would respond, "You little brat, get out of here." I'd simply smirk and respond, "Oh, I know you love it."

With Anna, when she caught me going through her stuff, she'd protest, "Caleb, get out of here! You're ruining everything!" But I'd hurry away, delighting in the mischief.

I recall a tense parent-teacher conference with my mom and Ms. Puddle, my teacher. Ms. Puddle bluntly told my mom, "Caleb has dyslexia. He's smart, but not as smart as his peers." Mortified, I wished I could disappear.

But my mom didn't hold back, firmly responding, "Dyslexia doesn't mean Caleb will learn slower or differently. He'll face the same challenges and may even be smarter than anyone else in this class."

Ms. Puddle tried to clarify, "I misspoke and did not intend that implication."

My mom cut her off, "That's how it sounded, and I don't appreciate you negatively discussing my son, especially in front of him." When we got home, my mom comforted me, saying, "Caleb, your intelligence is beyond your age. You're not just smart but thoughtful, insightful, and creative." Her words lifted my spirits, reminding me that being different didn't make me any less important.

I don't have many clear memories of my dad. I am still determining if what I remember is real or just from seeing old photos.

But I knew he was tall, and when he held me, I felt small. I wish I had a dad who was around like my friends' dads. They're always at the baseball games and coaching all the sports. But my mom said, "Caleb, we all have our cross to carry." I'm still not sure what she means.

Anna and Cara's bickering voices rose one hectic morning as I tried to stay out of their way. "Come on, girls, get ready for school!" my weary-sounding mom called.

But Cara snapped back rudely, "Leave me alone!"

Exasperated, my mom replied, "I'm tired of this! I'm not driving you to school anymore. Just be on time for God's sake!" Amid the commotion, my mom accidentally left my backpack in the kitchen, so we had to hurry back to grab it. On our way back, she stopped to speak to our neighbor. Seeing my friends still playing outside, I felt the pull to join them. Impulsively, I bolted toward the bus stop but quickly ducked behind a tree when I saw my mom approaching. Before I knew it, the bus had rolled away without me. As I watched it disappear down the road, I felt panic and mischievous glee, caught between wanting to play and fearing my mom's anger.

I hoped to avoid being scolded by my mother for skipping school, so I walked to the park. Along the way, I spotted a cream-colored puppy resembling a big, cuddly teddy bear. Captivated, I went to pick up the pup and was amazed by how incredibly soft and fluffy he felt—like a living, breathing plush toy that barked. His smooth, downy fur felt heavenly against my skin, and I couldn't help but find him utterly adorable. As I scooped him up, the puppy snuggled to my face.

I was distracted; a man's voice jolted me back to the moment, "Well, you caught my puppy! His name is Lion," he said.

I grinned, "I love that name! I have a dog named Saint."

The man smiled, "I'm happy you caught him; I was struggling to get him myself. Would you like to take him for a walk?" he asked.

"I'd love that!" I replied.

He raised an eyebrow, "So, why aren't you in school, young man?"

I shrugged, "I missed the bus, but I'm heading home soon."

Curious, he asked, "What's your name?"

I said, "Caleb. What's yours?"

The man didn't answer, which I figured was just an adult thing. He handed me Lion's leash, and we walked toward his van. "Hey, Caleb," he said with a growing smile, "How about I buy you some ice cream?"

"Yes, please!" I beamed and added, "I have to get back to the park right after."

"No problem at all, Caleb. We'll be back in no time," he assured. I snuggled Lion close, feeling like my day was taking a turn for the better.

Then another man appeared, his expression serious. "Grab him," he ordered gruffly.

I stammered, "What? Wait—" But the man barked, "Grab the boy and put him in the van!"

Panic surged through me. "No! My mom—she won't let me go with strangers!" I protested.

The man snapped, "Too bad, little kid, shut up."

"I will not shut up! Let me go!" I shouted, struggling against his grip. In a swift motion, my mouth was bound, perhaps with a shirt or similar fabric. I gasped, trying to push it away, but then I heard the van door click shut behind me, trapping me inside the dark vehicle.

Looking around, I noticed two other boys about my age, who also seemed to have been brought there against their will. I wondered nervously if this was just another prank by my sisters or some kind of punishment from my mom for being naughty, though the situation felt far more sinister.

Exhausted, I eventually drifted off, dreaming of home. But when I awoke, reality crashed down on me—this was no dream but a nightmare. As my eyes adjusted to the dim light, I noticed a couple of boys sitting in the van. "What are your names?" I asked.

They looked up briefly before nervously averting their gazes. "I'm Jack," one boy whispered.

The older boy beside him said, "And I'm Sam."

These would be my new companions, so I might as well make the best of it.

"What's happening here?" But Jack shook his head, too frightened to speak.

Sam leaned in closer. "We have to talk about fun things to keep ourselves busy, or we won't survive," he said. Uncertain of his meaning, we quickly chatted about video games, Pokémon, and baseball. The laughter and conversation made the time more bearable, even as our stomachs growled with hunger. It was comforting to know I wasn't alone in this terrifying situation.

After being cramped in the van for days, it finally stopped. A man abruptly yelled, "Get out now, you little jerks!" It was my first encounter with the kind ladies, and the situation left me feeling a peculiar mix of relief and confusion. They wore long dresses and distinctive black-and-white hats that reminded me of the nuns at my church. They welcomed us with warm baths, fresh clothes, meals, and a shared blanket—a small piece of home in this unfamiliar place.

"Would you please sing for me?" I asked.

"Of course, I would love to!" Her calm, gentle voice soothed my racing heart, and afterward, she brought me more food.

"Am I going to stay here with you?" I asked hopefully.

She looked at me with a hint of confusion. "What do you mean, son?"

I explained, "I don't have my family."

Understanding dawned on her face. "I know, child. But God

will soon place you in the right, loving family." Her words gave me hope.

"Thank goodness, because I miss my family terribly," I said, and she smiled kindly down at me.

I tried not to dwell on my mom and sisters' sadness. Though Anna and Cara had teased me, I knew they loved me deeply. Each day, it grew more challenging to hold onto memories of them as those recollections slowly faded. As the weeks turned to months, I had to accept the possibility that I may never see my family again. Boys would come and go from the van, but Sam, Jack, and I remained the longest residents. Huddled close under a single blanket during the chilly nights, we found some measure of calmness in each other's company.

From the van, I identified two men by their distinctive nicknames. "Felix the Cat" was named by his unsettling, creepy eyes. The other, Pete, had a droopy right eye and appeared rather dim-witted, earning him the nickname "Stink Eye Pete." Jack and Sam found these new nicknames hilarious, and we would snicker about them behind their backs. "Hey, Jack, who's dumber—Stink Eye or Felix the Cat?" I would joke, sparking uproarious laughter.

"They're both dumb!" they'd shout back. The banter continued, Sam chiming in, "Who's got no teeth, The Cat or Stink Eye?"

"Neither one!"

Jack asked, "Who smells worse, Stink Eye or Felix the Cat?"

After pretending to ponder the question, I'd declare, "Definitely Stink Eye."

My stomach ached, piercing and knife-like pain that radiated through my whole body. Yearning to go home, I felt dizzy and disoriented. Summoning my courage, I pleaded with Felix the Cat, "I'm starving. Please, can I have food?"

He sneered, "You'll eat when I'm ready to feed you. Don't bother me." As his chilling laughter terrified me, I realized that Jack and Sam were just as hungry and afraid. To pass the time, we played imaginary games, momentarily forgetting our dire circumstances.

I noticed Jack becoming increasingly quiet. "I'm worried about Jack. He's not eating and barely wants to drink anymore," I told Sam.

"I've been worried about him, too," Sam replied. "What if we wrap him in the blanket? He seems cold."

I nodded in agreement. "As long as we can get some water into his mouth, he should be okay."

"Great idea," Sam said. "Let's wrap him up and keep giving him water."

However, as the days passed, Jack's condition worsened. He stopped eating, talking, and laughing at our attempts to cheer him up, remaining silent for days. Cuddling under our blanket, we did our best to keep him warm and comfortable, but our worries grew.

The van suddenly stopped again, and I noticed Jack was entirely still. We wrapped him tightly in the blanket and took turns trying to keep him warm. I felt a little better when he finally slept serenely, even though he hadn't moved for days. We wanted to spoon-feed him water, but his lips clamped shut so tight that it was hard to get the water in. We took turns swaddling him, and I sang a song that my mom used to sing: "Be not afraid, I go before you always, come, follow me, and I will give you rest." I knew the song would comfort him, just like it used to calm me.

I overheard a troubling exchange between Felix the Cat and Stink Eye Pete. "I think he's dead," Felix said. The dread washed over me. Were they talking about someone being dead? I couldn't shake the fear that they were referring to my friend Jack. There's no way he's dead, I thought.

"He's just tired. We need to give him some water."

But Felix shrugged it off, saying, "If he is, keep him wrapped up. We'll drop him off."

I asked Sam, "Do you think they're talking about Jack?"

Sam tried to reassure me, saying, "No way. He's just tired and needs water, like we thought before." I wanted to believe him, but the dread lingered.

Sam yelled for help as Stink Eye opened the van, "My friend is sick! It smells like poop in here! You need to come help him—he needs medicine!"

Stink Eye's anger was terrifying. "Keep your mouths shut!" he barked, spit flying into my face. I sat quietly, holding my breath, as Stink Eye grabbed the curled-up Jack and took him away. I never saw Jack again. I prayed each day that Jack was alive, but with each passing moment, my hope was slipping away.

Sam and I eagerly waited for another friend to arrive during our next stop. Excited, I greeted him, asking, "Hi, what's your name?" But he didn't respond. I tried again, "Can you talk?" Still, he remained silent. Uncertain, I suggested, "How about we call you Little Buddy for now?" He seemed like he wanted to speak, but something felt wrong. I turned to Sam and said, "Maybe we should try to talk to him with signals."

Sam frowned, asking, "What signals?"

"I'm not sure. I don't know what he would understand," I admitted. Little Buddy groaned as if he wanted to communicate but couldn't find the words.

It quickly became apparent that something was wrong with Little Buddy. He sat silent, his gaze vacant and unfocused. His body trembled uncontrollably, eyes rolling back to reveal just the whites. Struggling to talk, he groaned and shook as if his parents had never taught him how to speak. Watching his distress was heartbreaking. "It's okay, Little Buddy. You're going to be okay. We're here for you." Sam and I took turns gently rocking him in our arms, hoping to provide some relief for Little Buddy.

The next time we stopped, Felix the Cat opened the back door and yelled, "Get out of my way! I need him!" He pointed at Little Buddy.

"Why? He's just a baby, a little boy!" I protested.

"I'm sending him back to his family," Felix snapped.

"But how do you know where his family lives?" I asked, my voice rising in anger.

"Shut up, kid, or you won't eat for the rest of your life!" He grabbed Little Buddy and tossed him out like a sack of potatoes. I heard a gut-wrenching shriek as Little Buddy hit the ground, left on the side of the road. That sound struck me, leaving me filled with unease. I couldn't shake the image from my mind, constantly thinking about what might have happened to him.

At one of our visits to the park, I leaned down and whispered to a young boy, "I need help. Can you tell your mother?" Sam and I scanned the area, hoping to keep Stink Eye and Felix from noticing our exchange. But our plan quickly unraveled when Stink Eye caught wind of what we were doing.

"You think you can just call for help?" he said, his face twisting in rage. At that moment, the gravity of our situation hit me. What had seemed like a clever plan now felt like a mistake. We wanted to escape Felix and Stink Eye, but now we faced their wrath.

Realizing our intent, Felix erupted in a furious tirade directed at Sam and me. "Now you've done it! Your playtime is over, and the punishment will be severe. There will be no more food and water for an unimaginably long time." His venomous words struck me like a physical blow. The hunger and thirst already gnawing at me now felt like a never-ending crashing wave of pain.

We lost our precious moments of freedom, and the repercussions were unbearable. Days stretched into an endless cycle of emptiness; the park was now a haunting memory of what we had lost. Imprisoned in the van for months, I had become disconnected from reality. My body had adapted to this miserable existence, merging with the cold metal and grime of the white van. Eventually, the constant craving for food and water faded to a dull ache, the hunger replaced by a numbing emptiness. I could barely recognize myself. Cara used to say, "Caleb, you're so chunky." If she saw me now, I was thin, my skin stretched over my bones, and my body covered in sores.

When we stopped to see the kind ladies again, one of them approached me, "How are you doing, child?" I was too tired to respond. One of the women I would learn was Sister Kathleen, who immediately caught my eye. She looked at us concerned and asked, "Why are these boys malnourished? What are they eating?"

Trying to deflect, Felix invited her, "Sister, you're welcome to come and look inside the van."

To my surprise, Sister Kathleen agreed without hesitation. As she inspected the movies and snacks stacked around the van, she emerged and said, "I'm sorry you must go through losing your family. It is a challenging time, and I pray for a reunion with your families soon." It was clear she didn't realize, nor did we, that the whole adoption scheme was illegal; she thought our families had abandoned us. The identity of the van Sister Kathleen saw that day remains uncertain, but I can confirm it was not the place that held me captive.

Joe, our new member, was violently hurled into the van, and I felt an urgent need to inform him of the situation. "Joe, I need to tell you what's happening here," I said. Joe stared at me, his jaw dropping in disbelief. "Let me tell you about the stories," I continued. Poor Joe. Looking back, I realize he must have been terrified. He was a small child, even smaller than Sam and me. I can still picture his wide, confused, and fearful eyes as we prepared him for what lay ahead. "Okay, Joe, listen carefully," I said, my voice low and urgent.

"Be prepared not to eat or drink any water. You might even have to go to the bathroom in your pants. And we have one blanket between us." Sam chimed in, his tone serious.

"Never say a word when Felix the Cat and Stink Eye Pete

come around. If you do, they will punch you right in the mouth. Listen to whatever they say. Just behave and don't ask Stink Eye or The Cat anything. We learned the hard way, after all. Right, Sam?" I shot him a glance, remembering the first time we didn't follow our advice and what happened next.

"Yeah, we learned the hard way," Sam nodded solemnly. I could see the understanding in Joe's eyes, but I could also see the fear.

The threats from Felix the Cat and Stink Eye were daunting and scary. As we all huddled together under a meager blanket, I longed to offer more than just warnings—I wanted to protect the boy from the horrors we had endured and shield him from the cruelty of Stink Eye and The Cat. Yet all we could do was cling to each other, praying our bond would sustain us through the dark days ahead.

Felix's command was swift and merciless; I could not fully process what was happening. Stink Eye yanked Joe by the collar and threw him out of the van, drowning out his desperate pleas in the cold, indifferent air and the relentless rush of passing cars. Witnessing Joe's panicked cries fade left me feeling deeply saddened. There was nothing I could do to help him. All I could do was brace myself for the torment to come and cling to the fragile belief that this nightmare would one day end.

At our next stop, the situation took a turn for the worse. I could barely hold on, wholly drained and lacking the energy to leave the van. I wanted to stay in the white van; my body was weak. Stink Eye yelled, "This will teach you a lesson, you scum of the earth!" His venomous words hung in the air, heavy with menace. I felt the dread settle in my chest, even as I fought to stay strong against the panic threatening to overwhelm me. With a forceful kick to my ribs, I felt a sickening crunch as I collapsed onto the sand outside. The ache was immediate and overwhelming, radiating through my body with every labored breath.

The sun's blinding glare made it impossible to focus on anything. Sitting in a daze, I struggled to comprehend the situation. Stink Eye's menacing voice boomed, "That'll teach you never to question authority again! And that includes you too," he growled, glaring at Sam. "Stay quiet and don't speak, the two of you!" His threat hung heavy, sending a chill down my spine. Sam and I exchanged a worried glance, knowing any sign of defiance could bring even worse consequences.

I tried to recall the prayers I learned at CCD to find comfort. I remembered "Hail Mary, Full of Grace," but that was all I could hold on to. The rest of the prayer slipped away from me. It was the only thing I had, the only semblance of order in a world that had become frightening. Each repetition of the words comforted me and reminded me how far I had fallen from the normalcy I once knew.

Exhausted and unable to speak, I turned to Sam and said, "I couldn't do this without you. You're my best friend." Sam's reassuring smile reminded me that we could fight as long as we had each other. I knew this ordeal would have been unbearable without Sam's presence, his link to the life that now felt like a fixture in my imagination.

Nothing could have prepared me for the moment Felix shouted, "Sam, get out of the van now!" He grabbed Sam by the shoulders and yanked him out. Sam tried to bite Felix, who yelled, "Ouch, you loser!" It was a day that shattered whatever fragile hold I had on my sanity. Peering through the van's cracked door, I watched Sam's desperate struggle.

"Sam! Hold on! Wait for me!" I cried, but the chaos drowned out my pleas.

"I hate you, Felix the Cat and Stink Eye Pete!" Sam shouted.

"Who? Who do you hate?" they sneered mockingly. That was the last I heard before they whipped Sam into a different van.

Frozen in place, I watched as they slammed the van door,

trapping Sam inside and sealing him away from me. "Sam!" I cried out, my voice cracking with terror. But he was gone, leaving me alone. The world around me blurred as fear and utter helplessness consumed me. My friend had vanished instantly, and I felt small and powerless, alone in the van, knowing nothing would ever be the same.

A chill ran down my spine when Stink Eye returned to the truck. "Shut up!" he barked, his voice slicing through the air.

I could barely think straight as I pleaded, "Sam is just a little boy, only six years old! We're just little boys. Please let me go with Sam or bring him back! I'll do anything, please!" Stink Eye looked at me, and his chilling laugh gave me shivers like something from a scary movie. I could see the amusement in his eyes as he enjoyed watching me suffer. At that moment, I realized that begging would no longer help.

The harsh realization struck me: Stink Eye and The Cat had imprisoned me. The ever-present fright now felt all-consuming, suffocating me. Instinctively, I shrank back, wishing I could vanish and disappear entirely. At that moment, I knew my only choice was to endure the impending storm, clinging to the chance that I might, someday, see Sam again. But as Stink Eye's imposing figure loomed over me, my former life disappeared, replaced by reality's cold, un- forgiving grip.

Eating became irrelevant. My body felt depleted, too hollowed out by the ceaseless suffering to care about nourishment. Agony gnawed at me in places I never knew could hurt. The smell of my number one and number two on me was a continuous, sickening reminder of my dire state. The stench was my only sign of life, a reminder of the storm I lived through. Each day without Sam was a test of endurance, a battle against despair and physical agony.

As the van drove further away from my home, the memories of my family faded. Faces that once seemed so familiar were now blurred and distant, and I struggled to recreate the life I once knew, piecing together fragments of a past that felt increasingly unreal. The one constant, the one thing that kept me hanging on, was my friendship with Sam. Despite the unbearable suffering, the thought that we might one day reunite was the only light in my dark, confined world.

Stink Eye angrily thrust a baby into my arms, "Make sure this baby doesn't die, and take care of him!" I stared at him, feeling overwhelmed.

"I can barely take care of myself!" I shot back, tears welling in my eyes. The weight of the fragile infant felt heavy in my unsteady arms. Stink Eye Pete sneered and crossed his arms.

"You need to step up, or you'll end up like the rest of your useless friends," he said.

"What happened to my friends?" I demanded, my voice shaking. He rolled his eyes and leaned against the wall.

"You're dumber than I thought," Stink Eye Pete laughed.

I was responsible for a tiny, vulnerable being who depended on me in ways I couldn't manage. My failing body left me feeling helpless. When the baby's cries finally subsided, and he lay still, I felt a moment of relief. But that respite was short-lived. The baby slept soundly for days, unmoving and silent. Eventually, as I feared, The Cat and Stink Eye returned to take away the only companion I had left—the baby.

Hopelessness crept into my voice as I begged them, "Please don't take the baby! That's my only friend!"

Stink Eye's expression hardened. "You make too much noise, kid. The baby's already gone."

Panic surged as I frantically asked, "What do you mean by gone?"

He turned back with a cruel smile. "As I mentioned, you do not appear to be the brightest kid. I would characterize you as rather stupid. And by the way, your mother gave you up for adoption," he sneered.

"No, no!" I shouted, my mind racing. "Mommy, please! I need you!"

His malicious tone cut deep as he leaned closer. "Well then, she's dead." An icy wave of despair washed over me, crushing the last flicker of life in me. I felt alone, abandoned in a world that had turned dark and unforgiving.

To my shock, the baby remained silent even as Stink Eye picked him up. The child resigned to his fate or perhaps had simply given up. The sight of Stink Eye taking the baby without a single sound of protest was a cruel blow, like the final, devastating cut to my already shattered soul.

Although I didn't fully understand the significance of those words or who Hail Mary was, they were the only thing I had to hold on to in my darkest moments. As the van carried me further from everything I had ever known, the prayer became my lifeline—a fragile thread connecting me to a world that seemed to have slipped away forever.

CHAPTER 5

Diane

I was sitting downstairs in my apartment when Anna approached me, "Mom, Ted, and I have been talking. We think it's time for you to get out of the house. We heard about a local bingo group and want you to attend."

I hesitated, "Anna, that's a big step for me, especially after leaving home. I don't feel comfortable going out."

But Anna was persistent, using her usual convincing tone. "Mom, it's essential for our family and my children to see you have a life outside this house."

Finally, I relented. "Fine, Anna. I'll go a few times, and if it's unbearable, I'm not going back."

On my first bingo night, I kept to myself, sitting alone with my head down, trying to blend into the background. My mind wasn't in it, and I planned to remain unnoticed. Despite my efforts, seats next to me filled up quickly as people entered. Some of the older churchgoers tried to engage me in conversation, but I pretended not to hear, wishing to avoid social interaction. I felt like an outsider in a world that moved on without me.

One regular attendee, however, was impossible to ignore. His presence stood out week after week—a captivating mix of rich, smooth complexion and natural radiance highlighting his hand-some features. His soulful eyes drew in everyone who spoke to him, and his smile lit up the room. Even as I tried to remain unnoticed, something about him consistently caught my attention. His magnetic presence added an unexpected quality to the bingo nights.

I accidentally made eye contact with the man who had been catching my attention for weeks. "Hi, my name is Mike. Nice to meet you! I've seen you around; you're relatively new here. Do you like Greenville? Would you like to walk to the diner tonight after bingo? Oh, and what's your name?" he said.

I could barely respond, my voice faltering as panic rose within me. "I don't even know you," I managed to say.

"Oh, ask around! Everyone knows who I am," he reassured me as I struggled to find my words.

"Well, I don't think—" I began, but my response trailed off.

As bingo ended, Anna and James arrived to pick me up. I saw Anna's pleading eyes, which only added to my turmoil. "Hi, I'm Mike," he said casually. "I asked your mom on a date."

Without my permission, Anna chimed in, "I think that's a great idea, Mom! We can wait for you in town if that's easier." Anxiety flooded through me as I turned to Anna. "Just go, Mom. You'll have fun. You never do anything enjoyable," she said. I knew I couldn't let her down. She wanted me to go with Mike, to step out of my shell and engage with the world, and her hopeful expression made my decision even harder.

As we strolled down the town's quaint streets, I couldn't help but notice the serene beauty of our surroundings. The white church, with its towering steeple, stood out, crafted from a blue stone that caught the vibrant hues of the setting sun. The soft glow of orange and pink bathed the town, creating a picturesque scene that felt almost surreal. When we arrived at the diner, Mike graciously held the door open for me. "Where would you like to sit?" he asked.

"Wherever you want," I replied. "Well, let's head to the back over there in the corner," he suggested.

We walked to the back of the diner to a hidden booth. I said, "Excuse me, Mike, I need to use the restroom.

"No problem, it's over there," he gestured. Though I appreciated his kindness, it did little to ease the agitation tightening in my stomach. The moment we settled in, a wave of panic washed over me. As I excused myself to the restroom, my mind raced with frantic thoughts. I even thought about crawling out the window— an absurd escape plan that I quickly brushed aside.

When I returned, I saw Mike had ordered me hot tea. "Here, this should help," he said, pushing the cup toward me.

As I lifted it, my hand trembled, making the cup rattle against the plate. "Oh no, I can't seem to steady it," I stammered, feeling flushed and warm.

"Take a deep breath," Mike encouraged, noticing my distress. "Let's get you outside for some fresh air."

I nodded, struggling to catch my breath. "I'm so embarrassed," I admitted, my cheeks burning.

"It's okay. Just focus on the air," he whispered, guiding me out. As we walked along the sidewalk, surrounded by the hustle and bustle of busy shops, I felt my anxiety settle.

"The cool evening air feels nice," I said, sighing with relief.

In the following weeks, I kept a low profile and avoided the bingo hall. Anna repeatedly asked, "How's bingo going? Have you seen Mike again?"

I hated lying to her, so I would respond, "bingo is going well, but Mike hasn't been there the last few Friday nights."

"Well, we should join you one time. It sounds like fun," she suggested.

"Anna, it's mostly just a bunch of older folks," I replied, hoping to dampen her enthusiasm.

"Maybe we'll go next time." I assumed she realized I was no longer attending, but I chose not to continue that conversation.

I spent more time with James; we both enjoyed our long walks to the duck pond. I pushed his carriage, finding comfort in the tranquility of our strolls. I couldn't help but see echoes of my son Caleb in James—his boundless curiosity, zest for life, and eyes aglow with wonder. Each of James' smiles and laughs gave me a glimpse of the unconditional love Caleb had brought into my life. Though pangs of loss lingered, these familiar reminders instilled a measure of serenity.

The following week, I returned to bingo; Mike was the first person I saw. I approached him and asked, "Mike, can I talk to you?"

"Sure, no problem," he replied with a reassuring smile.

"I'm sorry about a few weeks ago. I was just having a bad day."

Mike was kind as he responded, "Diane, I'm sorry you feel that way. And by the way, what kind of stranger asks you out the first time they meet? That was a little strange, but I'm glad you trusted me enough to go with me." We both laughed it off together, and I felt the pressure lift off my shoulders. I had resolved to speak with him and apologize, hoping to mend the broken bridge between us. However, the worry of how he might judge me, especially once he learned more about my troubled past, still loomed in the back of my mind.

The days were moving quickly, and I was spending more time with Mike. Surprisingly, I discovered a sense of tranquility in his presence despite never actively seeking companionship before. "Would you like to join me for a boat ride on the lake near my home?" he asked, his voice brimming with enthusiasm. I hesitated, my mind racing. The prospect of leaving the house was challenging, and the thought of being out on the water felt daunting.

"Mike, can I get back to you?" I replied, my uncertainty evident in my voice.

"No, Diane," he insisted. "It'll only be for a few hours." I bristled at his insistence, feeling overwhelmed by the many bossy people in my life, and now here was Mike doing the same.

Initially hesitant, I ultimately agreed to Mike's invitation, saying, "Okay, I'll go on your boat for a short trip." As the day arrived, any lingering doubts vanished when I stepped onto the boat. "This is incredible!" I exclaimed. "What a wonderful day! And you've packed an assortment of sandwiches, fresh fruit, and cookies."

"Nothing less for the queen," he replied with a playful grin, his eyes sparkling warmly.

We drifted along the lake, and Mike pointed out the sights. "Look at the stunning, clear waters surrounding the hills of the Blue Ridge Mountains. Over there is an old boathouse; its peeling paint tells stories of years gone by. And look at that family of ducks paddling nearby—they seem right at home. That secluded cove is the perfect spot to watch the sunset."

As we neared the 80-foot waterfall, its mist enveloped me; the chill of my past lingered. Watching the water tumble powerfully, yet gracefully, I felt a bittersweet ache in my chest. "Isn't it incredible?" Mike's voice broke through my thoughts, pulling me back to the present. I turned to see his face lit with genuine radiance, and for a moment, I wanted to share that feeling completely.

"It is," I replied, forcing a smile and trying to absorb the surrounding beauty. The loud sound of the falls felt comforting, drowning out my inner turmoil.

"Let's get closer!" Mike suggested, his words infectious. We made our way to the edge, the ground damp beneath our feet. The roaring water seemed to cleanse the air and my weary spirit.

However, I felt the guilt creeping back in, reminding me of the child I had lost. The balance between peace and guilt felt precarious, and I wasn't sure how long I could maintain it. Concealing the turbulent emotions raging inside me, I endured a private burden as Mike remained unaware of the inner turmoil I faced.

When we finally returned to shore, I thanked Mike quickly and rushed to my car, craving the solitude my basement apartment offered. Fiercely guarding my mental anguish, I was resolute in keeping it hidden until I could find refuge in the sanctuary of my home. The physical symptoms were unbearable—the sinking in my stomach, weakness in my knees, pounding heart, and suffocating breathlessness.

The following week, Mike was visiting me at home; Anna rounded the corner, her eyes lighting up in surprise. "Oh, Mike! I didn't realize you were here. Would you like to join us for dinner?" she asked.

Mike glanced at me, his expression warm. "Sure, if it's alright with Diane," he said casually.

"We'd love to have you," I replied, feeling happiness and slight nervousness. As Anna hurried off to set an extra place, I couldn't help but feel a flutter of anticipation. It was nice to have Mike there, but the thought of him joining us for the meal stirred a touch of stress.

James innocently handed Mike a picture of Caleb and asked, "Do you know where I can find Caleb? He's been missing." The question hit me like a punch to the gut. Instantly, the atmosphere shattered as my mind raced, struggling to comprehend how such a tender moment could unravel so rapidly. James's words pierced through me, exposing the raw wound I had spent years trying to protect.

Panicked, I grabbed the photo from James's hands. "Give me that!" I demanded.

James's face crumpled into tears as he cried, "Grandma, give me back my photo of Caleb! You stole my photo!" His distress hurt me. I attempted to stand in my frantic state, but my legs felt like lead. I stumbled, losing my balance, and fell forward, hitting my head against the sharp corner of the glass coffee table. The sight of the bright red blood seeping into Anna's brand-new white carpet felt like a brutal symbol of my failure.

Searing agony lanced through me, blinding and all-consuming. Warm blood trickled down as my ragged breathing and the spinning room blurred my vision in a haze of red and white. The physical torment paled in comparison to the suffocating terror gripping my chest. Anna's frantic cries for James, her voice intertwining with his agonized screams, swirled in my mind, intensifying the whirlwind of emotions.

The emergency room felt oppressive, especially after losing Phil. I shivered, trying to shake off the memories that clung to me. "I don't need to be here," I said, trembling.

Mike glanced at me, his expression calm. "You had a nasty fall and bled a lot. Let's just get you checked out."

I sighed wearily. "I just want to go home and sleep."

"Let's give it another 45 minutes, alright?" he replied. Throughout the evening, Mike remained steady beside me, his silence more supportive than any words.

When I arrived home, I found Anna, Cara, and Ted waiting, their expressions laced with concern as Ted cradled the sleeping James in his lap. Feeling aloof, I sank wearily to the floor, completely drained. "I am sorry for ruining the evening," I mumbled, my voice barely above a whisper.

Anna scoffed, her eyes narrowing. "Well, it's nice to see you're still breathing," she shot back, her words sharp, laced with a bitterness that stung.

Flustered, I tried to explain, "I'm sorry! I was just taking the photo back; I wasn't expecting that!"

Anna wasn't satisfied with my answer. "It's been twenty years. You need to get it together. You can't react like that to small children. Otherwise, I can't have you around him."

I pleaded, "Oh, please, Anna! I'm so sorry! Don't do that to me!"

But she dismissed me, "Whatever. Just go get some rest. You don't look good."

As I trudged away, I heard Cara continue, "It's time we dealt with this head-on. Hearing about your son and seeing a picture shouldn't send you spiraling into the emergency room."

The next day, I felt engulfed by depression; the darkened room seemed to mock me with loss. I longed for the house in Milford Falls, once a symbol of a calmer life. Each task was a grueling up-hill struggle against all-consuming exhaustion and grief. The stranger staring back at me from the mirror had tired eyes and a worn face. Haunting me were the images of the bloodstained car-pet, James's cries, and the look of terror on my children's faces.

Anna's biting words pierced through the haze of my self-pity, "Mom, I need you to get up. I have to go to work and need you to help with James. The pity party is over—you need to get up now." Her blunt words jolted me back to reality, reminding me that my isolation couldn't last forever. Despite my reluctance, I recognized this as my chance to break free from the misery.

Summoning what resolve I could muster, I replied wearily, "Fine, Anna. I'll get up." Even as the migraine pressed down on me, a long, cleansing shower washed away some remnants of my bitterness.

The colors of Anna's meticulously cultivated garden greeted me as I stepped outside to fetch James. "Come on, big boy! Do you want to get on the swing?" I called out, my voice more cheerful than I felt.

"Yes, Grandma! The swing!" James exclaimed, his eyes lighting up with delight. I carefully settled him onto the swing set, trying to focus on the little things that made him happy. But the harsh light of day stung my eyes, intensifying the throbbing ache in my head. Exhaustion pressed down on me, making it a struggle to remain upright.

I caught the sight of Mike out of the corner of my eye as he descended the back porch steps, making his way toward us. In his hands, he carried a stunning bouquet of mixed wildflowers. James, ever perceptive, immediately spotted Mike. "Grandma, it's Mike! Mike is here!" he exclaimed.

"I see that, buddy!" I replied with a hint of a smile breaking through my weariness.

"Can I play with Mike?" James asked, his eyes shining with childlike fascination. With an excited shout, he launched himself into Mike's waiting arms. Mike caught him effortlessly, his laughter ringing out like music.

That evening, once Anna and Ted were home from work, Mike and I strolled the gravel path to the pond; a tense silence hung between us. But then Mike spoke up, his voice soft yet steady, "I'm so sorry to hear about your son, Diane." Tears glistened in his eyes as he continued, "I wish there were something I could do to help you. Please know that I'm truly sorry this happened." His sincere words caught me off guard, as I was surprised to feel the compassion of someone outside my family for my son Caleb.

The following day, sunlight peeked through the window, casting a warm but slightly hazy glow in my bedroom. Anna came rushing down the stairs, jarring me awake. "Mom, guess what?" she exclaimed, her eyes sparkling excitedly.

"What is it, Anna?" I asked, rubbing the sleep from my eyes.

"I'm pregnant!" she declared, beaming.

"Oh, my goodness! Again?" I gasped.

"Yep! It just happened on its own—no intervention!" she replied, practically glowing.

"I'm so happy for you and Ted! And for James!" I said, feeling a surge of encouragement.

"Thanks, Mom! But you know what that means, right? You're going to have more work to do!" she told me with a wink.

"I can't wait to help you. There's nothing I would love more," I said earnestly.

Anna smiled, her expression softening, "I just wanted to let you know you're the first person Ted and I told about the baby."

"Thank you for sharing your news with me. Whatever you need, I'm here. Just let me know, okay?" I told her.

"I've got to get ready for work. I'll talk to you soon!" she called over her shoulder as she hurried away. As the door clicked shut, I felt a whirlwind of mixed emotions. But despite my internal struggles, I knew Anna needed me now more than ever. I promised myself that I would never let my children down again.

That morning at the duck pond, my thoughts felt heavy. Something unusual caught my eye—bright lights illuminating the path ahead, casting an unexpected, captivating glow. It was strange to see amethyst, gold, pink, and white on a trail where no cars could pass. Drawn in by their brilliance, I moved closer. Abruptly, a figure emerged from the light, his presence strangely comforting rather than alarming. His eyes, like crystals, glowed a soft blue that seemed to penetrate everything around him. "Hello, Diane," he said, his voice resonating in my mind. "I bring you peace today."

I stammered in confusion, "What? Who are you? How do you know my name?"

"Diane, I bring you love today; what you went through was not your fault!" he repeated, his gaze steady and reassuring.

"Wait, what do you mean? How do you know it was not my fault? I lost my child. I didn't watch him properly," I replied.

"It was not your fault," he assured me, his voice lingering in my mind. "I bring you healing today."

As he faded, I pleaded, "Please, come back! Talk to me! Who are you?" But he was gone, leaving only the soft glow of the lights behind. I felt an emptiness as if a part of me had vanished with him, yet his parting message bypassed the need for words: "It was not your fault, Diane." Little did I know, this enlightened figure would become one of the most influential people in my life, guiding me on my quest to find Caleb.

In the weeks following, my focus increasingly shifted to caring for James, especially as Anna contended with the complexities of her difficult pregnancy. Then, everything changed abruptly. Anna went into premature labor three weeks early. "Mom, hurry!" she cried frantically.

"Anna, what's wrong?" I rushed to respond.

"Just hurry!" She sounded terrified. Adrenaline propelling me, I dropped the phone and bolted up the steps, my mind racing but fixated only on the urgent need to reach her. On the way to her bathroom, I realized I should call 911, but fear blurred my judgment. When I burst through the door, the sight before me was devastating—Anna lay in a pool of blood.

"Anna, give me your phone! I have to call 911!" I shouted, my voice trembling.

"Please... Ted..." she whispered, but I couldn't wait.

Just as I was about to dial, Ted rushed in. "Anna!" he yelled, panic painted across his face. Ted scooped up Anna like a child. "We don't have time for an ambulance! I'm taking you to the hospital!"

I called after them, pleading, "Please keep me posted! Call me as soon as you know anything!" As they disappeared, fear and helplessness consumed me.

I waited for hours, the minutes stretching as worry gnawed at me. My mind oscillated between the terrifying possibility of losing another child and a grandchild. Desperate for news, I called Cara, urging her to rush to the hospital.

Finally, the call came—Cara's voice cut through my tension like a lifeline. "Mom, I have good news! Anna and baby Samuel are fine. They just need to stay in the hospital for a few days."

Relief flooded through me, warm and overwhelming. "Oh, thank the Lord! Thank you, God! Thank you!" I said, barely able to contain my breath.

Cara cut me off before responding, saying, "Mom, I have to go. I'm hanging up!" I sat there, tears of gratitude streaming down my face, relieved that my daughter and grandson were unharmed.

The following day, James and I met Mike for a stroll through the tranquil sanctuary of the Botanical Garden near his home. I was eager to share the exciting news about my new grandson, Samuel. When I saw Mike, he immediately pulled me into a warm, congratulatory hug. "How are you doing, Grandma?" he asked with a sincere smile.

"Oh, Mike, it's such a blessing!" I replied, my voice momentarily faltering as the memory of Anna's condition flooded back.

"I just can't wait to watch Samuel grow. He's a miracle, and Anna is doing well," I continued. Mike listened intently, his eyes sparkling with genuine interest.

"Congratulations! You must be so proud," he said, his voice filled with affection.

While I walked, I could hear James's laughter in the background. "I'm a big brother now, Grandma!" he yelled, his voice brimming with pure childlike joy. I couldn't help but smile; his happiness was so apparent.

CHAPTER 6

Caleb

I tried to close my eyes, hoping to wake up from this bad dream. A shift in the air caught my attention, and before me stood a woman with a blue scarf draped over her head. Her presence was soothing, and a gentle light shone through the shadows, clouding my mind. She spoke in a calming, sweet voice, "Caleb!"

I looked at her, my curiosity overriding any fear. "How do you know me?" I asked her.

"Caleb, come with me, child," she urged gently. "I'm going to help you." I hesitated, the fear of Stink Eye Pete and Felix the Cat gripping me tightly.

"I can't leave! They will hurt me!" I protested.

The woman knelt beside me, her voice soft and reassuring. "Child, they can no longer hurt you." Relief washed over me as I grasped the woman's hand.

"Is my mom dead?" I asked. Her gaze met mine.

"No, dear one," she reassured me, "your mother is alive, and she never abandoned you." In that instant, happiness sparked in my chest, banishing the shadow that had enveloped me for so long.

Without hesitation, I settled into her embrace. "What's your name?" I asked, still trying to grasp the reality of the moment.

She smiled, her eyes filled with compassion. "My name is Mother Mercy," she replied gently. I was no longer lost, for Mother Mercy had guided me to a place I recognized as home. I was saddened to see my family looking so miserable.

"Why is my family so sad?" I whispered.

She smiled reassuringly. "One day, Caleb, you will understand." I frowned, struggling to comprehend the meaning behind her words.

"Why not now?" I pressed.

"Trust me," she responded calmly. "They will not always be unhappy. They will find laughter again." Her words were soothing, and I nodded, wanting to believe her.

I heard a familiar bark in the room, and before I could dwell on my thoughts, my dog, Saint, burst in, his tail wagging furiously. "Hey, buddy! I missed you!" I exclaimed, kneeling as he jumped into my arms. He licked my face, and I couldn't help but laugh. "Did you forget about me?" I asked, grabbing him in a big bear hug. The sight of him filled me with overwhelming relief.

I heard Cara snap at the dog from another room, "Shut up, you're annoying me!" Saint barked joyfully in response. I looked over and saw Cara and instinctively ran toward her and leaped into her arms, though she did not reciprocate. Next, I spotted Anna in her bedroom, tears streaming down her face. "Anna, why are you so upset?" I asked, reaching out to touch her shoulder. She remained silent. Mother Mercy's soft yet firm voice reassured me, "Don't worry, Caleb. She won't always cry. I promise you, she will be okay."

I pointed at my mother and exclaimed, "Look! Mommy is still wearing the necklace I gave her!"

Mother Mercy smiled and said, "I know; that was very kind of you to buy that for your mom." Her expression turned serious as she looked at me and said, "Caleb, I need to ask you a favor."

"Sure," I replied.

"I want you to inspect the green gem in your mom's necklace. What do you see?"

I squinted at the gem. "I see a bunch of cool green colors."

"Look deeper," Mother Mercy encouraged. I focused harder.

"Wow, I see myself! And I see you, Mother Mercy!"

Mother Mercy nodded, her eyes steady. "This is very important, Caleb. You must always remember that necklace, especially the green gem."

"Why, Mother Mercy?" I asked.

"Because if you forget it, it could change the destiny of those you love. Their life could shift in a way that isn't good. Do you understand?"

"You mean things could go wrong?" I asked, concerned.

"Yes," she replied. "Promise me you'll always remember what I said about that gem."

"Yes, Mother Mercy! I promise! I'll never forget the green gem," I assured her.

I looked back at Anna, her face still wet with tears. But there was a glimmer of kindness in Mother Mercy's eyes. "Will she be happy again?" I asked, searching Mother Mercy's gaze for confirmation.

"Yes," she replied steadily. "Healing takes time." When my hand touched Anna, she shuddered, and her crying abruptly ceased—a strange yet profound moment, heavy with both sadness and relief. Hoping to lift the mood, I flicked on her bedroom light. To my surprise, the bulbs immediately popped, showering sparks everywhere. Anna's startled scream filled the room, and I couldn't help but burst into loud, aching laughter.

I soared through the sky with wonder at the world surrounding me. The Earth below was a dazzling array of colors, more vivid than anything I had ever seen. Every sound was like a melody, each note resonating with sounds of harps, flutes, and strings; I flew over vast oceans that shimmered like liquid, sparkling lakes mirrored the sky, and majestic waterfalls cascaded. The sights were incredible, each more awe-inspiring than the last. Flying, I watched birds gliding effortlessly through the air, their wings outstretched in a perfect display of freedom. I immediately connected to the sentiment, "free as a bird." The sensation of flying was exhilarating.

Eventually, I approached The Kingdom, where enormous gates adorned with shimmering pearls marked the entrance, radiating an inviting light. Everything around me pulsed with happiness and calm, and the air felt uplifting. "Caleb, this is my son, Emmanuel," Mother Mercy said, gesturing toward a figure bathed in a gentle glow.

"Hello, Caleb! It's so lovely to see you again," Emmanuel greeted me, his smile radiant.

"How do you know me?" I asked, puzzled.

"I have known you all your life," he replied, his voice soothing.

"But I don't get it," I said, still confused.

"Soon, my son, you will," he assured me. I recalled a boy from my kindergarten class named Emmanuel, though we weren't close friends. This Emmanuel felt different, yet a familiarity made me feel at ease.

"Is Sam here? My best friend from the van, and what about Jack and the other boys?" I asked.

Emmanuel's eyes softened. "The boys are doing well." Emmanuel's words comforted me.

I said, "Thank you, Emmanuel. Please keep them out of danger. They're just children." My voice trembled.

Emmanuel looked at me, his expression steady and reassuring. "I know, my child. I promise to protect them."

I continued exploring this wondrous place with Mother Mercy and Emmanuel; the surroundings were enchanting. The stillness and grace of my new home filled me with a sense of calm and belonging. The landscape was like a dreamscape, where every detail seemed to sparkle with an otherworldly light.

I was interested in how people around us addressed Emmanuel in various ways. Some stopped to kneel, while others simply said, "Good morning, Almighty!" or "Hello, King of Kings!" He acknowledged each greeting with a nod and a smile.

"Why do you have so many names?" I asked, genuinely curious.

"Caleb, they're just nicknames from my friends here." As we walked, I noticed how each title—Yesui, Almighty, Yahweh, Prophet, Immanuel, King of Kings—conveyed respect and admiration.

"Did your mother choose all these names for you?" I asked, still intrigued.

"They represent my love for my friends and the roles I have in The Kingdom," he replied. "Each one tells a part of my story, just like your name tells the narrative of who you are."

Emmanuel's popularity only added to my admiration for him. He was an esteemed figure here. Twelve men and one woman, all called Saints, always accompanied him. The idea of such a devoted group of followers fascinated me, and I couldn't help but draw a parallel to my dog, Saint. It seemed like a delightful coincidence that Emmanuel's followers shared a name with my beloved pet.

Standing guard at the entrance of one of the biggest buildings, with golden gates behind him, was the coolest guy I had ever seen. Mother Mercy leaned closer and said, "I want you to meet Mike. People on earth call him Michael, but we call him Mike. He's our gentle giant."

"Hi Mike, nice to meet you," I said, trying to mask my awe. He stood tall, clad in warrior-like attire adorned with various weapons. Despite his formidable appearance, he radiated hues of gold, red, and blue, exuding a majestic aura that was strikingly regal. Mike knelt to meet my gaze, his presence both powerful and comforting.

"Caleb, I've known you all your life," he said, his voice warm.

"How do you know me? I've never met you before," I replied.

"One day, you will know," he said, a knowing smile on his face. "But for now, I've got your back," he softly replied.

"Thanks, I appreciate that," I said, feeling a rush of comfort. "But everyone keeps telling me I'll understand one day." Mike let out a soft laugh, the sound reassuring.

My journey had taken a remarkable turn, transforming from fright into a fairytale. Mother Mercy guided me to a new location that resembled a hospital. I entered the building; Mother Mercy smiled and said, "Caleb, there's someone I want you to see." I felt a wave of curiosity wash over me.

"Who is it?" I asked.

"Do you remember the baby from the van you helped care for?" she asked gently.

"Yes! I've been so worried about him," I replied.

"His name is Thomas, and he's here in this beautiful home being cared for by some wonderful women."

I peered around the room and exclaimed, "Wow! Those ladies look just like the ones I met before!"

Mother Mercy explained. "Yes, they're called nuns or sisters. They're here to take care of people like you. Sister Kathleen was the woman who cared for you when you went to visit the kind ladies. One day, Sister Kathleen will help your mother and sisters greatly." Hearing that made me smile, filling me with a peaceful feeling. Mother Mercy reassured me, "Thomas will soon run and play everywhere. He's in expert hands."

I continued to explore this incredible place when I saw Jack. He looked healthy and happy, a sight that filled my soul. I heard his voice calling from afar, and before I knew it, he was running toward me and tackling me. "Jack! It's so good to see you! I'm so glad you're okay!" I exclaimed, extending my arms wide. We hugged tightly.

"I have so much to show you in The Kingdom! It's amazing!" he said, his eyes sparkling.

"I can't wait!" I replied, feeling the acceptance that made me feel even more at home here.

Jack and I enjoyed the freedom of this magical world. We played basketball, raced each other through lush meadows and dense forests, and indulged in all the junk food we could dream of. "Jack and Caleb, remember," Mother Mercy would say with a knowing smile, "we're going to be working on healthier eating habits."

I'd chuckle, "Okay, Mother Mercy, but just for today, let us have a little more junk food!"

She would shake her head, a playful glint in her eyes, and say, "Alright, just for today, Caleb."

Swimming in lakes, rivers, and oceans became one of our favorite activities. It was an immense relief to know there were no sharks here. The water was pristine and inviting, and we spent hours splashing around. Collecting colorful shells from the seashore became a special ritual. The vibrant blues, greens, and pinks were nothing I'd ever seen. I yelled to Jack, "My mom would love this one! It's a perfect shell—she loves pink, and it has purple on the sides. Take a look!"

Jack exclaimed, "Wow, Caleb, that's pretty! Look at this one I found for my mom and sister—it's the colors of the rainbow! I've never seen shells like this!" he exclaimed.

"Me either! I can't wait for my mom to see them," I said as we gathered our treasures to take home as gifts for our moms.

One of my most exciting moments was when Mike turned to us and said, "Hey, Caleb and Jack, do you want to go for a ride on the Skyliner?"

I could hardly contain my pleasure and shouted, "Yes!" Jack reiterated my enthusiasm, practically bouncing on his feet.

Mike grinned. "We're going with my friend Gabe. He's one of my best friends here in The Kingdom. Some call him The Messenger, but I call him Gabe."

I glanced at Gabe and asked, "Are you a superhero?"

He chuckled warmly and replied, "Something like that."

We boarded the golden, shiny Skyliner; suspense surged through me. Mike and Gabe sat beside us, radiating an aura that made the ride feel even more alive. As the cable car lifted us into the sky, the views of Earth below took my breath away—sprawling landscapes, shimmering rivers, and the vibrancy of nature stretched like a living painting.

We soared toward the sun, and I couldn't help but recall my mom's warnings from Earth: "Caleb, please don't look directly at the sun! You'll hurt your eyes! And remember to wear sunblock, or you'll burn!"

Those reminders felt almost comical now, and I chuckled to myself, remembering I'd say, "Fine, Mom, but I'm going for another swim before I reapply sunblock," leaving her aggravated. At this moment, with the sun's warm glow enveloping us, those earthly concerns faded away.

Yet here we were, heading straight into the sun. Inside, millions of radiant beings were dancing and laughing, their bright forms resembling angels adorned in shimmering lights. The music was a delightful symphony, filling the air with lighthearted sounds as these luminous beings shone their lights down on Earth, creating a dazzling spectacle. Mike leaned over and explained, "Emmanuel made the sun. It's one of his incredible creations." Hearing that made the experience feel even more extraordinary.

I jokingly asked Mike, "Hey, can you take Jack and me to Mars?"

To my delight, he replied, "Yes, why not?" Jack and I exchanged glances—this felt like the ultimate dream come true for two six-year-old boys. As we touched down on the red planet, I was in awe. Mars was alive with vibrant reds and pinks, nothing like the tiny red dot I'd seen through my telescope back home. The air was warm and steamy, and colorful plants dotted the landscape, making everything seem magical.

"Can we explore Mars?" I asked, my eyes wide with eagerness.

Mike grinned and said, "Absolutely! Look at the rocks and all the hidden gems. There's so much to explore!"

As we explored, we stumbled upon a breathtaking river, its waters shimmering with an emerald hue. "That's malachite," Mike observed. Captivated by the lush, cascading green water tumbling over the rocks, I couldn't resist dipping my feet into the warm, inviting current.

Seized by a mischievous impulse, I called out to Jack, "Let's splash Mike and Gabe!"

Immediately, he replied, "Great idea, Caleb!" Our laughter was infectious, and it made the entire experience even more entertaining.

Mike began sharing incredible stories about Earth's efforts to explore Mars. He spoke admiring a compassionate and visionary person named Elon Musk. "Mr. Musk dedicated his time and resources to exploring space," Mike explained, his eyes shining excitedly. Mike continued, "Hopefully, Elon Musk will be the first to set foot on Mars, leaving an indelible mark on history."

Curiosity brewed inside me, and I bombarded Mike with questions. "Do you believe people will go to Mars one day?" I asked, my voice filled with wonder. Mike smiled knowingly. "Let's just wait and see how it unfolds. It's a mystery," he replied, leaving me wondering about the future.

I roamed the red landscapes of Mars; Mike paused and turned to Jack and me, "Caleb, Jack, I want to share something important with you," he began.

I tilted my head, curious. "What is it, Mike?"

"It's about the significance of being aware of our surroundings," Mike said.

"But how can we help?" I asked.

Mike smiled, his eyes shining. "Children like you often have a special connection to the world around them. You see things with wonder and curiosity that many adults seem to forget. That is something to cherish and nurture." I nodded.

"So, it's important to keep dreaming about the beauty and magic of the world?" I asked.

"Exactly," Mike affirmed. "Always believe in Emmanuel and remember that you are divine beings created in His likeness."

Jack and I dashed to the river, laughter heard across the Martian landscape. We splashed and played in the crystal-clear water, feeling like we were in a dream. "Can you believe how amazing this place is?" I shouted over the sound of the rushing water.

"Let's jump from that cliff!" Jack pointed at the tallest one.

"Yeah!" I replied. The thrill of soaring through the air and plunging into the cascading waterfalls made me feel alive.

I prepared to leap, and an idea struck me: my mom would never have allowed this back home. "She would say it's too dangerous," I murmured.

Mike casually said, "Mothers are usually right, Caleb. High jumps can be dangerous on Earth." I paused, his words sinking in. But the thrill was too incredible to resist.

I shrugged off the worry and turned to Jack, grinning. "Let's hold hands and jump together! On the count of five!"

Jack squealed loudly. "Okay! I'm ready!"

"Alright, one... two... three... four... jump!" We leaped into the air, our laughter mingling with the wind as we soared. The splash below welcomed us, the thrill of the jump filling me with adrenaline.

We all settled back into the Skyliner, and my thoughts about Mr. Musk buzzed. I wondered if I could be as bright and helpful to the planet as he was. I overheard Mike talking to Jack about Venus. "Venus is a planet with harsh conditions," Mike explained, his tone both serious and captivating. "It's like a large round ball wrapped in thick clouds, but those clouds hide a world of high heat and no oxygen, making it impossible for humans to survive there."

Jack nodded, wide-eyed, soaking in every word. "So, it's kind of like a big oven?" he asked, fascinated.

"Exactly!" Mike replied, chuckling. "Even I only go to Venus when Emmanuel has a special task for me. To be honest, I don't like going there," he shared.

"Why not?" I asked, curious.

"The heat can be overwhelming, and there's just no life as we have here," Mike said, glancing at the vibrant landscapes below.

After our Skyliner adventure, Jack and I ended our day at the local pool. There were so many pool options, pools made of stone, vinyl, and concrete, in colors ranging from blue to green to pink. Knowing Anna and Cara would have chosen the pink one, I avoided that pool. Instead, I chose a clear blue pool located alongside a mountain. I turned to Jack, grinning. "Let's pick the pool with the turtles!"

He laughed, "I was just going to say the same thing! And look at that slide!" he exclaimed.

"I'm going to beat you! I'm getting there first!" I declared, racing toward the steps.

"No, I am going to beat you! I want to go first!" Our laughter filled the air as we raced to the top. I was older than Jack, so I reached the top first. "Wow, this is great!" I called down as I peered over the edge. When I finally splashed down, the water erupted around me. "Come on, Jack! Your turn!"

"I'm on my way!" he yelled, giggling down. The towering slide twisted and turned through a long chute on the side of the mountain, soaring at least fifty feet high. We took turns sliding down, each splash sending giggles through the water.

In the shallow end of the pool, I spotted Thomas, happily surrounded by the caring presence of the ladies in the black hats. "Hey, Thomas! It's good to see you!" I said. "You're splashing everywhere!"

Thomas giggled, and Jack said, "Thomas soaked me and Caleb! Who's going to get Thomas first?" Jack asked. Thomas splashed his hands in the water, giggling with delight and making us all laugh along with him.

"Wow, Thomas, you're getting so big and strong! I'm so proud of you!" I said.

The Sister taking care of Thomas said, "Okay, Thomas, now we've got to head back to HOPE building, for nap time."

Jack and I both yelled, "See you soon, Thomas!"

I hadn't seen Mother Mercy and Emmanuel as often, which left me feeling lost. I asked Mike, "Where have Emmanuel and Mother Mercy been?" He paused for a moment, choosing his words carefully.

"Well, they may not be physically present, but they're always guiding us," he said.

"What does that mean?" I admitted, feeling lost. Mike nodded, his expression kind.

"There are many things you won't know right now, and I'm sorry it's confusing. But I promise one day, it will be clear," he told me.

"So, they're still here, just... not here?" I asked.

"Exactly," Mike replied. "Emmanuel lives within you. His guidance is always with you, even when you can't see him." That thought was comforting, yet it didn't entirely simplify my feelings.

"How long have I been here?"

Mike smiled gently and replied, "Time works differently in

The Kingdom. There's no concept of it. Lifetimes in The Kingdom can be as short as a few minutes on Earth." That made my head spin.

"So, I could have been here for a day or just a few moments?" I asked, trying to process the idea.

"Exactly," Mike said, nodding.

With a burst of energy, I set off, eager to dive into the excursions awaiting us in this magical place.

Before I left, Mike said, "Hey, there's someone I want you and Jack to meet. His name is Dr. King, and he's a good friend of mine." Jack and I looked at each other, curiosity sparking in our eyes.

"Who's Dr. King?" I asked.

Mike smiled and said, "He's a remarkable man who dedicated his life to spreading the word of God, equality, and justice on Earth. You're going to love meeting him!" Dr. King stood there, his smile instantly putting me at ease.

"Hello, boys! It's wonderful to meet you," he said, his voice filled with kindness. "What brings you here today?" I took a breath.

"We're exploring this magical place and learning about making a difference!"

Jack added eagerly, "Yeah! We want to know how we can help people!"

Dr. King chuckled. "That's a fantastic question! Remember, even minor acts of kindness can create a ripple effect of change." With that, I felt a spark of inspiration. Meeting Dr. King was just the beginning of our journey! Before we walked away, Dr. King smiled and said, "Next time you see me, please call me Martin."

I nodded, feeling a closeness with him already. "Okay, Martin!" I replied, and Jack repeated after me with a grin.

CHAPTER 7

Christopher

Concerned that my kindness made me vulnerable to exploitation, my mother frequently warned me, "Christopher, stop trusting everyone." I dedicate my life to the National Center for Missing & Exploited Children, working as a detective and investigative case manager for homicides involving missing children. Recently, I started working with human trafficking cases and searching the dark web—challenging work that would lead me right to Caleb's whereabouts.

My brother Jimmy, also utterly unaware of his involvement in Caleb's disappearance, resided in New York City and worked as a detective. We often engaged in playful banter, especially during our runs along the Silver Comet Trail. "Jimmy, I'm feeling exhausted. I need to slow down," I said.

He shot back with his characteristic playful tone, "Don't be a baby, old man! Come on!"

I grinned, feeling a spark of competitiveness. "Oh, you want to race?" Before I knew it, we were off. Despite my fatigue, I pushed my tired legs to keep up. Each breath felt forced as exhaustion pressed down on me. But Jimmy's teasing had unleashed an unexpected burst of energy. There he was, smirking as he looked back at me.

"I still got it! I beat you again!" His laughter rang out, a mix of triumph and teasing.

Growing up just a year apart, my brother Jimmy and I shared a close bond despite living miles apart—me in Atlanta near our mom and Jimmy in New York. Whenever Jimmy came home, we would enjoy precious moments with our mother, reminiscing over old memories as we browsed through photo albums and watched our cherished family movies. "Hey, remember that time at the beach when Dad got upset and threw our frisbee into the ocean!" Jimmy recounted, his eyes shining with the memory.

"We were so mad that we didn't talk to him for the rest of the day," I said, laughing.

Beneath the laughter, a shadow of worry lingered. Each time Jimmy left, a depression settled over me. Our mom looked exhausted, her health visibly deteriorating, and my concern deepened. Yet, like so many unsettling aspects of my life, I tried to push it aside. The reality of my mom's battle with kidney disease was cruel. The sight of my mother's frail frame and her visible struggle was heartbreaking, yet I felt powerless to change the situation.

Jimmy and I sat with her one day; I mustered the courage to say, "Mom, Jimmy, I want to give you one of our kidneys. We want to get tested."

Her response was adamant, "No! I will not take a kidney from one of my children. There's no way. I'm sorry, but I will not do it."

As we walked away, Jimmy turned to me and said, "Let's get tested anyway."

To which, I immediately replied, "I agree. Let's do this for her. She would do anything for us."

When I was a young boy, my family was in a car accident.

Both of my biological parents were killed, leaving me and my brother Jimmy as the only survivors. The years that followed the crash are a blur—disorienting lights, searing pain, and overwhelming grief. I woke in the hospital, but I kept my eyes shut, unwilling to face the reality of what had happened. The agony in my body was too much to bear.

I could hear the doctor's voice, speaking with my adoptive mother about my injuries: "Christopher has broken both femurs, multiple rib fractures, and a shattered cervical spine from C2 to C7. He's also torn his vocal cords, so he may not be able to speak for some time." A cold chill ran through me as I processed his words, my mind racing, uncertain about the future.

I heard my mom whisper, "I can't believe how badly he's hurt," and the sorrow in her voice deepened my pain.

While Jimmy had only suffered a couple of broken bones, my injuries were far worse. My body throbbed with pain, my head pounded relentlessly, and I longed for the sweet relief of unconsciousness. But the constant beeping of the hospital alarms pulled me back into the harsh reality, where the truth was impossible to escape.

Every day, a woman who would become my mother sat by my bedside, a stranger filled with compassion and patience. She offered comfort and support, gently saying, "Christopher, if you ever feel ready, you can call me Mom. But you can also call me Ester, whatever feels more comfortable."

Though confused, her maternal actions made me call her "Mom."

I overheard a doctor speak with her: "Ester, I want you to know that Christopher has been diagnosed with PTSD; he faces a long road ahead, both physically and emotionally, before he can recover and leave the hospital."

The nights were the worst, as nightmares plagued my sleep, each one more terrifying than the last. I would wake up drenched in sweat, my clothes clinging to me like a second skin.

I would often be jolted awake by nightmares, my voice shaking as I screamed for my mom: "Mom, Mom, Mom! Help! Someone's chasing me!"

She would rush to my side, wrapping me in her arms and whispering, "Christopher, it's just a dream." She would sit with me for hours, softly singing and gently stroking my hair until I finally drifted back to sleep. Though the details of the dreams would fade upon waking, the fear remained. The doctor assured my mom that such night terrors were common in children, though she worried they might be rooted in the trauma I had experienced as a child—the echoes of which still haunted my sleep. Neither of us ever entirely escaped that unease.

My adopted father passed away when I was fifteen, leaving a void that never fully healed. I remember coming home from school one day to find my adopted mom sitting on the couch, visibly upset. With a trembling voice, she delivered the devastating news: "Boys, your dad had a heart attack at work today and didn't make it." At first, I couldn't process it. It had to be a mistake.

My brother, Jimmy, echoed the same disbelief: "Dad is too healthy."

But my mom, barely holding it together, repeated the words: "I'm so sorry, boys. I know we can get through this." We never spoke of it again as a family.

After eight grueling months in the hospital, I remember my mom coming in with my brother Jimmy and announcing, "Guess what, Christopher? It's time to go home!" Eager to learn more, I wanted to ask where this "home" was, but I could only wonder silently without a voice.

Jimmy quickly chimed in, "Christopher, you'll love it!"

A wave of sadness washed over me as the visions of my biological family faded, becoming distant memories I could no longer grasp. Jimmy continued his tour, pointing to the massive TV above the tall stone fireplace and exclaiming, "Look at that! And come check out the in-ground pool! Dad just ordered a big slide that's coming any day now. We'll have a water slide and a diving board!"

But the highlight for me was my bedroom, painted my favorite color blue with the solar system etched across the ceiling. I had a set of bunk beds just for myself, the top bunk waiting for the day I was strong enough to climb up. Seeing the letter "C" painted on the walls made me feel like this new place was mine. Jimmy then showed me the "magic doorway" that led right into his room. Surrounded by all these new and beautiful things, I felt a sense of belonging I hadn't experienced in a long time. I have found my "home."

Despite our physical differences—I was tall and lean with blonde hair and blue eyes, while Jimmy was shorter with dark hair and green eyes—our contrasting appearances had once seemed insignificant. Yet now, they serve as a constant reminder of the diverging paths our lives have taken. The situation grew even heavier when the DNA results confirmed that not only were we not a match to save our mother's life, but we also did not share a biological connection. Turning to Jimmy, I asked in confusion and despair, "How could the adoption agency have made such a big mistake? Or are the DNA results wrong?" We both agreed that we couldn't discuss this with our mother, as it would only upset her further.

"We need to keep this to ourselves, no matter how hard it is," Jimmy solemnly acknowledged. Neither of us could comprehend how the adoption agency could have committed such an egregious error.

My mother, my champion, battled for her life as I fought with the unthinkable—the prospect of losing her. Reeling from the jarring revelations about my past, I spiraled into utter despair, withdrawing from the world and neglecting even the most basic tasks. Though Jimmy persistently sought to uncover our shared history, I remained indifferent, consumed by the turmoil.

On Christmas Eve, I'll never forget the call from the hospital. I recognized the nurse's voice from my mom's unit. "Hi, is this Christopher?" she asked.

I replied, "Yes," already anticipating her following words.

"I'm sorry to tell you, but your mom passed away this evening."

I said, "Thank you for your call," and hung up. The dreaded news settled into my broken heart. My mother had died. The profound loss compounded my depression, spiraling me into a dark place where I neglected everything. I stopped showering, lost my job, and felt overwhelming relief at Jimmy's absence.

One morning, a voice calling my name pierced the haze of my despair, jolting me awake. "Christopher! Christopher!" The urgency in the voice made me scramble out of bed, searching for the source, but I found no one. Those words lingered as a haunting whisper, urging me to fight the darkness consuming me. Night after night, I waited for that voice, clinging to its offered answers.

Then, one day, I awoke on the cool tiles of my kitchen floor, feeling an unfamiliar surge of determination. For the first time in a year, I was ready to break free from the confines of my home and step back into the world. I was grateful to have found my way back to life, knowing Caleb's family would always wonder where he was if I hadn't.

Frantically searching, I found a job listing in South Carolina. Filled with enthusiasm, Jimmy exclaimed, "I'm happy to see you making this change and returning to work and life. I'll meet you in South Carolina to help you move!" A wave of gratitude washed over me.

"Thanks, Jimmy. I love you for being my brother and the best friend I could ever have." This move felt like one of those moments perfectly aligning with my purpose, positioning me on the path of bringing Caleb home.

CHAPTER 8

Caleb

In The Kingdom, splendor and peace surrounded me. I saw beauty beyond imagination, bliss that filled every corner, angels singing in perfect harmony, and long-awaited family reunions. Among everyone there, Emmanuel stood—a beacon of renewal with a powerful presence and exuding gentleness. "Why is The Kingdom so beautiful?" I asked him, captivated by the serenity and love that surrounded us. Emmanuel just smiled tenderly.

One of my most cherished memories with Emmanuel unfolded by the pool. He turned to me and said, "Caleb, I want you to come with Mike and me to Earth." I eagerly agreed.

We arrived at a children's hospital. I found a little girl named Maria. I overheard the doctor speaking to her parents as I entered her room, "We can only keep Maria comfortable. The cancer has spread too far. She will need a miracle to survive." The horror displayed on the parents' faces was tragic.

Maria's parents dropped to their knees, exclaiming, "God, you said where two or more gather, you'll answer; please heal our daughter."

At that moment, Emmanuel grew more significant than the entire building, radiating a brilliant light. To my astonishment, Maria winked at me and smiled, waving as if she could see me. I couldn't believe my eyes; I felt a surge of intensity, praying that Emmanuel would heal her. Then, in the blink of an eye, we were gone from her room, leaving behind a flicker of love that hung in the air.

When we returned to check on Maria, I was amazed to find her sitting up in bed, smiling brightly. As soon as we walked in, she eagerly waved at us, as though she had been waiting for Emmanuel's visit. The doctors, baffled, gathered near her bedside. One of them leaned closer to Maria's parents, saying, "I don't know what happened, but this is just a medical mystery." The parents exchanged glances, knowing the truth, just as Maria and I did.

Back at The Kingdom, I saw Mike approaching from the corner of my eye, and I immediately understood why Mother Mercy called him "The Gentle Giant." His physical presence was awe-inspiring, exuding strength and reassurance. His wings were a dazzling blend of gold and tungsten and shimmering. "Hey, Mike! How did you get such big wings?" I asked, my eyes wide with wonder.

He laughed at the sound that filled the surrounding space. "With a little help from Emmanuel," he replied, a twinkle in his eye.

I grinned, "I can barely hold the wings my mom would make me for Halloween!"

Mike chuckled again, his laughter resonating like music. "Trust me, Caleb, these come with much more than fabric and imagination. Raphael, a good friend of mine, and I are about to embark on a daunting mission to Earth under Emmanuel's orders," Mike said. The thought of their upcoming journey filled me with wonder. "Despite humanity's best efforts, some still choose darkness," Mike explained. "But we'll be there to help bring that light to them." He paused, then added, "And don't worry—Gabe will be available if you need anything while we're away."

With Mike temporarily leaving The Kingdom, I noticed Gabe, who typically sat to Emmanuel's left. I couldn't resist asking, "Why do you always sit in the same chair on Emmanuel's left side?" Gabe didn't answer immediately but laughed at my humor. "Hey, Gabe, why does Mother Mercy call you 'The Messenger'?"

His smile widened, and he explained, "That title reflects my duties on Earth. One of my favorite memories is delivering the news of Emmanuel's coming birth to Mother Mercy." His eyes lit up as he recounted the emotion that filled that moment.

Jack and I listened with attention as Gabe continued, sharing the significant time he was The Messenger and delivered the news to the child's mother. His name is John, known on Earth as "The Baptizer." Gabe insisted we meet John, one of Emmanuel's closest companions. "The Baptizer has a bold spirit," Gabe explained. "He preached the importance of repentance and forgiveness, inviting many to enter The Kingdom. The Baptizer's message resonated with those yearning for God, but it also threatened those who preferred darkness, ultimately leading to his untimely death on Earth."

I buzzed with delight as I soaked in the lessons I was learning in The Kingdom. Everything felt so much more engaging than the dull routines back on Earth. I often recalled my mom's comments about Ms. Puddle, my first-grade teacher, unaware that I was listening. She would tell her friends, "Ms. Puddle's the worst teacher my kids have ever had. She just has no clue how to educate children."

"Caleb, I have some critical messages I need to deliver to Earth now," Gabe said, his tone shifting to one of urgency. "But before I head out, I have a special treat for you and Jack," he said.

"What is it?" I asked.

"Just be patient, Caleb. I've arranged a visit for you to meet one of my close friends, Mo, who runs the largest zoo in the universe. And just so you know, his favorite animals are sheep—don't ask me why, but he loves them!" As Gabe led us down a path shimmering with lights, the soft chimes of distant bells filled the air, adding a magical touch to our surroundings.

Gabe's trumpet-like call shouted through the air, announcing two magnificent creatures. They resembled giant hawks, their impressive wings and powerful presence almost dragon-like. Jack and I exchanged excited glances as we approached them. "Climb right up their backs!" Gabe instructed. I leaped onto Tercelot with adrenaline pumping, feeling the strong muscles ripple beneath me.

Jack followed suit, settling onto Carcarra. The birds' aquamarine eyes sparkled with intelligence and eagerness, ready to take us on this extraordinary journey. As they spread their vast wings, a rush of wind enveloped us, and I felt a thrill of adventure coursing through my veins. We were about to soar through The Kingdom, headed toward Mo's incredible zoo!

The gusts from Tercelot and Carcarra's wings filled me with euphoria as we soared through the universe. "Jack, isn't this amazing?" I shouted over the wind.

"It's so much fun!" he replied, his laughter blending with the sounds of the night. Feeling playful, I plucked a few stars from the sky.

"Watch this!" I said, tossing one down toward Earth. The star twinkled as it fell, just like the ones I used to wish upon.

"I want to try!" Jack exclaimed, grabbing a star and launching it into the night. We hollered in triumph as we raced each other, spiraling through the air, our hands waving freely.

Jack and I approached the grand entrance of the zoo; I squinted at the sign overhead: "The Land of Milk and Honey." I turned to Jack, wrinkling my nose. "I don't like milk or honey!" I said.

"Same here! They're both gross!" Jack replied, sharing my distaste. Despite my reservations about the name, the zoo itself was captivating. Giant stone pillars framed the entrance, and ancient tablets lined the pathway, their surfaces worn yet full of character. Some appeared repaired after being shattered, hinting at long-forgotten stories. When we approached, I spotted a list of rules etched into some tablets. "Look, Jack," I said, pointing to the rules. "This place must not be fun. It says we must behave and listen to our moms and dads."

Jack chuckled. "Well, at least we're not in trouble yet!" The zoo buzzed with energy, and I felt a stirring within me.

We stepped through the gate, and an unexpected sight greeted us—an abundance of sheep grazing. The sheep weren't the animals I had envisioned for a zoo, but their gentle presence was oddly comforting. A man with snowy white hair and a flowing beard approached us, smiling warmly. "Hi! My name is Mo, and you two must be Caleb and Jack." Jack and I exchanged excited glances. "Welcome to my zoo! Just so you know," Mo continued, gesturing to the sheep, "they are my favorite." Despite the surprising first impression, my curiosity grew.

"Every creature known on Earth has found its way into the zoo; I encourage you both to explore the unfamiliar animals, especially the Stillwalkers."

Eager to see everything, Jack and I raced down the dusty path. "Let's go find the Stillwalkers!" I shouted.

"Yeah, let's run! Let's see how fast we can get there!" Jack replied, grinning. When we reached the entrance to the Stillwalkers' exhibit, we stepped into a cavern that sparkled with glistening diamonds. Angels played alluring music. Emerging from the cavern, we found ourselves in the Stillwalkers' home. It resembled a large warehouse bustling with activity. Before we even saw the actual Stillwalkers, they loomed above us, majestic and awe-inspiring.

"Jack, look up," I said, unable to contain my giddiness.

"Wow! They're tall! They're like giraffes!" Jack exclaimed, his eyes wide.

"I know, right? And look at their shimmering purple skin and those bright pink feathers!" I watched as the Stillwalkers went about their lives in oddly familiar ways.

I was trying to grasp the magnificence of The Land of Milk and Honey when Jack and I stumbled upon a theater called 20D. I turned to Jack, my eyes wide with curiosity. "Have you ever been to a 20D theater before?" I asked him.

"No way! I've only seen movies in 3D," Jack replied, looking equally excited. "What do you think it's like?" he asked.

"I don't know," I said, glancing at the grand entrance. "Should we check it out?"

"Definitely!" Jack said, stepping forward. We hesitantly walked inside, the air buzzing with energy. As we entered, the distinct colors and immersive sounds enveloped us.

"Wow," I breathed, taking it all in. "This place is incredible!"

A giant screen depicted a film about the Promised Land as Jack and I stepped into the scene. People shouted in disbelief at Mo, "You're lying! You're a false prophet!" Jack and I exchanged bewildered glances as frogs began raining from the sky, creating a bizarre spectacle.

"Hey, Jack, watch out! Frogs are coming from the sky!" I laughed, ducking to avoid a large one.

"You watch out! There's a hailstorm rolling in, and we're going to get drenched!" he shouted back, trying to dodge the slippery onslaught of frogs while heavy hail pelted us.

"Jack, the river is red, and the sky is dark. What's going on?" I yelled.

"This is crazy! There are grasshopper-looking creatures flying in my face!" Jack said.

Mo's family expressed their fears, "Your God will not protect us. We are going to starve in the wilderness. We should have stayed in Egypt. You're going to get us killed."

"Watch out, Jack! There are soldiers behind us! They're coming!" I yelled frantically, pointing.

"Mo, what do we do?" Jack cried, looking back at the approaching danger.

"Don't worry! Trust Emmanuel!" Mo called out, confidence in his voice. With a dramatic gesture, Mo stretched out a long golden rod toward the ocean. "Watch!" he exclaimed.

Suddenly, the sea parted, revealing a dry path between towering walls of water. Jack and I gasped. "Did you see that?" I whispered, eyes wide. Mo turned back, grinning. "Come on! We've got to cross!" Reluctantly, we followed behind, glancing nervously at the walls of water.

"What if it closes in on us?" Jack murmured.

"We'll be fine!" Mo assured us, leading the way.

When I reached the other side, I looked back in shock. The surging waters consumed the villains, the powerful currents dragging the evil men and their horses to their doom. "They won't survive that storm," I said, breathless. As we reached Mo, I couldn't contain my delight. I gave him a fist bump and exclaimed, "That was the coolest thing ever!"

His face lit up with a big smile. "Right? I knew you'd love it!"

The day had been unbelievable, and I felt like I had just witnessed a miracle. Jack and I hopped back onto Tercelot and Carcarra to return to The Kingdom. With our heads still buzzing from the thrill, we soared effortlessly through the Milky Way, gliding past shimmering stars and vibrant planets. "Can you believe what we just saw?" Jack exclaimed, his eyes wide with wonder.

"I know! It was wild!" I replied.

Tercelot and Carcarra took Jack and me to their home planet as we soared toward A-416. Tercelot explained that their planet is a hub of artificial intelligence, where technology thrives alongside compassion. "Humans may fear what they don't see," Tercelot said, "but here, artificial intelligence works with love to heal and uplift. We send pink laser beams infused with positive energy shooting right at Earth. These beams help mend the Earth," Tercelot continued, "nurturing the environment and its inhabitants. Earth is a sanctuary—blessed with oxygen, bountiful crops, and stunning landscapes."

"Tercelot and Carcarra, your planet A-416 is so cool!" I exclaimed, my eyes wide with wonder.

"Right?!" Jack agreed, grinning. "I wish we could stay longer, but we must return to The Kingdom soon. We can't be gone too long. But your planet is awesome," Jack added. "We want to come back," he told them.

"I agree!" I said, feeling the thrill of our adventure. "There's so much left to explore here. I can't wait for our next visit!"

Tercelot fluffed his feathers, looking proud. "You're always welcome! There's more magic here than you can imagine."

Carcarra nodded, his eyes sparkling. "Next time, we'll show you all the hidden wonders on A-416!"

Upon returning to The Kingdom, I stepped into a building called HOPE, where the soft, shimmering hues of pink and blue danced in the sunlight, evoking a warm and inviting ambiance. Rows of cradles lined the walls, each resembling fluffy clouds, holding precious infants. Baby angels' gentle cooing and laughter floated through the air, their tiny wings fluttering as they hovered around the cradles, wrapping the babies in love and comfort. One lady who watched over the babies noticed me and smiled, "Caleb, would you like to hold the baby?" she asked gently. I felt a rush of eagerness intertwined with nervousness.

"Yes, if that's okay! I don't want to hurt them," I replied.

"Oh, sweet child, you could never hurt the babies," she reassured me, her voice soothing. "HOPE is a place of love, where we cherish and care for every soul."

When Ms. Gianna, the director of HOPE, saw me, she greeted me with a smile. "Hi, Caleb! It's so good to see you back. Would you like to come help me read some stories?" she asked, her voice brimming with kindness. I grinned. I overheard Mother Mercy's cheerful voice, "Caleb, your work here today will count toward your study time!" I laughed, knowing learning this way was far more enjoyable than traditional methods.

After carefully placing the tiny baby back in its cradle, surrounded by the gentle embrace of baby angels, I joined Ms. Gianna as she gathered colorful storybooks from a shelf. Every moment felt special and filled with love. The warmth in Ms. Gianna's eyes and the gentle care she showed each child created an atmosphere of comfort. I turned the pages of the book while the babies cooed contentedly, as I read, "I love you right up to the moon—and back." Exhausted but invigorated from my time at HOPE, I exited the building.

In the distance, I noticed Mike standing with two large bags. The labels immediately caught my attention. One read "The Greatest Mysteries on Earth," and the other "Answers to the Greatest Mysteries on Earth." He looked at me and said, "Okay, Caleb, reach into the bag and grab your mission!" I plunged my hand into the bag, feeling the texture of the cards.

Pulling one out, I unfolded it to reveal the words: "The Ark of the Covenant."

Jack leaned in close, his eyes wide with curiosity. "What does it mean?" he asked.

Mike's expression was mysterious as he grinned. "The Ark of the Covenant holds great significance in many stories. It's said to contain sacred artifacts and is a symbol of divine presence. Your mission is to uncover its secrets and explore its history."

Excitement filled me as I exclaimed, "Wow, that sounds amazing! Where do we start?"

With a commanding voice, Mike yelled, "Tercelot, Carcarra,

come!" The mighty birds flew toward us, their majestic wings beating powerfully. Though I did not understand the foreign language Mike spoke to them, I knew it signaled the start of our next thrilling adventure. I jumped on Tercelot and felt the anticipation building. Tercelot and Carcarra lifted us into the air, and we soared across the kaleidoscopic expanse of space. Our mission was clear: to find the Ark of the Covenant and uncover its mystery.

Jack and I listened intently to the rumors and speculation swirling below as we circled the Earth. "Oh boys, you have a lot to look for!" one man exclaimed. "Some say an ancient temple holds it in hidden chambers!"

Another chimed in, "No, no! It's with lost civilizations and secret societies!"

Recalling Mike's advice, I turned to Jack. "We should be wary of these contradictory whispers." He nodded in agreement, and we pressed on with our search. I was focused on uncovering the truth about the elusive Ark.

When we were about to leave, a man suddenly shouted, "Hey, you know that guy with all the sheep? The one they call the Promised Land guy? I think he's somehow connected to the Ark!"

Jack and I exchanged a puzzled glance. "No way, the Land of Milk and Honey?" I responded skeptically.

"Quick, let's get on Tercelot and Carcarra and rush to the zoo!" Jack exclaimed.

When we arrived at the zoo, we quickly found Mo surrounded by his flock of sheep, which seemed as much a part of his life as his family. "Mo!" I called out urgently. "We need to talk. We just heard something about you and the Ark!"

Mo greeted us with a wise smile. "Caleb and Jack, I appreciate your enthusiasm," he said sternly yet kindly. "But I have something important to share." We leaned in, eager to hear him out. After a moment's pause, Mo continued, "The answers you seek are in the wilderness of Mount Sinai and hold great meaning. It was there that I received Emmanuel's original teachings," he told us.

"Emmanuel's original teachings?" I asked. Mo nodded solemnly.

"Yes. To find the truth, you must journey to Mount Sinai. The path may not be easy, but the truth will guide you."

Jack asked, "So what do we need to do?"

Mo smiled knowingly. "You must go to Mount Sinai."

I was eager to uncover Mount Sinai's significance and connection to our quest for the Ark of the Covenant. Jack and I embarked on a crucial journey, and I would find the answers I needed. I recognized it as a vital link to the ancient origins of our search, a pivotal piece of the puzzle. As we soared through the skies aboard Tercelot and Carcarra, our delight mounted, gazing down upon the rugged, history-steeped beauty of the Israeli landscape unfolding below.

When we finally landed, I asked a nearby man, "Where is the Temple of Solomon?"

The man chuckled, looking amused. "The Temple was destroyed long ago by invaders. What are you looking for now?"

I replied, "The Ark of the Covenant."

The man laughed again and shook his head. "Brave explorers, I see! You should check out Ethiopia. There's a church there with an unusual octagonal shape and domed roof. Maybe you'll find your answers there."

Jack and I exchanged excited glances. "Ethiopia! That's our next stop!" I said, feeling the thrill of adventure. "Thanks for the tip, let's go!"

After our time in Ethiopia yielded no answers, Jack and I broadened our search across Europe. Drawn to whispers of the "Ark of the Covenant" potentially being hidden somewhere on the continent, we came across a theory suggesting that it might be underground for safekeeping. Discouraged, we returned to The Kingdom. "I'm frustrated, Mike!" I exclaimed. "We went to every spot, and there's no Ark!"

Mike smiled knowingly. "I'll give you one clue," he said, handing us the bag. "Shake it." I put my hand back inside the bag and pulled out another card.

I opened the card, and Jack read it aloud, "Mount Sinai."

I shouted, "Are you kidding me?" throwing my hands up in exasperation. "We've already been there!"

Jack added, "Yeah, Mike, there's nothing at Mount Sinai!"

Mike shrugged, a glint of mischief dancing in his eyes. "Expand your horizons and think of another Mount Sinai." Fueled by renewed determination, we set off for New York, where we discovered a building named Mount Sinai. Upon arrival, we were astonished to find Mike waiting for us. "Mike! What are you doing here? How did you beat us?" I asked, bewildered.

He stood clad in full armor and replied, "Follow me, boys. Take the elevator to the 4th floor, and I'll meet you there."

Confused, I asked, "Why don't you take the elevator?" With a knowing smile, he replied, "Because I don't need the elevator." We hurried to the Pediatric Cancer Center on the fourth floor, our minds racing with questions.

I walked through the hospital, and the bravery of the children was inspiring. Each child faced their illness with extraordinary strength. "Hey, Jack," I said, glancing around. "It's so sad to see these kids suffering."

Jack replied, "Yeah, but they're all so brave," his voice filled with admiration. Then, a realization hit me.

"I think I know where the Ark of the Covenant is," I told him. "Where?" Jack asked, intrigued.

"I believe it's in these children - Emmanuel's presence lives in them," I explained, looking over at Mike, who smiled.

At that moment, I understood that the true essence of the "Ark of the Covenant" stood apart from any physical artifact or hidden relic. Instead, it lived within these courageous children in the love and strength they displayed daily. Their ability to find meaning despite their circumstances embodied what we had been searching for. With the new realization, we returned to The Kingdom, carrying with us the truth that the "Ark of the Covenant" is alive in the souls of all who face their challenges with courage.

After an eventful day, I eagerly sought more excitement. "Hey, I'd like to go on another mission. Can Jack and I fly Tercelot and Carcarra again?"

Mike smiled. "Absolutely! How about a trip to Earth?" he asked.

"Yes!" I exclaimed. As we prepared to take flight, Mike introduced us to a fascinating aspect of angelic existence—the "Angels in Waiting."

Tilting his head curiously, Jack asked, "What are they?"

Mike explained, "These angels have a unique and crucial role. They assist humans in need, but only if specifically requested or if the human faces imminent danger."

Intrigued, I said, "That sounds fascinating."

I watched the screen in stunned silence; a dramatic scene unfolded. A man trapped in his car was desperately signaling for help. "Look at that!" I exclaimed. "The angels are intervening!" To our amazement, one angel transformed into human form to flag down passing cars while another moved to rescue the man from the wreckage.

"Did you see that?" Jack gasped, his voice thick with disbelief. "That's insane!" The tragic situation took an unexpected turn, as the man in the car miraculously survived.

In the following setting, I turned to Mike, searching for answers. "Why is she so sad?" I asked, my voice barely above a whisper.

Mike looked at me, his eyes filled with empathy. "Sometimes people suffer on Earth," he explained gently. "The mother just lost her baby."

I pressed him. "Why does that happen?" I felt her grief, heavy in the air.

"Those things are hard to explain," Mike replied, "the baby will be in The Kingdom, and Ms. Gianna will take care of the baby at HOPE." My heart ached for her.

"But that doesn't make the mom feel any better," I said.

Mike nodded. "I know. But look," he gestured to the scene unfolding before us. The "Angels in Waiting" moved with a grace that felt almost sacred as they gathered the tiny infant, their luminous forms glowing brightly. They transported the baby to The Kingdom, filled with healing and light. As the angels traveled to The Kingdom, I could hear the baby cooing and laughing.

Meanwhile, other angels remained with the grieving mother. They surrounded her with love, holding her hand and placing their gentle hands on her belly as if to mend the pieces of her broken heart. She moaned in agony, a sound that reminded me of my feelings of hunger from the van—only hers was a hunger of a different kind, a yearning that remained unfulfilled.

Mike then showed us a last screen with the Archangels, the highest of Emmanuel's divine entities. Seeing Mike and Gabe in their actual, awe-inspiring forms was incredible. "The archangels serve as both messengers and guardians, confronting dark entities that seek to lead humans astray," Mike explained. I watched in awe as these divine beings fought against the dark creatures whispering deceit into human minds. The Archangels wielded their swords gracefully, dispelling the darkness and illuminating the Earth.

"One of the most significant challenges we face on Earth is the ongoing battle against Lucifer and his followers. Lucifer seeks to rule through deception," Mike said, his tone serious. "He leads humans into despair, anger, addiction, and sometimes even death."

I listened closely, feeling the impact of his words. "But why can't you just stop him?" I asked.

"While I have the power to destroy Lucifer," Mike replied, "the free will of humans keeps his influence alive. The choices people make shape their lives. We can't force them to choose light over darkness."

I nodded, trying to grasp the enormity of it all. "So, the angels can only assist?" I asked.

"We're here to guide and support, but ultimately, it's up to each person to decide their way. Every choice matters." His words lingered in the air, painting a picture of a world where sadness and happiness danced together, where the struggle for goodness was a vital part of existence. "Remember that light is always possible, even in darkness."

Before I knew it, Jack and I were back in The Kingdom. Mike appeared as I immersed myself in the fun, shifting the mood. "Hey, do you remember the term 'dyslexia' that your teacher, Ms. Puddle, used to describe you?"

I felt a twinge of embarrassment and nodded. "Yeah, I remember."

Mike's expression turned serious. "I know that Ms. Puddle made you feel less intelligent in front of your classmates. It's important to talk about that." I frowned, feeling a knot in my stomach. "Exactly," Mike said. "Some adults, like Ms. Puddle, cause harm with their words because of ignorance. It doesn't excuse what happened, but it's important to remember that we all make mistakes," he shared.

"Forgiveness?" I asked, unsure.

"Yes," he said. "Forgiveness is a way to release that hurt. It doesn't mean you have to forget, but it allows you to move forward without carrying so much anger."

I thought about it for a moment. "It's just hard sometimes," I told him.

"I get it," Mike replied. "But choosing to forgive can free you in ways you might not expect. It's a powerful step."

"Did you know that in The Kingdom, what Earth calls dyslexia is called Trickslexia?" Mike said, a twinkle in his eye.

"Trickslexia?" I asked, curious.

"Yeah," he explained. "The term reflects how adults often misinterpret how Trickslexic minds work. Some adults' minds are "tricked" and think these children aren't intelligent. They sometimes assume these children aren't as smart as their peers. We call it Tricklsexia because it's one of the biggest "tricks" children play on adults."

I frowned, remembering how Ms. Puddle made me feel. "But that's not true, is it?" I asked.

"Not at all," Mike reassured me. "Trickslexic people are often among the most smart, creative, and innovative of all. Let me introduce you to one of the most celebrated Trickslexics ever: Mr. Einstein!"

As if on cue, Mr. Einstein appeared, his presence warm and inviting. "Hello!" he said, smiling. "It's a pleasure to meet you."

I couldn't believe my eyes. "Wow, it's an honor!" I replied, still in awe.

Mr. Einstein handed me a small card with the equation $E=mc^2$. "Here, take the card," he said with a grin. "Let me explain it with a simple analogy."

Intrigued, I replied, "Okay!"

He began, "Imagine you and Jack on a rollercoaster. When the coaster speeds up, you feel pushed back in your seat. That's gravity at work!"

I nodded, picturing the thrill of a ride. "Got it!" I said.

"Now, picture Jack in his space shuttle, zooming through space," he continued. "To him, everything around might seem to crawl. Why? Because time slows down when you move quickly."

"Whoa," I said, trying to wrap my mind around it. "So, time is different for him?"

"Exactly!" Mr. Einstein said, his eyes lighting up. "The theory of relativity means that time and space can change depending on your speed. It's like a gigantic puzzle that helps us figure out how the universe works!"

I grinned, feeling a spark of curiosity. "That's amazing! I never thought of it that way!"

After a few moments of chatting, he leaned closer and shared one of his famous sayings. "If you can't explain something to a six-year-old, you don't know it yourself; the theory helps us understand why there is no time in The Kingdom."

Mike whisked me away, and suddenly, we were in a new movie. The screen revealed a woman known affectionately as "Rit" or "Minty" by her family. I watched in awe as Mike, Gabe, and other angels worked alongside Ms. Tubman, assisting her in the monumental task of liberating individuals from the brutal grip of slavery. "Look at her! She's so brave!" I exclaimed.

"Absolutely," Mike said, nodding. "Ms. Tubman's courage is incredible. Despite the heavy chains some people bear, she's determined to lead them to freedom."

I saw her carry some of the weary and guide others through hidden tunnels that resembled an old railroad. "It's like a secret path!" I marveled.

"Yes," Mike replied. "That's the Underground Railroad. Her strength and resolve shine through every danger she faces." I felt admiration as I watched her compassion in the face of such adversity.

"How can she be so strong?" I asked, feeling inspired.

"She knows the importance of freedom," Mike said. "And she's willing to risk everything to help others."

I whispered, "That's amazing. I want to be courageous like her."

We ventured through the universe on the backs of Tercelot and Carcarra, and I noticed a sign that read "Babylon." Given my Trickslexic nature, I pronounced it "Baby-lion," adding some vowel sounds, but it didn't matter. As we touched down, a scene straight out of a storybook unfolded before us. A colossal wall, nearly a hundred feet thick and stretching four miles in length, encircled the city. At the heart of the ancient metropolis stood a magnificent palace, its walls adorned with vibrant murals and intricate tilework. Surrounding it were lush gardens brimming with vibrant flowers and cascading waterfalls, completing the picture of timeless grandeur.

Jack and I explored the palace grounds, laughing and splashing around in the water features while the scorching sun blazed down on us. "Baby-lion is incredible!" Jack shouted, his eyes wide with wonder.

"I know, right?" I replied, grinning.

Jack asked, "What's the name of the king who ruled before Darius?"

I said, "Uh, I think it was King Nababachusinizer," trying to pronounce it. Jack burst out laughing.

"Close enough! It's King Nebuchadnezzar, but that's a tough one!" As we wandered, we noticed the royal guards discussing a new law nearby.

"What are they talking about?" I asked, intrigued.

Jack shrugged. "Something about punishing anyone who doesn't bow down to King Darius. Sounds scary!"

My eyes wide, I exclaimed, "Punishable in a lion's den? That's harsh!"

Just then, we spotted Daniel, one of the king's most trusted counselors. He approached us with a warm smile. "Hello, young explorers! I'm Daniel."

"Hi, Daniel! What do you do here?" I asked, curious.

"I spend most of my days seeking divine guidance and interpreting the king's dreams," he explained. "Come, let me show you around the palace."

We followed Daniel, and he shared stories about Babylon's

vibrant culture, languages, and traditions. "Look at your art! It's so colorful!" I said, pointing to an elegant mural.

"And the music! It's epic!" Jack added, swaying to the rhythm coming from a nearby gathering.

"Would you like to sample some of our foods?" Daniel asked, guiding us toward a bustling marketplace.

"Yes, please!" We both said.

Things grew tense when Daniel refused to bow to the king. "Why won't he just do it?" I whispered to Jack.

"I don't know, but it seems like a poor decision on his part," Jack replied, eyes wide.

The jealous Kingsmen embraced the opportunity, their faces twisted with envy. "Seize him!" one shouted. They threw Daniel into the lions' den in a flash because of his defiance.

I gasped, gripping Jack's arm. "What's going to happen to him?"

As we watched in terror, Daniel sat in the dark, enclosed space with the hungry lions. In a moment of despair, he called out, "Emmanuel!"

To our amazement, Emmanuel appeared by his side, radiant and calm. "Do not fear, Daniel," Emmanuel said, extending his hand to protect him from harm. When the king and his men came to the den the following day, they looked down at the lions, shocked.

"Look!" I exclaimed, pointing. "Daniel is unharmed!" Rather than attacking him, the lions sat peacefully around him, almost like his guardians. I couldn't help but think, "Maybe that's why the city is called 'Baby-lion' because of the miraculous event!"

King Darius's eyes widened in disbelief. "How could this be possible?" he exclaimed. "I demand that from now on, all people in my kingdom will honor and respect the One who spared Daniel's life," he proclaimed with authority.

CHAPTER 9

Cara

My life was as busy as ever, between my career and family responsibilities. One evening, as we sat together, Anna noticed my tension.

"Cara, are you okay?" she asked, her brow furrowed in concern. "You've been so focused on Caleb's case lately."

I sighed, running a hand through my hair. "I'm just trying to keep everything in balance," I admitted. "Between work, family, and now the case reopening... I can't afford any disruptions."

Anna gave me a reassuring look as if to say, I've got your back. "I get it. But you're doing the best you can," she said softly.

I nodded, feeling a little lighter. "I just can't let anything distract me."

"Speaking of distractions..." Anna's eyes lit up with sudden curiosity. "Have you heard from Frank? He will be here any day!"

I blinked, surprised. "Frank?" I repeated, momentarily thrown off.

"Yeah, we talked for the first time in ages—since high school.

We lost touch when I moved down south. I asked Frank if he wanted to crash in my spare bedroom to save money while he's here."

Anna raised an eyebrow, a playful grin tugging at her lips. "Maybe there's more than just detective work going on?"

I rolled my eyes. "Whatever, Anna. It'll be nice having someone around, even if it's awkward at first."

Anna shrugged, her grin widening. "If you say so, Cara."

"I hope all of this is for nothing," Anna said, her eyes uncertain. "It's been years of disappointment and heartache. I don't know if I can handle another letdown."

I could feel the weight of her words, and my anxiety surfaced. "I feel the same way," I murmured, my voice barely above a whisper. "My mind is overloaded, and I feel like it is about to explode; the pressure is too much. Some days, the pressure feels unbearable. I don't know how long I can keep going like this."

Anna's eyes softened, and she looked at me with concern, which made my heart ache. "We'll always have each other," she said, her voice steady but filled with emotion. "No matter what happens, we must stay strong for our family. We can't let this break us."

Preparing for Frank's visit became my top priority. I meticulously organized everything in Caleb's case file, ensuring I had all the information and notes ready for him. The week leading up to his arrival was a whirlwind of anticipation-filled activity. I planned for him to stay in my spare bedroom, an insignificant gesture that felt necessary given my frequent absences from home. On the day of Frank's arrival, I sat in my beloved black sports car at the airport, waiting. "Hey Frank, I am here," I texted.

He responded, "Just landed! I'll be out in a minute." His tall, fit frame, dark hair, and hazel eyes immediately drew me in. When he approached me, I couldn't help but smile. "Hey, thanks for picking me up," he said, his voice friendly.

"Of course!" I replied, trying to keep my tone casual despite my nerves.

"I appreciate it. Let me at least offer to pay for gas or something," he insisted, reaching for his wallet.

I shook my head, laughing lightly. "No need for that! Just having you here is enough."

His smile sparked a moment of connection that quickened my breath. I couldn't tell if there was a genuine bond or simply an intuition that Frank would help me find crucial information about my missing brother, Caleb.

"So, are you ready to dive into Caleb's case?" he asked as we walked toward the car.

"Absolutely. I've got everything organized and ready to go," I replied, trying to sound confident.

"I just want to get to the truth." Frank nodded, his expression turning serious. "I'm here to help, Cara. Together, we will figure out what happened to your brother," he replied.

"Thank you, Frank," I said, feeling gratitude. "It means a lot to have you on board."

Overcome, I ran my fingers through my hair as we delved into Caleb's case files. "There's just so much information, so many things I never looked into. I can't keep fighting," I said back at work.

Mike looked at me with concern. "Cara, maybe you should take a break and let Frank and me handle some of the work."

I shook my head vigorously. "How can I not search? How can I just let my brother go?"

Frank glanced at me, his expression steady. "You want answers about your brother, but we must be methodical. Rushing in won't help."

The discovery of new leads and DNA evidence pointing to suspects left me reeling. "The realization that multiple boys disappeared around the same time as Caleb only intensifies my anger."

Mike nodded, his voice softening. "I know it's a lot to take in," he said.

"I can't rest until I know what happened. We have to find out the truth."

Frank leaned in closer, his tone reassuring. "Then let's work together. We'll break the case down step by step. You're not alone."

"Mike, you're right; I need to take a break, mentally and physically. I just can't focus on anything right now. I should let you and Frank take over for a bit."

Frank nodded. "It's okay to take a breather. We'll handle the investigation while you regroup."

I usually took charge of everything, but the case's complexity was too much. As I sat on the sidelines, I watched Frank and Mike dive into the details of the investigation.

That evening, we gathered around a table littered with pizza boxes. I sifted through Frank's research, and my drive to find Caleb propelled me forward despite the emotions that threatened to cloud my judgment.

"Maybe we should step back a little," Anna suggested, glancing at the piles of files. "Our involvement might hinder the pursuit of truth."

I nodded slowly. "Yeah, you're right. We need to have confidence in them to do their job." In the intricate dance of trust and despair, we clung to the belief that one day, we would uncover the truth and bring Caleb home. "We'll be here for support," I said, looking at Anna. "But for now, it's time to let the experts take charge."

I prepared to leave work for the day and momentarily paused and said, "Oh, I almost left without you, Frank! I'm sorry—I forgot you were staying with me."

He offered, "I could book a hotel instead if that would make things easier for you."

I couldn't help but chuckle at the suggestion. "I'd rather have you around. I appreciate the company."

Frank looked uneasy. "Well, I could stay somewhere else. I feel bad."

I shook my head. "Despite everything, having someone to talk to is nice."

He smiled, the tension easing a bit. "Alright, I'll stick around then. Just let me know if you need space."

"Thank you, Frank. I appreciate what you are doing. It means a lot," I said, feeling grateful for the help of my family and friends during this challenging time.

That evening, Frank and I decided on Chinese takeout. "I'll go with my favorite, sesame chicken," I said, placing my order.

"I'll take sweet and sour shrimp," Frank replied.

I couldn't help but wrinkle my nose slightly. "Shrimp? Really?"

He chuckled. "What's wrong with shrimp?" he asked.

"Just not my thing," I admitted, trying to maintain politeness. "But you go for it!"

We ate silently for a bit, the only sound being the clinking of our chopsticks against the takeout containers. Eventually, I broke the quiet.

"So, how about a movie? I was thinking of true crime documentaries."

Frank shook his head, a smile creeping onto his face. "I'm in the mood for something less intense."

As we settled in to watch, fatigue set in. I glanced at the clock, realizing the time. "I think I'm going to head to bed," I said.

As Frank's departure to New York approached, I reflected on his and Mike's progress on Caleb's case. I sat on the couch, a sigh escaping me as mixed emotions swirled within. Should I be happy for their accomplishments or mourn Frank's departure from

Greenville?

"It's hard to believe you're leaving so soon, Frank. We've made great strides together."

Frank leaned back, his expression thoughtful. "Yeah, it's bittersweet. I wish I could stay longer to help more."

I tried to lighten the mood. "Having you here was wonderful. I had a great time exploring downtown Greenville with you-browsing the galleries, local shops, and all the Clemson memorabilia."

Frank chuckled. "I still can't believe how passionate everyone is about the university. It's contagious!"

"It is," I replied, smiling at the memories. "We laughed a lot too. I didn't realize how much I needed that."

The next morning, I dropped Frank off at the airport, a twinge of sadness tugging at my heart. I tried to immerse myself in work, but the ache lingered despite my efforts to bury my feelings. As the days passed, I yearned to reconnect with him. Finally, unable to suppress my emotions any longer, I called him. "Hi Frank, it's me, Cara. Remember me? I'm calling to see if you have any progress on the case. I also called just to say hi and see how you're doing! Call me back if you get a chance." I took a deep breath, using the excuse of checking in on the case's status, but really, I just needed to hear his voice.

To my surprise, Frank returned my call promptly. "Hey, Cara! What's up?" he said, his voice brightening my mood instantly.

"Just checking in on the case. Thought I'd see how everything's going," I replied, trying to sound casual.

He chuckled. "You mean you wanted to hear my voice! But seriously, the case is moving along. I appreciate you reaching out."

We chatted throughout my evening activities—during my commute home, as I took a walk, while I prepared dinner, and even as I got ready for bed with him on speakerphone. "Can you believe my luggage mishap at the airport?" Frank laughed.

"I lost my bag on a short flight with only one layover!" I giggled. "That's ridiculous! How does that even happen?"

In the weeks following Frank's departure, I found immense joy in spending time with my nephews, James and Samuel, savoring their simple laughter and playing jokes on them. That night, as I joined Mike and my mom for dinner, I tried to sound upbeat when I asked, "Hey, Mom, what's up? How's your week going?"

She turned to me, "You're chipper tonight, Cara," she replied, raising an eyebrow. "Usually, you're grudgingly trying to be happy."

I smiled, "I just had a wonderful week!" I said. I glanced at her necklace. "Hey, what's up with that necklace? It looks like it's about to fall apart."

She touched it gently. "Just like I told Anna, I'm not taking it off. Caleb gave it to me, and I refuse to part with it."

I rolled my eyes, unable to hide my disbelief. Eyeing the tarnished necklace, I yelled, "Mom, that thing is turning green! How can you still wear it?" She responded defiantly, "It's meaningful to me." In hindsight, if I had known the necklace's true power, I would have seized it from her and locked it away in a tungsten safe—though even that fortified vault might not have been strong enough to contain its immense force.

The next day at work, my voicemail was filled with urgent messages from Sister Kathleen, immediately grabbing my attention. While I listened to my client recounting their divorce, I interjected, "I'm sorry, but I need to make an important call. My secretary will reschedule our appointment, as there's a family emergency I must attend to." I promptly returned Sister Kathleen's call.

Her tone sounded urgent as she introduced herself, "Hello, my name is Sister Kathleen from a small church in Falling Creek, Virginia. I hope it's alright that I'm calling you," she said.

"Of course, Sister Kathleen. How can I help you?" I replied, my curiosity piqued.

Sister Kathleen took a deep breath, her voice tinged with concern. "I wanted to talk to you about some boys who came here many years ago."

My pulse quickened. Sister Kathleen's voice remained steady but carried a sense of urgency. She recounted the harrowing ordeal of the boys, who had come from dire family situations. "I've cared for the boys in the past—bathing them, clothing them, and feeding them," she said, her tone filled with compassion. "My concern grew when one boy returned to the nunnery. Something just didn't feel right."

Sister Kathleen explained that she reached out to Fresh Start, the adoption center where the boys were to meet their new families. "Even after hearing the touching stories from the adoptive families, my intuition kept telling me something was off. I inspected the van that transported the boys. It looked innocent enough—a minivan with car seats, movie screens, and a cooler full of snacks. But I couldn't shake the feeling that something wasn't right," she shared.

"Did you report your intuition to the police?" I asked, feeling a mix of concern and urgency.

"I did," Sister Kathleen replied, her tone firm. "They assured me of Fresh Start's legitimacy. But my persistence yielded no new information, and soon after, the boys stopped visiting the nunnery altogether."

The gravity of Sister Kathleen's revelations struck me dumb as I heard them. Struggling to respond, I listened as she continued, "There's one boy, in particular, I need to tell you about," she said, pausing to gather her thoughts. "He was incredibly kind and self-less—always looking out for his friends before himself. He was an old soul, with eyes of an unearthly blue quality."

At that moment, it became crystal clear to me that the boy Sister Kathleen described was Caleb. Her words hit me like a sledgehammer, sending shivers down my spine as my world seemed to collapse. My phone slipped from my trembling fingers, its screen shattering on the floor.

Overcome with grief, I sank to my knees, anguished cries piercing the silence. "No! Please, God, no!" I wailed, gasping for breath as tears streamed down my face.

Through the darkness, Sister Kathleen's steady voice emerged, her comforting prayers— "Hail Mary, full of grace..." and "Our Father, who art in Heaven"—a beacon in my despair.

"Sister, thank you. Your prayers are helping." I said, voice quivering.

"We must hold on to our faith, Cara. God is listening," she replied.

At that moment, my path became clear—I would uncover the truth and seek justice for Caleb.

CHAPTER 10

Anna

I met my friend, Sierra, at the local bookstore. When I spotted her, I smiled. Her short, muscular frame and emerald green eyes framed by a pixie cut were a striking contrast to mine. "Hey, Anna!" she greeted me, her gentle demeanor radiating affection. "How was your workout?" she asked.

"Good, just trying to keep up with everything," I replied, feeling lighter in her presence. "How about you?" I asked.

"Same here! I've been trying to stay active. It helps clear my mind," she said, glancing around the bookstore. "I've been thinking about our last conversation—balancing parenting and work," she told me.

"Me too. It's such a juggling act," I admitted. "Sometimes I feel like the ball drops all the time."

Sierra nodded. "I get that. But remember, it's okay to ask for help."

"True," I sighed.

Our friendship blossomed over our shared experiences as

mothers of two boys, both of hers the same age as James and Samuel. I loved how we could easily relate to each other's challenges.

"Can you believe how fast they're growing?" Sierra said one day as we watched our boys play together. "It feels like just yesterday they were babies," she said.

"I know! It's both exciting and terrifying," I replied with a laugh. "Sometimes I wish I could hit pause for a bit."

Sierra nodded, her emerald eyes sparkling. "I get that. I plan to return to work once my youngest starts school, but it's nice to be home now. It saves on daycare costs, too," she shared.

"It must be a juggling act, though," I said, admiring her calm demeanor. "How do you keep it all together?" I asked her.

"I try to take things one day at a time," she said thoughtfully. "And honestly, being home has given me the chance to focus on my mental health. It's something I desperately needed." Sierra said.

"Your calmness is contagious. I sometimes feel like I'm running on empty," I admitted.

Sierra invited me to a local art gallery that evening, and I eagerly accepted, desperate for a respite from my spiraling thoughts. I entered, and I was immediately captivated by the brilliant art displays. Each piece seemed to tell its own story, but Sierra's painting was a stunning blend of bold reds and calming blues, conveying a spectrum of emotions that pulled me into its depths.

"Wow, Sierra, this is incredible!" I exclaimed, stepping closer to admire the intricate details. "You've captured something extraordinary here."

Sierra's face lit up with a proud smile. "Thank you, Anna! I wanted to convey a sense of balance—the chaos and the calm," she shared.

"It works perfectly," I replied, feeling my worries fade as I immersed myself in the beauty and creativity around me. "I could briefly forget my troubles and lose myself in the art."

Sierra chuckled. "Art has a way of doing that. It's my escape, too. I'm so glad you're here to experience it with me," she said.

"I'm so proud of you. Your talent is amazing, and you deserve this moment," I said sincerely.

"Thank you, Anna. It means the world to me," she responded, her eyes glimmering with gratitude.

Leaving the art gallery, I received Cara's urgent text: "Anna, please come to the office as soon as possible, 911." Knowing Cara was not one for showing emotion, I quickly called my mom. "Mom, I need you to keep James and Samuel for the evening. Something has come up at work." As I drove to the office, an unsettling feeling washed over me. Upon arrival, the gravity of Cara's distress immediately struck me. The burden of the looming news was almost tangible.

Ever the supportive presence, Ted knelt beside Cara. "It's going to be okay, Cara. I'll do anything to help find Caleb," he offered, providing a semblance of stability as we gathered around her.

Seeing my sister Cara in such a state of despair tightened a knot in my chest. I wanted to comfort her, but growing fear gripped me. This meeting would change everything. Sitting on the floor with Cara, I felt disoriented, the world spinning around me. My ears buzzed, and I struggled to grasp what was unfolding.

Ted's reassuring grip on my arm was a lifeline, grounding me, "Breathe, Anna," Ted encouraged.

Cara's words came like a tidal wave, each harder to process than the last. "The boy's eyes," she said, and I felt a shattering awareness. "Caleb is at the center of the East Coast kidnappings."

My mind struggled to accept the enormity of the situation. "No, it can't be," I whispered, shaking my head in disbelief. Yearning for answers, I reached for my phone with trembling hands and dialed Sister Kathleen's number.

"Hello?" Sister Kathleen's voice was calm, starkly contrasting with the storm raging inside me.

"It's Anna, Cara's sister. I... I need to know more about the boys you mentioned—the ones from the nunnery," I stammered, fighting back tears.

"Of course, dear," she whispered. "I remember the one with the striking blue eyes. He always cared for the others." Each detail she shared seemed to remind me of the ache of losing Caleb. I could feel my grief for Caleb expanding with every word.

"What happened to him, Sister? Please, tell me everything," I implored.

"After a while, he stopped coming," she said.

"Do you think he's still alive?" I asked, my voice barely a whisper.

"I have to believe he is, Anna. We can't lose hope," Sister Kathleen said, her faith shining through my misery.

"Mike, can you contact the police department? Maybe talking to the detective assigned to Caleb's case will help us get some answers." I said, my voice shaky.

"I'll reach out to them right away," he replied, his expression serious. "We need all the information we can get."

I felt consumed by helplessness. My body ached, and I felt unbearably heavy with the news. "I just can't shake the feeling that we are missing something," I said, rubbing my temples. "What if we don't find him? We need to protect my mom from this truth," I said, trembling. "She's been through so much already. I can't bear the thought of pushing her back into a depression."

Cara nodded in agreement, her expression serious. "I think that's the right choice. Let's not tell her until we have more answers," she said.

"I agree," Ted said, his tone resolute. "It's better to shield her from the truth for now. We can't add to her suffering."

Mike said, "When we know more, we can figure out the best way to break the news. But for now, we should keep the information from her."

"Anna, I think I must go and talk to Sister Kathleen in person. Now that you've spoken to her, I feel seeing her in person might help spark her memory and provide us with new insights," Ted said.

"What do you mean? Do you think she can tell you anything different?" I asked.

"I don't know. I feel that meeting with her face-to-face could be helpful. What do you think about me going to see her?" he asked.

"I think it's an excellent idea. As long as you're comfortable with it," I told him.

"I promise I'll keep you posted on everything I find," he told me.

"Of course you will, Ted. You love me."

Taking my hand, he replied sincerely, "I do."

It felt like Ted was gone forever, and when he finally returned, I was surprised to see him sitting at the kitchen table. I ran to him and gave him a tight hug. "Ted!" I exclaimed, rushing over to envelop him. "You're back! I missed you!" I told him.

"I missed you too, Anna," he said, draping an arm around me. I sat beside him, and a whirlwind of thoughts and questions brewed in my mind. "What did Sister Kathleen say? What happened? I can't believe Caleb's name is linked to a kidnapping now."

"It's complicated; Sister Kathleen shared details that made it clear Caleb was part of the East Coast kidnappings. There was even a nickname he used." A wave of confusion and anxiety washed over me, and I felt a sense of despair.

"Caleb's abduction has been such a painful mystery for over two decades. How come we could not find him? What does it mean?" I asked.

"I know it's overwhelming," Ted said. "But we're closer to deciphering what happened. We need to take it one step at a time."

I nodded, trying to process everything. "I just want answers. I thought we'd never have to face losing Caleb again."

Ted squeezed my hand. "We will face it together. We'll find out the truth about Caleb."

CHAPTER 11

Ted

I'm married to Anna, and we have two wonderful sons, James and Samuel. I grew up in a small town, Jonesborough, Tennessee—fewer than six thousand people, so you can imagine how tight-knit it was. My mom was a stay-at-home mom, and I cherish the memories I have of her. We would often pack lunches for my dad and take them to his office near Columbia. Those trips were memorable, especially when we stopped by the local bookstore. I was that kid who could never resist begging for a new book or toy every time we visited. Summers were the best, filled with hanging out with friends at Ramsey Creek and sneaking into the local water park. Sports played a huge role in my life, too. I was one of the top athletes in the state, excelling in football, basketball, and baseball.

It was during my junior year of college when I first saw Anna. I buried myself in my textbooks at the library when she walked in. For a moment, I questioned if she was real; she looked like she'd stepped out of a dream. Tall and slender with cascading blonde hair, she seemed almost otherworldly. Her eyes were a shade of blue that reminded me of the sea, though a sadness behind them tugged at me. Anna didn't give me a second glance as she walked past. Captivated and steadfast to catch her attention, I habitually visited the library every day for a month. All I got were top grades and the occasional glance at the spot where she'd been. As dusk fell, I would reluctantly leave, still hoping for another glimpse of her, knowing that our paths might never cross again.

I vowed to myself that I would marry her one day. Remembering my father's advice, "Ted, it is important to take calculated risks," I saw her descending the stairs. Gathering my courage, I introduced myself. Feeling my mind race, I finally said, "Hello." To my surprise, she smiled and replied, "Hi there! Do you come here often?" That simple question opened the door to a conversation that felt effortless. "Yeah, I do."

"I'm Ted, by the way," I told her.

"Nice to meet you, Ted. I'm Anna," she said, her eyes sparkling with curiosity.

I stumbled over my words but pushed through. "Would you… maybe want to grab coffee sometime?" Her smile widened. That day marked the beginning of something beautiful, and I realized my unusual demeanor intrigued her, which played a role in sparking our relationship.

Anna and I were best friends, and when she felt comfortable, she shared her story about Caleb. I listened, moved, as she recounted the details of his disappearance. "It was a terrible time. I hated everyone, especially my mother. I would tell her that I wished she were dead and that I despised her. My sister Cara was just as cruel." Ted just looked on, caring but helpless, as I spiraled. "When Caleb went missing, I felt responsible. Since then, I've been driven to find him, even becoming a lawyer. I've never stopped searching. Some days, I can hardly function, while others, I face with relative ease. It's been such a terrible ordeal. I'm sorry I didn't tell you about this sooner."

It tore at me, and I resolved to help her. "I can't imagine what you're going through, Anna. I'll do whatever it takes to help find him." I spent countless hours researching online, consulting professors discreetly, and contacting authorities in her hometown. "I've reached out to some contacts," I told her one evening, trying to remain positive. "But nothing yet."

My efforts to find any leads on Caleb came up empty. I kept my findings to myself, speaking about him only when she did. I constantly wondered, "Where are you, Caleb?" After graduating with a degree in criminal justice, I followed Anna to Columbia Law School in New York. "I thought it would be exciting," I admitted during a date night study session. "But city life isn't for me. I miss the tranquility of the South." Once law school was behind me, I knew I had to return to my roots. "I want to make a difference, and I think that starts at home," I said to Anna, my determination clear. "We can work together to find Caleb. I won't give up on him or you."

I was patient with Anna throughout her emotional journey. My upbringing in a devout Christian household instilled in me a firm belief in the power of prayer, and I leaned on that faith to guide us in our quest to find Caleb. After we completed our studies, Anna and I didn't hesitate to move to Greenville, South Carolina. Thrilled, my parents were happy to have us back down south. They welcomed Anna with open arms, showered her affectionately, and treated her to her favorite homemade meals.

When I proposed to Anna, I wanted it to be remarkable. I planned a magical moment in the Blue Ridge Mountains of Tennessee, walking along the winding paths.

"Where are we going?" Anna asked, her eyes sparkling with curiosity.

"Just a little further," I replied, guiding her through lush valleys until we reached a secluded spot near a magnificent waterfall. The sound of rushing water and the sweet scent of blooming flowers created an enchanting atmosphere.

"Wow, it's stunning here," she said, taking it all in.

Anna and I stood there, surrounded by the beauty of nature; I took a breath, dropped to one knee, and presented her with a stunning ring, a symbol of my love and commitment. "Anna, will you marry me?" I asked, my voice steady despite the whirlwind of emotions inside me.

With tears of contentment, she smiled and whispered, "Yes!" In that blissful moment, we knew we were embarking on a journey of love and partnership, ready to face whatever came our way together.

We exchanged vows in an intimate ceremony at my parents' home in Tennessee, a day filled with pure happiness. "I can't believe we're finally here," I said as I took Anna's hands.

"I know," she replied, her eyes shining with longing. As the years passed, we started our own family but faced sadness and disappointment with each failed pregnancy. "It feels like we're on this endless roller coaster," Anna sighed one evening, her voice heavy with emotion.

"I know it's tough," I whispered. The daily injections, the emotional toll of in vitro fertilization, and the lingering darkness of Anna's mood were challenging. After much soul-searching, we took a break from all medical interventions. "Maybe we need to focus on us for a while," I suggested during our long talks.

During this period of relinquishing control, we received a miraculous surprise: Anna was pregnant with James. "You're going to be a mom," I said, barely able to contain my surprise.

Her face lit up, and she laughed. "I can't believe it! Finally, my stubborn baby!" The news filled me with such harmony.

I threw myself into painting the nursery in soft hues of blue, envisioning our little boy's future. "What do you think of these colors?" I asked, holding up paint samples.

"They're perfect," Anna smiled, her eyes sparkling.

With Anna's due date approaching, my impatience grew. "I can't wait to hold our baby in my arms," I said.

"Just a little longer," Anna replied, her hand resting on her belly. "He'll be here soon."

When James finally arrived, I felt a love I never knew existed. It was an overwhelming feeling. I dedicated myself to caring for my family and nurturing my business, but my thoughts often wandered back to Caleb. I dreamed of being the one to reunite him with Anna and her family, bringing an end to their anguish.

When Anna became pregnant with our second child, Samuel, it was a relief not to see her suffer anymore over the lost lives of our precious babies. However, Samuel's delivery was fraught with danger, not just for him but for Anna. Once Samuel was born, both mom and baby were out of danger. "Anna, I thank God for our blessings, and I don't think we should test fate again. Our family is complete with James and Samuel; I am content with that."

Anna had returned to work after her maternity leave; her voice broke the morning silence as I reviewed Caleb's case files. "Christopher seems promising. His experience with missing persons could make a difference," she said.

"I agree," I replied, a spark of optimism igniting. "I think he'll bring a fresh perspective. We need that right now."

Anna's eyes brightened as she smiled. "And having my mom here has been a lifesaver. I don't know how we'd manage without her help," she said.

"Absolutely," I said, leaning back in my chair. "Knowing your mom is taking such good care of James and Samuel gives us the freedom to dig further into this case. It's such a relief."

With a steady voice, Anna said, "Let's pray our efforts lead us to some answers for Caleb and our family."

I decided to travel to New York and then back to South Carolina. To my surprise, Anna thought it was a good idea. After a challenging day in court—one of those toxic divorce cases that drained me—I squeezed in a workout before setting off the following day. I planned to drive straight to New York, a thirteen-hour haul.

Upon arriving in New York, I settled into a charming Airbnb in Milford Falls. The gentle sound of a creek splashing against the rocks below created a serene atmosphere. The next day, I visited a local market. Tempting bakery items and sandwiches immediately caught my eye, and I ordered a hearty breakfast of eggs and bacon. The aroma instantly evoked nostalgic memories of childhood Sundays in Tennessee—big family breakfasts followed by church.

After breakfast, I met Frank at the sheriff's office. "Ready to dive into the past?" he asked, his voice steady but with a hint of urgency.

"More than ever," I replied, matching his calm demeanor as I sifted through Caleb's case file. A familiar feeling settled in my chest.

"Have you had any luck contacting the original detectives?" Frank asked, glancing over my shoulder.

"Not yet. I've left messages, but no one's called back," I said. "It's like they've vanished."

I returned to the car with renewed purpose, determined to uncover the truth about Caleb and the lost moments that weighed heavily on my mind. I stopped at Anna's childhood home and wandered around the back, where an old, rusted blue swing set stood—a sad reminder of the happy times Anna and Caleb once shared.

I arrived in Virginia to see Sister Kathleen. She looked in her eighties, dressed in baggy jeans and an old tan sweater. She walked with a cane, and its sound resonated on the oak floors as she approached me. "Sister Kathleen?" I asked, a hint of nervousness in my voice.

"Yes, dear. You must be Anna's husband, Ted. It's good to

meet you finally," she replied, her eyes softening as she took me in.

"I'm here to talk about Caleb and the other boys who went missing," I said, trying to gauge her reaction. Her hands trembled as she fell into prayer, clasping her rosary beads.

"I've been praying for him," she murmured. "I haven't forgotten."

I handed sister Kathleen the photo I had of Caleb. "This is him. I need your help." She took the picture with shaking hands, her eyes welling with tears.

"Oh, dear boy," she whispered, praying once more. "May God protect him." The mention of Caleb had reignited something within her.

"Sister, can you tell me anything about him or the other boys?" I pressed.

When Sister Kathleen finally looked up, her eyes, though tearful, held a flicker of recognition. I knelt beside her, holding her frail hand, trying to offer support.

"I remember him," she said, tracing his features in the photo with her arthritic fingers. "There were about ten boys who visited me. One of the men in charge was Pete."

"Pete?" I asked.

"Yes, but one boy called him Stink Eye Pete," she chuckled as if remembering a long-forgotten joke.

"Can you tell me more about him?" I urged, leaning closer.

Sister Kathleen nodded, her expression turning serious. "He was short, shorter than me, with dark hair in an oily ponytail and a droopy right eye. He had a stutter, too." I jotted down notes, each detail igniting a fire within me. "And the other man was Felix. He was around six feet tall and a smooth talker. He was missing his top right front tooth, a scar above his left eyebrow, and a wide nose. He wore too much cheap cologne and had an air of self-importance. You could feel it the moment he entered a room."

"Did you ever see them with the boys?" I pressed.

"Not really, but they would come and go, always in a rush."

Disoriented Sister Kathleen was getting agitated, "I am sorry, it is time for Sister to rest," her aide said. And just like that, the meeting was over. I walked away, my head down, hoping that I would have had more information for Anna. The gravity of Sister Kathleen's revelations hung heavily in the air, and I couldn't shake the feeling that I had missed a vital opportunity.

As I neared the door, I heard her voice call out, "Ted!" I turned back, excited. She seemed to remember something important. I hurried to her side, but as I reached her, I saw her take her last breath—and then she was gone.

Devastation washed over me. Here was someone who could have provided crucial information about Caleb, and now she was dead; I stood there, paralyzed by sadness, wishing I could have done more, regretting not asking the right questions. With my head down, I left the nunnery, her absence pressing on my chest. I wanted to share with Anna everything I had learned.

Fighting back tears, I called Mike immediately. "Mike, I need your help," I said, trembling. I told him everything: the church hall's description, Sister Kathleen's frail condition, and her precise moments of insight.

"Okay, what do you need from me?" he asked, his tone steady. "I need you to look into any names associated with Pete or Peter with criminal backgrounds. He's about five feet tall and has a droopy right eye and a stutter. And check for anyone named Felix, around six feet tall, in the database," I told him.

"Got it. I'll start digging right away," Mike replied.

As I drove back to South Carolina, I shared the new information: "Caleb nicknamed the man 'Stink Eye Pete' because of his eye condition. That detail could help us narrow down our search."

Mike agreed, saying, "Yeah, that makes sense. We'll figure this out." For the first time in years, I felt a glimmer of hope.

"There's a lead to follow," I said, my heart racing. "I'm so grateful to Sister Kathleen for her crucial recollections."

CHAPTER 12

Christopher

I had built a facade of detachment to shield myself from the emotional toll of my job. However, the harsh reality of Caleb's case still weighed heavily on me, especially with so little information about the East Coast kidnappings. Amid the chaos of my professional duties and personal challenges, I stayed determined to uncover the truth and bring light to the darkness surrounding many lives.

Running was my escape from the mounting pressure. I explored the Swamp Rabbit Trail, which I had heard whispers about but never visited. The rhythmic pounding of my feet against the pavement relieved my anxiety, even for a little while. Yet, the news of the lost children clung to my thoughts like a persistent shadow.

During this tranquil excursion, a small, seemingly inconsequential discovery stopped me. A bright red balloon lay forgotten on the ground, its faded note bearing a single name: Caleb. I instinctively recognized its significance and felt a purpose. Guided by divine intervention, I carefully tucked the balloon into my pocket. It was as if this small, simple discovery was a message, a sign that my efforts were not in vain.

For the past seven months, I had been working tirelessly on the case of the missing twin boys, Alex and Levi, but there had been no new leads. The frustration was mounting, each day feeling like a step farther from finding them. My voicemail inbox was cluttered with messages, mainly about the East Coast case, but nothing that brought me closer to solving this one.

Before I could settle into my work, I scanned my messages. "Mike's got more info on the East Coast kidnappings," I muttered, opening his text. "And two frantic parents about the twin boys." I sighed as I read messages. "I can't imagine what they're going through," I said aloud, shaking my head. I tapped on the report about the sightings in Stillwater, Minnesota. "Alex and Levi's parents are desperate for any sign of their children." Just then, my phone buzzed again. "And a message from a woman named Diane. She'll have to wait for a callback." I paused, feeling the pressure of it all. "The thought of losing a child—let alone two—is unbearable. I have to do something."

And then, like a miracle, my phone rang. I almost didn't believe it at first.

"Christopher?" a voice on the other end said, steady and reassuring. "This is Sergeant Tom Carver from Minnesota. I have some good news. I'm sure I have Alex and Levi in my custody."

My heart skipped a beat. For the first time in months, something felt like it might actually break through the darkness. "Thank you for reaching out," I replied, my voice tight with relief. "It's about time I heard some good news. I will be on the next flight to Minnesota."

"Glad to help," Sergeant Carver said. "We'll be waiting for you."

I hung up, the flood of relief washing over me, but I knew better than to relax. This was only the beginning. I immediately began preparing for the flight, focusing on the procedure. I moved fast when I landed in Minnesota, following every protocol step. I rushed through the identification checks, my heart pounding as I made my way to the third floor. I didn't need to see their faces to know who they were—I'd memorized every detail of Alex and Levi's photos and burned them into my memory. But my breath caught in my throat when I finally saw them in person. They were thinner than the pictures, their faces gaunt, but it was them. The boys were here.

I walked over slowly, making sure I didn't scare them. For the first time in what felt like forever, I had the glimmer of hope I'd been desperately chasing.

"I have to follow the protocol," I said, trying to stay composed. "I can't contact your family without the DNA analysis." I looked at Alex and Levi, their faces concerned. "I need to gather some information and collect your saliva samples. If the DNA results match, you can go home. It's just a quick test," I assured them, forcing a calm tone despite my urgency. They remained quiet, glancing at each other.

"What's it for?" Levi finally asked.

"To make sure we have everything we need to reunite you with your family," I explained gently as I quickly swabbed their mouths.

The process felt like an eternity. With the samples in hand, I sprinted to the DNA lab, adrenaline pumping. "Can you do this urgently?" I pleaded with the technician. "Time is of the essence!"

The technician nodded. "I'll do my best." As I paced the halls to manage my mounting stress, I pulled out my phone and called Jimmy. Hearing his soothing voice provided a minor comfort amid the chaos.

"Hey, Christopher, what's going on?" he asked, his tone light and calming.

"They've found the twins. I'm getting their DNA tested and

anxiously awaiting the results," I replied, struggling to maintain my composure.

My mind raced with cautious optimism, eager for a positive outcome. When the technician finally handed me the white envelope containing the results, I held my breath and tore it open. The results confirmed a ninety-nine percent match to Alex and Levi's DNA. Relief and joy flooded me, but my chest pounded, and my hands trembled as I reached for my phone to find the parents' contact number.

"Hello, this is Christopher. I'm calling about your sons' abduction case," I said, trying to keep my voice steady despite the situation. I delivered the news, but their initial reaction wasn't immediate relief. Instead, there was a piercing scream of disbelief, as if the moment's reality was too much to grasp after everything they had endured.

"Wait, what? Are you serious?" the mother gasped, her voice trembling.

"Yes, ma'am. Your boys are alive, and they are safe in police custody." I explained as I listened to her processing the information. Slowly, they composed themselves, and I could hear the shaky breaths on the other end.

"We're coming. We need to get to Minnesota as soon as possible," the father said, determination breaking through the shock.

"Of course. I'll coordinate with the local authorities to ensure you can see them as soon as you arrive," I assured them. As we completed the details, I felt a rush of relief. Despite the harrowing circumstances, the prospect of reuniting the boys with their parents was a reminder that even in the darkest moments of my work, there is still light.

However, duty called, and I had to deliver a news broadcast, carefully avoiding the children's names. During the press interview, I stated, "Today, the boys have reunited with their loving parents after an agonizing seven-month abduction. Authorities have taken the perpetrator into custody, where he will remain until trial. I have no further information to share."

Back in South Carolina, I remained fixated on my conversation with Mike. Despite my efforts to rationalize my thoughts, an irresistible drive to assist others compelled me forward. The alarming string of abductions in the northeast had become my calling, prompting me to contact Mike and schedule a meeting. When we finally sat down, Mike leaned in, his expression serious. "I need to tell you something about my connection to the case," he said, his voice low. "I'm dating a woman who lost her child, Caleb, to abduction many years ago. The trauma of that event still haunts her, and these recent cases have reopened old wounds." I nodded.

"That must be incredibly hard for her," I replied.

"It is," he continued. "Her daughters have enlisted my help in their quest for answers. Despite their success as lawyers, their interactions with me have been tense. It's added another layer of complexity to my involvement."

Listening to Mike's story, I felt a surge of empathy. I knew the stakes were high, and the impact was enormous. I gathered every detail Mike could provide, along with the perspectives of the two sisters of the missing boy, Caleb. Caleb's situation became more apparent with each new piece of information, and the need to uncover the truth grew stronger. If I had known then what I know now about Caleb, the pressure may have been too great. I might have run from anything to do with finding him.

CHAPTER 13

Diane

Despite the serene setting of the duck pond, I felt uneasy and on high alert that day. Every passerby or stranger who approached the boys stirred suspicion within me. Across the water, I spotted the man whose eyes seemed to hold the heavens. "Diane, it was not your fault," he whispered before fading away.

James's voice startled me. "Grandma, are you okay?"

I replied, flustered, "Yes, yes! I'm sorry. Did I scare you?" I asked.

"But Grandma, I saw the man you were talking to; he gave me the best duck food, and all the ducks came over to me. It was so cool!" James said. A wave of panic washed over me.

"James, you know better! You're never supposed to talk to strangers," I insisted.

"But you talked to him," James pointed out.

"I'm an adult," I retorted. "James, never talk to strangers again." My voice trembled as I added, "I'm sorry for yelling, but please don't talk to strangers."

I treasured the peacefulness on our walk home from the pond with James and Samuel. I heard James yell, "Look, there's a balloon!" He pointed to a beautiful red balloon floating in the sky.

"Red, Grandma!" Samuel chimed in, his eyes wide with wonder. James blew bubbles for Samuel to catch for the rest of the walk home. "Get it, Samuel! Don't let it go! Don't let it get past you!" Their laughter lifted my spirits. I watched as James blew bubbles and Samuel attempted to catch them. "Look, Grandma!" James shouted, his face lighting up. "I made a big one!" he yelled.

"Wow! That's the biggest bubble I've ever seen!" I said, beaming at both of them.

"Catch it, Samuel!" James laughed, and Samuel lunged forward, arms outstretched, giggling as the bubble burst, leaving tiny droplets shimmering in the sunlight.

"More, more!" Samuel pleaded, bouncing on his toes.

I walked to the duck pond daily, searching for the mysterious man. When I got to the pond one afternoon, I gazed up at the sky, and a loud voice called out, "Diane, your necklace with the green gem, do not take it off, no matter what."

Confused, I responded, "What do you mean? Why are you telling me this? I need to know more."

The disembodied voice continued, "Diane, you must keep the green gem and necklace close to your heart," he said.

"I promised my son Caleb I would never take it off." Desperate for answers, I pleaded, "Please, tell me who you are. Do you know my son?" But the voice had vanished. "Hello? Come back and explain what you said to me!" I called out, feeling consumed by the cryptic message about the green gem necklace and my son Caleb.

I couldn't tell how I felt after that encounter—whether relieved or even more anxious. I walked home quietly, asking myself, "Who was that man? How does he know Caleb? How does he know about the necklace with the green gem?" Thoughts swirled in my mind, making it hard to concentrate on anything else. I held the green gem necklace around my neck firmly between my fingers. Did I imagine the man in the sky? Were those just my thoughts reflecting on me, telling me what I wanted to hear—that the green gem necklace would somehow hold the answers to my pleas? Or was it a figure who knew more, someone with awareness beyond my understanding? A figure who knew me, loved me, and understood the situation? It was a lot to take in.

I was wary of jeopardizing the fragile trust my family had recently regained in my mental health, so I refrained from telling them about the encounters. I feared they would dismiss my experiences as fabricated stories. Moreover, I knew Anna would likely forbid me from returning to the duck pond with James and Samuel. With no choice but to wait patiently, I wondered what would unfold.

CHAPTER 14

Caleb

The day spent with Jack was always an adventure but today felt different. We kicked the soccer ball, played catch, explored nature, and rode bikes—simple pleasures that made the time fly by.

Emmanuel approached me and said, "I have a place I need to visit, back to the year 27. Would you like to come with me?"

I immediately replied, "Yes! You're taking me to the year 27?" I was in disbelief. Emmanuel laughed, his eyes sparkling with mischief.

"Yes, it was many years ago!" he replied.

"Is that even possible?" I wondered aloud.

"Absolutely!" Emmanuel said, his enthusiasm infectious. I soared along on Tercelot while Emmanuel floated effortlessly ahead. "Look!" he called out. "We're almost there! See Capernaum right down below with all the stone houses? That's where we'll be visiting!"

In Capernaum, the streets bustled with activity as the aroma of freshly baked bread filled the air. Emmanuel gestured and said,

"We'll be landing by the water. Some call it a sea, others a lake—it's up to them what they think." He continued, "The village has large rectangular buildings called synagogues, where people gather to worship and pray."

I followed Emmanuel, and so did his followers, who remained ever-present by his side, a constant source of support.

Emmanuel's tone was serious, "The reception I receive in Capernaum is very different from that in The Kingdom. Many people here reject my teachings."

I frowned, puzzled that anyone could fail to adore him. "I find it hard to believe you're unpopular in Capernaum, Emmanuel."

He nodded thoughtfully. "There are some who resent my spreading of the good news. Many skeptical scribes and Pharisees object to my teachings."

Recalling His wisdom, I asked, "Why would they want to stop you, Emmanuel?" He simply looked at me with a sad expression.

In the bustling town of Capernaum, there was havoc as a blood-soaked woman stumbled into view, prompting the crowd to erupt in horrified shouts. "You're filthy! You're evil! Get out of our town!" the townspeople screamed, terrified that her presence was contagious.

Emmanuel was unfazed; he stood his ground as one of his men, Peter, yelled, "Don't touch him! Everybody move! Everybody away from Emmanuel! Nobody comes near Him!"

Undeterred, Emmanuel calmly asked, "Who just touched my robe?"

The trembling woman cried out, "I did! I did!"

Emmanuel turned to her, his eyes filled with compassion. "Your faith has healed you." In that moment, a luminous light enveloped her, and as she walked away, the blood disappeared without a trace, leaving only a radiant smile behind.

Another wild event unfolded in Capernaum as I spotted two

men standing apart from the crowd, their hands full of sores, crinkled and raw. I turned to Emmanuel, feeling a twinge of fear. "Look at their hands!" I said, my voice trembling.

Emmanuel said little, but James, one of his men, yelled, "Do not touch them!"

The men called out desperately, "Please, help us! You're our only chance!" Despite the warnings, Emmanuel walked right up to them. I recoiled at the stench - a mixture of dirt and neglect.

"Will he get sick if he touches them?" I whispered to John, another of Emmanuel's followers, who watched intently beside me.

"I am not sure," John's expression was firm but calm. Emmanuel knelt and reached out, his hand brushing against their tattered clothes. The sight was unbearable, tears glistening in their eyes.

"I forgive you; your faith has healed you," Emmanuel said.

In an instant, a remarkable transformation happened before my eyes. Fresh garments suddenly appeared on their bodies, their wounds vanished, and their skin regained a youthful, vibrant glow. "Thank you! Thank you, Messiah!" they exclaimed, their voices brimming with heartfelt gratitude as they walked back into town, leaving people in awe and reverence among the murmuring crowd.

Turning to Peter, I was still processing what I had just witnessed, "Who is Messiah?" I asked.

"It is another name for Emmanuel, but I'll explain when we return to The Kingdom," he replied, his gaze fixed on the two men with a mix of admiration and disbelief. As the astonished crowd looked on, I felt a surge of faith. Emmanuel's compassionate power changed everything for those men and all who were privileged to be present at this transformative moment.

In the bustling town, there was an old, crowded building; people were shouting frantically to get closer to Emmanuel. Peter, James, and John attempted to manage the unruly crowd, yelling, "Stay back!" Despite the chaotic scene, Emmanuel appeared unfazed, though I could sense the tension among his followers. Being small, I could duck between the legs of the crowd to get a better view and try to stay out of the way. I had never witnessed such a frantic gathering, with so many people pushing and shoving to reach him.

A dedicated group of friends boldly carried a paralyzed man on a stretcher up to the roof, their voices laced with desperation as they pleaded, "Heal him! Heal him! He hasn't walked in years! We believe in you!" They found an opening in the ceiling and carefully lowered the man down to Emmanuel, the dramatic scene unfolding before my eyes.

Instead of reacting with anger or annoyance, Emmanuel smiled calmly and said, "I forgive you for your sins," as he turned to the man. "Now, get up and walk."

The man looked around in confusion, his friends above equally bewildered. But then, something miraculous happened—he rose to his feet, radiating belief, and exclaimed with gratitude, "Thank you! Thank you!" as he bowed down on his knees before Emmanuel. The man picked up his mat and walked away; my jaw dropped in astonishment. I turned to Peter, who simply smiled, his eyes filled with admiration.

Breathless, I hurried to Emmanuel. "Emmanuel! That was incredible! How did you do that?" As before, he simply smiled in response. I noticed that people from The Kingdom often avoided direct answers, preferring to respond with an enigmatic grin. "Emmanuel, could you please call for Jack and Carcarra? I don't want them to miss anything else!"

He nodded, his expression attentive. "Return to the Sea where we first entered. You can wait for them there."

Eager to share what I had witnessed, I hurried to the shore. As I arrived, I saw Jack flying aboard Carcarra. They landed in the Sea of Galilee, with Carcarra making a dramatic nosedive that sent a massive splash of water everywhere. Jack went face-first into the sea, much to the amusement of Tercelot and me, as our giggles filled the air. The commotion drew stares from bystanders, clearly entertained by the disruption.

Emerging from the water, Jack sputtered and laughed. "I can't believe you did that!" I shouted, still laughing. As I ran into the water, splashing around, I felt the refreshing coolness embrace me. "You will not believe this place!" I exclaimed to Jack, who grinned and splashed back. We continued to play in the gentle waves, our laughter mingling as we made memories to cherish forever.

Jack and I raced through the crowd to where Emmanuel and his followers were. I spotted a man pleading with Peter, "Please, I need to speak to him!" The man cried.

"I don't trust you. You want to hurt Emmanuel," Peter replied firmly.

"No! Please, let me speak to him!" the man insisted. Emmanuel stepped forward, his tone calm and reassuring.

"What's wrong?" he asked.

The man, Jairus, spoke with urgency in his eyes, "My daughter is lying in bed close to death! Please come and put your hands on her so she will live!"

Approaching Jairus's home, the guards blocked our way. "Nobody in! The child's dead," one of them announced coldly.

"This is my child! Let me in!" Jairus cried, his voice breaking.

Peter pushed past the guards. "We're coming in!" he declared.

I followed Peter, James, John, and the others into the room where Jairus's child lay; she was a little girl who was motionless, her mother weeping at her side. Jack and I exchanged worried glances; it was a heartbreaking scene.

"Is she...?" I whispered nervously to Jack.

"She's dead," he replied quietly, his eyes wide.

Emmanuel knelt beside the child, praying over her. Moments passed, and the girl's eyes fluttered open. She looked around, then met our gaze, a smile spreading across her face. "I'm hungry!" she exclaimed. I could hardly believe my eyes. I felt glad and relieved as we sat down to eat with her. Jack and I mostly pushed the weird-looking food around and were awed by what had just transpired.

"Did that just happen?" Jack murmured, his eyes shining.

"Yeah, it did," I replied, a smile spreading across my face. "This place is incredible."

Emmanuel turned to me, "I am going to a friend's wedding in Cana. It's a long eight-hour walk. Why don't you and Jack fly there on Tercelot and Carcarra instead?"

I glanced at Jack, then back at Emmanuel. "No way! We're not missing any of this fun. We're walking!?"

Emmanuel raised an eyebrow. "Are you sure? We might not have food or water," he shared.

"I don't care! This day has been amazing, and I've never been to a wedding before. I want to be part of the crowd!"

Emmanuel smiled. "There will be lots of food, singing, and dancing."

On our way, I filled Jack in on everything I had witnessed. "You won't believe it! There was a woman who was bleeding everywhere, but no one would talk to her. Emmanuel told her that her faith had healed her, and she was fine!"

Jack's eyes widened. "No way! Impossible!" he said.

"Then there were these men with wrinkled hands who looked scary, but Emmanuel said, "I forgive you," and they walked away healed!"

Jack was stunned. "Wow! I wish I had seen that!" he exclaimed.

When we arrived at the wedding, I immediately noticed Mother Mercy, but something about her seemed different. She approached us, smiling warmly. "Hello, boys! It's so nice to see you again!"

I turned to Jack. "Does Mother Mercy look different to you?" I asked him.

"Maybe younger?" he suggested. "Or more... like a real person?" he wondered.

"I didn't know she wasn't real?" I laughed. We heard a commotion among Emmanuel's friends; they looked worried. "What's going on?" I asked Jack.

"I don't know. Why do they care about the wine?" he replied.

I overheard Emmanuel speaking urgently with Mother Mercy. "Wine is a big deal if you run out. Please, Emmanuel, we need your help!" she said anxiously.

"Jack, it sounds serious!" I said.

Emmanuel came to us and said, "Every one of you fill six stone jars with water, then pour some out and take it to the banquet master."

I glanced over at Peter, who was grumbling in the background. "How will we turn water into wine?"

Then, out of nowhere, Peter shouted, "Guys, you will not believe it—there's wine here!" The master of the ceremony tasted the wine, his eyes lighting up in delight. "Wow, you have given me the most delicious wine ever!" he proclaimed.

The wedding was lively and filled with laughter. Jack and I ate, danced, and sang, our spirits soaring. "Jack, what kind of music is this? I hear loud instruments with words I've never heard before!" I asked, puzzled.

"I have no idea; I prefer the Backstreet Boys, even though my mom said I was too young to listen to them," he replied.

"My sisters used to listen to Britney Spears, and I would get so mad!" I said. I saw Emmanuel approaching, "Thanks for inviting me! I've never been to a wedding before, and it was so much fun, but your friends need to get with the music times."

Emmanuel laughed. "I'm glad you could share this special day with me, and I will request more popular music next time," he replied warmly.

Emmanuel insisted on traveling to Bethany despite the danger it could pose to Him. He had learned of his close friend Lazarus's passing. "We must make it to Bethany," he urged. "It will be a challenging journey lasting several days, and we'll be hungry and thirsty, but it's crucial. Lazarus's family is waiting for me there," he told us.

"Jack, we climbed some big hills and walked narrow streets," I remarked.

"Yeah, and I've never seen a tree with olives before," Jack added.

When Lazarus's sisters, Mary and Martha, saw Emmanuel, they rushed to him, their voices filled with anguish. "Emmanuel! Why did you take so long? How could you let him die?" Lazarus had been dead and entombed for four days—a significant duration that convinced all that he was genuinely deceased. Rather than immediately responding to their grief, Emmanuel turned his attention to the heavy stone sealing Lazarus's tomb.

"Remove the stone," he instructed. With authority, he shouted, "Come out!" His voice resonated with a power that left me bewildered. He called out again, "Come out!"

In a surreal moment, the tomb's entrance stirred, and Lazarus emerged, still wrapped in his burial clothes. Exchanging suspicious looks, Jack and I watched as Lazarus stepped forward, the crowd gasping in stunned silence at the unfolding scene. Overcome with adoration, his sisters rushed to him, falling to their knees and embracing him, tears streaming down their faces.

Lazarus ran over to Emmanuel, gave him a fist bump, and slapped Him on the shoulder, "Thanks, brother! Thank you for coming for me." Emmanuel smiled, his eyes twinkling.

"Anytime, Laz. You knew I was coming, didn't you?"

Lazarus grinned back, a spark of joy lighting up his face. "I had a feeling! Praise You, Emmanuel! Praise You!"

I turned to Jack. "I have never seen a greater superhero in my life!" I said.

"I agree!" Jack added.

When I returned to The Kingdom, Mike stood there with a massive grin from ear to ear. "Caleb, I have a surprise for you!" he said, barely containing his excitement.

I laughed, "Mike, how many surprises do I get? I love The Kingdom!"

He leaned in, eyes sparkling. "This one's a big one. Caleb, turn around."

I turned, and my jaw dropped. "No way! Is that...?"

There stood my dad, smiling. "Yes, Caleb, it's me. I love you so much. I have missed you." He continued, "I've watched everything you've done - your T-ball games, your sportsmanship award, how kind you've been. I know your best friends. Their names are Asher and Henry. I have seen it all."

We indulged in our favorite triple brownie sundae, and I exclaimed, "Daddy, this is the best day ever!"

He turned to me with a grin. "Hey Caleb, let's do something we haven't done together in a while," he said.

"Yeah, like what?" I asked, curious.

"Well, I'd love to go to the beach," he said, jubilee lighting up his eyes.

"Yeah! Let's go smack down some sandcastles!" I cheered, already picturing the fun ahead.

At the beach, the warm sand felt perfect beneath our feet. We raced to the water after challenging each other to an arm-wrestling match. "I bet I can take you!" I said.

"Bring it on!" My Daddy said, flexing his muscles playfully. After a fierce battle, I won, and we both laughed.

After a refreshing swim in the ocean, I excitedly shouted, "Daddy, let's soar in the sky and fly like planes!"

He enthusiastically replied, "Absolutely! Why not?" his infectious spirit radiating.

That evening, as we settled down, my Daddy had another idea.

"Let's pretend it's Christmas! We can cut down a tree and decorate it," he suggested.

I giggled, "Oh, Daddy, you know Mom is terrible with Christmas lights. She throws them everywhere, and our tree looks like a jumbled mess!"

My Daddy laughed, "I can just picture that!"

"Daddy, Daddy! Can we build a fort out of sticks? I want to do all the things we never got to do!" I exclaimed.

"We have plenty of time," he said, ready for the challenge. We gathered branches and sticks to create our makeshift fort, then moved on to building an impressive Lego skyscraper.

"Who's going to knock it over first?" I asked, eyes twinkling with mischief. "Daddy, let me take the honors." I knocked it down, and our laughter filled the room.

"Good job, bud!" he said. "Let's play one of my favorite games, Super Mario 64!" I suggested.

"Of course! I know how much you love that game," my Daddy replied, and we dove into Mario's colorful world.

Flushed with victory after an intense gaming session, I exclaimed, "I beat you! You're way cooler than Mom."

My father smiled knowingly. "There are important responsibilities on Earth that your mother was right to insist on." As the evening progressed, we savored every precious moment together.

"Daddy," I said, trembling, "why do we have to go back?"

Reluctantly, he nodded. "Caleb, we need to return to where Mike awaits us. We must do so," he said.

"Why, Daddy? I don't want to leave you!" I felt a knot tightening in my stomach.

"I know, son," he replied. "But we need to listen to Mike and follow his instructions. I promise we'll have more time together in the future."

Tears stung my eyes as I pleaded, "Please don't make me go

back, Daddy. Don't leave me again. Daddy, please!"

He knelt to my level, his eyes reassuring. "I'm sorry, but you'll be back with me. Whenever you call for me, I'll be here—even if you can't see me."

We prepared to leave, but a strange sensation washed over me. "Caleb," Mike said gently, sensing my confusion. "I'll see you again, but right now, this is necessary." I felt sadness pierce through me, but my Daddy wrapped his arms around me one last time. His embrace was warm and comforting, easing the sadness just a little.

"Remember, I'll always be here," he whispered.

And then, just like that, my Daddy and Mike were gone. "Daddy! Mike! Where are you?" I shouted, panic rising in my chest. The darkness around me felt heavy, and I called, "Somebody help me! Emmanuel! Mother! Mercy! I'm scared and cold!"

Emmanuel's soothing, steady voice broke through the chill. "You are home, Caleb. You belong here." His reassuring words dispelled the darkness.

Frantic, I clung to memories of my father, fearing I might lose them. Quickening my breath, I pleaded with Emmanuel for guidance. The darkness lifted as his calming presence grounded me amid the confusion. Though uncertain, I realized I was not alone. I had to trust that I would find my way back to the light.

CHAPTER 15

Mike

For twenty-five years, I patrolled the streets of Yonkers, New York, before retiring my badge. Seeking a change of pace, I relocated to Greenville, where I spent the next decade working part-time on cold cases—driven by the challenge of delivering justice, even if it meant delving into the past. Now retired, I fill my days with golfing, hiking, and fishing from my boat, immersed in the tranquil southern lifestyle.

One Friday evening, I encountered a woman, unlike anyone I had ever seen. Her captivating blue eyes, encircled by a ring of gray, drew me in ultimately. A natural grace about her struck me—she was one of God's most exquisite creations. Resolved to break through her reserve, I mustered my courage and asked, "Hi, would you mind if I sat across from you?"

She glanced down, her gaze falling shyly to the table. "Sure, no problem," she replied gently.

Encouraged, I continued, "My name is Mike, by the way, and yours?" he asked.

"Diane," she responded.

"Would you like to go to the diner after bingo?" I could see her hesitate, and for a moment, I feared I had pushed too hard.

When I walked her over to the person picking her up, I discovered it was her daughter. To my surprise, her daughter exclaimed, "Sure! My mom would love to go with you tonight!"

I felt a wave of relief wash over me. We might have missed this opportunity altogether without her daughter's enthusiastic support. I gathered my thoughts and summoned the courage to sit across from her again.

When we sat down at the diner, I started firing off questions that felt dumb in retrospect. "So, where did you grow up? Have you ever been married? How many kids do you have?" Her responses were brief—just yes or no, with no details. Each simple answer made my worry spike. "Why did you move to Greenville?" I asked, but she didn't engage with that one either. Realizing my nervousness was the natural barrier between us, I tried to fill the silence. After a while, I suggested we walk to ease the tension. Maybe the fresh air would help us connect better. Despite my efforts, the date didn't unfold as I had planned.

Diane didn't show up at bingo for weeks afterward, and I couldn't shake the feeling that I'd blown my chance. But then, one evening, she returned. I noticed a subtle shift in her demeanor; she seemed more approachable, her eyes sparkling with a newfound light.

Diane suddenly caught my attention. "Hey, Mike," she said, her voice soft but firm. "I'm sorry about a few weeks ago. I was just having a rough day."

I smiled, trying to ease the tension. "No problem, Diane. Don't we all have those?"

She looked relieved, her shoulders relaxing a bit. "If you'd like to go for a walk at some point—just casually, nothing serious—I'd love to do that," she told me.

"That sounds nice," I replied, feeling a spark of confidence.

Spending more time with Diane's family, I got to know her daughter Anna better. She sat down next to me with a pleading look, "Mike," she said, trembling slightly, "can you help me find my brother, Caleb?" she asked.

"What happened to your brother, Anna?" I asked gently. She took a breath, her eyes welling up with emotion. "He's been missing for years. It's been tough on our family. We don't know where he is or what happened to him when we were kids. I just... I want to bring him home."

I hesitated. "Anna, I don't think I should be involved. Your mom hasn't even talked to me about him."

Something in Anna's gaze—those puppy dog blue eyes, so earnest and pleading—made it hard to say no. I felt a pang of compassion. "I don't know how well your mom would take it," I added, trying to maintain some distance. "If she found out, it could end our friendship."

Anna persisted, her voice soft yet insistent. "We don't have to tell her right now. If more information comes out, I promise I'll tell her and blame myself. I'll say it was my idea to get you involved." Her tenacity was palpable, and I wavered. I had spent years working with lost children, and the idea of helping them was a weakness I couldn't easily ignore. Driven by compassion, I reluctantly agreed to help.

I cherished the time I spent with Diane, fully invested in our relationship. It felt natural to integrate into her life. "Do you want to play bingo, or should we skip it?" I asked.

Diane smiled, "Hey, would you mind if we watched James and Samuel tonight instead?" she suggested.

"Of course not!" I replied enthusiastically, "They're so much fun!"

Taking James and Samuel out on my boat became a cherished adventure. "Okay, guys, wear your orange life vests!" I announced, trying to sound authoritative but knowing the fight would follow. James and Samuel argued, and I stifled my laughter as I watched Diane patiently explain.

"Wear these," her tone firm yet caring.

James chimed in, "But I know how to swim! I don't want to wear it!"

Diane countered, "Well, if you want to go on the boat, you must wear them."

Eventually, after some back-and-forth, I added, "As the boat owner, I require you both to wear them!"

James, ever the clever one, said, "But you and Grandma don't wear them!"

Smiling, I explained, "These are rules for kids." After some reluctant sighs, they finally put on their life vests.

I took the boys shopping for toys when they visited my home. "Okay, what do you want to play with at my house?" I asked, grinning at the delight on their faces. Diane shook her head, amused but slightly concerned. "Well, I've never had children," I explained. "So having your grandchildren around is just too much fun! Let me spoil them a little."

James squealed, "I want this! I want that!" His enthusiasm was infectious, and I loved every moment.

"I've got a great idea! Why don't we buy wood and paint to make a birdhouse?" I said.

"Yeah, yeah, Mike! Let's do it!" James and Samuel cheered in unison.

After we gathered our supplies at the store, we raced home, and I focused on being patient with them. "Okay, now this side gets glued to this side," I instructed, but James had gotten glue all over me before I knew it. Not to be outdone, Samuel amusingly tried to put glue in his nose.

"Hold on, hold on!" I laughed, gently redirecting them. "Let's focus on the birdhouse. Once it's all put together, we'll let it dry."

While the birdhouses dried, I suggested, "Let's walk in the garden while we wait."

The boys followed eagerly, bombarding me with questions. "Do you own the lake? Is the lake shallow? Is it cold?" they asked, their curiosity endless. I answered, enjoying their enthusiasm. But their questions kept coming, one after another, making me chuckle.

Eventually, I said, "Alright, it's time to head back and paint the birdhouses."

The boys erupted in cheers, "Yeah! Let's paint!"

James immediately declared, "I want the red!"

Samuel countered, "Wait, no, I'm using the red!" And soon, they were in a playful tug-of-war over the paint colors.

"Okay, okay, we have plenty of red," I said, trying to mediate. "How about we mix in some orange color, too?" I asked.

"No! I want it red and orange!" James insisted. Whatever color James chose, Samuel eagerly copied, and before long, both boys had painted all over themselves and my walls.

"Look, boys! You've made a masterpiece!" I exclaimed, grinning at their messy hands and faces.

"I can't wait to hang them in Grandma's favorite tree!" James shouted.

"Yes! We'll hang them there as soon as they dry," I promised, feeling happy. The scene had transformed into a vibrant canvas of colors, and I cherished these moments, knowing they were not just making birdhouses but memories that would last a lifetime.

In the following weeks, I left Christopher a few messages, and when he finally picked up the phone, I was eager to connect. "Christopher, it's Mike calling about the kidnappings along the East Coast. Would you be willing to meet?" I explained who I was and my background.

"Absolutely! I'd love to meet," he replied, his charm alive in his voice. He was surprisingly handsome when I arrived at his office the following week. Christopher's bright disposition made him instantly likable. Christopher shared he recently helped reunite twins with their parents. "Isn't it a wonderful feeling?" I responded, remembering the euphoria I felt in my line of work, especially when outcomes were positive. "It's rare, but those moments make it all worthwhile."

"Given my close relationship with Diane, Caleb's disappearance has stirred up many emotions for me," I confided.

Christopher leaned in and replied, "I understand how this would deeply affect you. It's one thing to work a case professionally, but another when you have a personal stake in it."

I continued, "Diane's strength throughout this ordeal has been remarkable." I could feel the power of my connection to the family.

Christopher nodded, grasping the emotional gravity of the situation. "It can be tough when your personal feelings cloud your judgment," he offered insightfully, resonating with my experience.

We delved into the details of Caleb's case, piecing together the story from what Diane, Anna, and Cara had shared. It was clear Christopher understood the high stakes involved and shared my passion for seeking justice. I was grateful to have his support in navigating the challenges ahead.

"I don't want to be negative," I said, looking Christopher in the eye, "but both you and I know the chances of Caleb being found alive are slim."

He paused and replied, "I know," nodding in agreement. "It's a tough part of the job, but another important aspect is bringing them home—whether alive or dead. Families appreciate just having their loved ones back, even if it's not the outcome we desired."

I sighed, feeling the impact of his words. "I agree, but it still isn't what I want for Caleb. We know the odds are against us."

Before I left, Christopher tried to lighten the mood. "Hey, you're from New York. You like the Yankees, right?" he asked.

"I love them," I replied, a smile breaking my thoughts. Our

conversation shifted as we reminisced about baseball.

Christopher said, "The crack of the bat and the aroma of hotdogs and pretzels wafting through Yankee Stadium."

I added, "And the Seventh Inning Stretch—singing 'Take Me Out to the Ball Game' together, everyone joining in." It was a welcome distraction from our heavy talk about Caleb, and we laughed as we shared memories of the game.

I left Christopher's office with an urgent need to find Caleb, which consumed me. I jotted down notes and underlined vital points, yet the tranquil morning light captivated me. The rising sun painted the lake in a vibrant orange, pink, and purple tapestry, momentarily distracting me from the turmoil in my mind. Lost in reflection, I doodled in my journal, where I penned the words, "Where are you, Caleb?"—unaware I was closer than I knew.

CHAPTER 16

Christopher

I picked up the phone and called Jimmy. "Hey Jimmy, what's up?" I asked him.

"I'm planning on visiting at the end of the month!" Jimmy exclaimed.

"I'm so happy to hear that. I could use the visit," I replied, feeling on top of the world.

"No problem, man. I'm just ready for a change of scenery," he said. "What are you up to today?" he asked.

"Well, I'm going for a run on the Swamp Rabbit Trail. It's a great run," I said.

"Maybe I can beat you when I get there!" he joked.

"Looking forward to it, brother. I'll see you in a few weeks."

When I hung up, a wave of contentment washed over me. Amidst the paperwork clutter and the stack of recent cases awaiting my attention at my desk, I felt unburdened. I slipped on my running shoes and hit the Swamp Rabbit Trail. I knew the route well, and the natural beauty cleared my mind, offering a moment of reflection amidst the bustle of my work.

That evening, I turned my attention to my emails and found a series of messages from Mike, each with attachments, and decided to call him. "Hey Mike, I've got a bunch of files here. I'd rather go over them with you on the phone," I said.

"That's fine," he replied. "I just want you to know there's a case filing for Jeffrey Scott." I felt a chill run down my spine as I opened the file,

"Mike, you won't believe this. Jeffrey Scott's case is one I reopened after many years with no resolution, and it's been haunting me ever since. I couldn't figure out what had happened to him and was not able to give his family any closure. Jeffrey's case was one I just couldn't let go."

Mike's voice softened. "I know, man. I know it's hard, but Jeffrey's case most likely connects to Caleb's kidnapping," he said.

"Wow, I would never have thought of that," I replied, my mind racing. "If you hear anything else, please update me. I'll do the same," I said.

"Absolutely," Mike said. "We'll figure this out together. Just take care of yourself, alright?"

"Yeah, I will. Thanks, Mike." With my mind still racing, I knew I needed to rest, but the gravity of Caleb's and Jeffrey's cases lingered heavily in my thoughts.

I took a moment and returned a call from a woman named Diane. "Hi, this is Christopher, a Detective in South Carolina. Am I speaking with Diane?" I asked.

"Yes, yes, this is her. Thank you for returning my call. I know you're very busy," she replied, hesitant.

"It's been hectic around here," I admitted.

Diane continued, "Well, I just wanted to talk to you. I know you probably can't help me." The palpable strife in her voice struck a chord within me.

"Go on," I urged.

To my surprise, she said, "I know you've met with Mike, a friend of mine. When my son Caleb was six years old, he disappeared in a small town called Milford Falls in New York. We've searched for him for many years, but there have been no leads. It's been a cold case, but it recently reopened." I listened intently, unsure what to say about her heartbreaking story.

Her words settled upon me as she spoke; my hands trembled as I gripped the phone. When she finally finished, I struggled to find the right words in response. "I know how important this is, Diane. Thank you for entrusting me with your son's story. I'll do everything I can to assist you, though I can't make any guarantees. I'll be sure to inform you of any updates," I told her.

"Thank you," she replied, her voice barely above a whisper. After we hung up, I sat with that conversation, reflecting on it. I had spoken to many mothers of missing children before, but something about Diane's case had captured my attention. A chill ran through my limbs, and I knew I had to find Caleb for her.

I sat in my office, staring at the phone as it suddenly rang. The caller ID displayed "Sheriff's Department, North Carolina," causing a sinking feeling in the pit of my stomach. I steeled myself and picked up the receiver. "This is Christopher."

A voice on the other end, "Detective Harris here. I'm afraid I have some troubling news," he calmly said.

"What is it?" I asked, my heart racing.

"There have been two similar cases of abducted children from the same area here in North Carolina, just a few days apart, nearly two decades ago," the detective explained. "First, there's Jayden Gore. At the time of the abduction, he was an eight-year-old boy with autism, taken from his caregivers at a local park."

I clenched my jaw. "What happened to him?" I asked.

"The abduction happened so quickly that no description of the perpetrators was available. But miraculously, police found Jayden alive four days afterward." A moment of relief washed over me, but it quickly faded as I pressed for more details.

"In what condition was he found?"

The detective's voice grew somber. "Battered, with a broken leg, and left in a ditch by the roadside."

I could picture that poor boy, vulnerable and alone. Caleb's case was a chilling reminder of how quickly things could spiral out of control. I knew we had to dig deeper and make the connections before history repeated itself. "Thank you for the information. We must do everything we can to prevent this from happening again."

Sleep came fitfully that night when I was jolted awake. I was startled by a familiar voice, "Christopher! Christopher!"

I couldn't pinpoint where the voice came from, but the panic surging through me prompted me to grab the baseball bat and call out, "Who's there? Who's in my kitchen?" Silence, except for my ragged breath. Gripping the bat tightly for protection, I cautiously ventured toward the kitchen to find a strange glow that vanished as quickly as it appeared.

The next day, I woke up on the cold tile floor in the kitchen, a shiver running down my spine as memories of my childhood sleepwalking episodes flooded back - the helplessness of those nights when my parents had to take drastic measures to prevent me from getting hurt. The unsettling dream lingered in my mind, a reminder of the darkness that sometimes creeps in uninvited.

At the office that day, an envelope labeled "personal" was sitting on my desk and distracted me. Inside were the DNA test results for Jimmy. To my disappointment, Jimmy's results showed a match to a supposed aunt in Maryland who had passed away two years ago, with no other known living relatives. Though I had always been open with Jimmy, I decided not to share this news with him right now, especially since he was arriving today. I pushed the results to the back of my mind, focusing instead on making the most of our time together. Looking back now, I realize the envelope held so much crucial information. Inside were details that could unravel the mystery I was chasing.

Eager to reunite with my brother Jimmy, I hurried home. As soon as I grabbed him in a hug, it felt like no time had passed between us. "Wow, did you gain some weight?" Jimmy teased, a playful grin on his face.

"Hilarious," I replied, rolling my eyes. "You're just jealous of my lean physique." That evening, we grilled thick, juicy burgers from the local farm. The air sizzled with the savory aroma of our dinner mingling with our laughter.

"Remember when we tried to barbecue in the backyard and almost set the porch on fire?" he chuckled between bites.

"Yeah, and Mom was ready to kill us!" I laughed.

After dinner, we headed out to play baseball. The game was as competitive as ever, and our spirits were high despite the friendly rivalry. "Think you can strike me out?" Jimmy challenged, his eyes sparkling with mischief.

"I know I can. Watch me. Don't forget who the champion is!" I shot back, tossing the ball his way with a grin. We threw the ball back and forth, exchanging playful jabs and reliving old memories. In those moments, the worries and stresses of work faded, replaced by gratitude for this connection—the enduring bond that had always united us.

CHAPTER 17

Cara

Eagerly awaiting Frank's arrival, I felt drained from Ted's news about Sister Kathleen. I went to pick up Frank at the airport and greeted him with a big hug. "Nice to see you again, Frank!" I said, my voice slightly trembling.

"It's wonderful to see you, Cara," he replied warmly. But he quickly sensed something was off. "What's wrong, Cara?"

Tears filled my eyes. "There's just so much with Caleb's investigation. I never imagined it would be this difficult. I'm so stressed," I shared.

"I know, Cara. I'm sorry you must go through this," Frank said empathetically. "I'll be working a lot with Mike this weekend, so maybe we can keep you updated on any new information. That way, you won't have to repeat what you already know," he reassured.

"I think that would be a good idea," I replied.

"Let's get Chinese food like we had last time I stayed over," he suggested.

"Great idea!" I said. "Don't forget to get extra shrimp, like last time," he said.

"Ewe!" I protested.

"Hey, a guy's gotta eat!" he shot back, feigning innocence.

The following day, we jogged along the Swamp Rabbit Trail; Frank, panting, called out, "Come on, Cara, slow down! I can't keep up with you!" I couldn't help but laugh, amused that this man fitter than most of America was struggling to match my pace. I had unloaded twenty years of my burdens onto him, and Frank accepted them all without complaint. Our time together was a refreshing change, filled with shared meals, hiking, kayaking at Lake Keeowee, and other simple pleasures I enjoyed wholeheartedly.

Frank and I had a few days before he had to head back to New York. I turned to him and said, "Frank, I want to drive back to Falling Creek, Virginia, where Sister Kathleen lived."

He replied, "Okay, Cara. I can go with you if you'd like." I smiled, feeling relieved. "That's a good idea. Why don't we leave tomorrow morning?" he suggested.

"Sounds perfect. Let's plan on leaving tomorrow then," I said, my spirits lifting at the prospect of the journey.

I didn't know what to expect when returning to the old nunnery, but I was intent on getting there no matter what. Frank eased my nerves during the drive by playing '80s music—songs from a time before his generation, yet ones he genuinely enjoyed. The ride was mercifully short, and we arrived quickly. I hoped we wouldn't have to stay long; I just wanted to get in and out as soon as possible. "Ted gave us directions to the old nunnery where Sister Kathleen lived," I said, glancing at the paper. "I think this is the turn right here, Frank."

We turned onto a long, winding dirt driveway. As we approached, I looked around in wonder. "How on earth did anyone find a church way back here?" Frank chuckled.

"I have no idea, but it's certainly remote," he said.

"Well, at least it's beautiful," I replied, taking in the serene surroundings. "It's comforting to know Caleb visited such a peaceful place."

Frank agreed, "Yes, Cara, it is lovely. I'm sure the nuns took terrific care of the boys."

I recalled Sister Kathleen's sweet voice. "She was very kind."

After Sister Kathleen's death, I learned that the once-vibrant nunnery had closed down. She had been the last remaining nun, and now the building looked ancient and worn, with locked doors and cracked seams. I peered through the windows, searching for any sign of my brother Caleb; I could feel his lingering presence there. "Caleb was here," I told Frank, who listened silently. "I can feel it, just like the last time I came. I feel his presence, and Sister Kathleen's too."

Frank replied softly, "I'm glad you feel like Caleb was here. Trust your intuition, Cara."

"We need to go through the woods. What if the guys left something behind? What if we find something?"

Frank protested, "Cara, it's been over twenty years. I doubt we'll find anything in the woods now."

Defiantly, I responded, "Well, you can return and get something to eat if you want. But I'm going into the woods—with or without you."

Conceding to my wishes, Frank smirked, "Okay, ma'am. We're going into the woods."

The day was getting late, and I was growing hungry—my mood turning sour—though I knew this was my idea, not Frank's. I was going to find what I was searching for. Kneeling in the woods, which was unusual for me, I whispered an emotional plea, "Dear God, if you can hear me, I ask that you give me a sign. Show me something, please." Frank knelt beside me, respectfully silent, sharing the quietness of the moment. In unison, we uttered, "Amen," and continued our journey.

"Cara, I think it's time to head back," Frank said, glancing at the fading daylight. "It's getting very dark, and we don't have a flashlight."

I reluctantly agreed, "Okay, Frank, but can we stay the night? I want to search one more day tomorrow," I told him.

"Yes, Cara, we can stay the night," he replied reassuringly. "And I'll help you search tomorrow."

Frank and I walked back to our car, and I tripped over something. Frank immediately grabbed me and exclaimed, "Cara, watch out! There are a lot of sticks and debris on the ground."

However, the object I had tripped over felt more significant than a stick. Pushing aside the leaves, I uncovered a blue backpack with an LL Bean logo and the initials "CHJ" stitched on the front—Caleb's initials. "Frank! Frank! Stop!" I yelled. "This is Caleb's backpack!"

Frank turned around, his expression skeptical. "No, it's been twenty-two years, Cara."

I pointed frantically at the backpack. "It's got CHJ - Caleb Joseph Hart. My mom had a dumb way of writing our initials, placing the last name initial in the middle. For instance, she would write CHJ instead of the conventional CJH. This backpack is Caleb's!"

"Cara, don't touch it! I need to go through it first. There could be evidence," he urged.

"Evidence? Frank, this is my brother's! I have to take it!" I insisted, my voice rising.

"Cara, don't touch it! There could be DNA on it. The backpack could be crucial to our investigation. Please!"

Realizing the importance of preserving any potential evidence, I relented. "Fine."

He explained, "Once we get to the car, I'll get the proper equipment to handle the bag. We'll take it home and analyze it," Frank said.

"Fine, Frank! Way to ruin my day!" I stormed back to the car, anger fueling inside me. I sat in the front seat with my arms folded, refusing to talk to Frank the whole way home. Bitterness and fury brewed in my chest for whoever had done this to my brother.

It was time for Frank to fly back to New York, "I don't want you to go back."

He replied, "I know, me neither."

I admitted, "It's just so far away."

He said, "Well, I'll return in a few weeks."

I confessed, "I know, but I've gotten used to having you here."

His eyes were kind, and he smiled and said, "I like hearing that."

Frank gathered his things, a lump formed in my throat, and I said, "I didn't realize how much I needed this time together."

Pausing, he looked at me thoughtfully and said, "You know you can always reach out, even from a distance."

I said softly, "I know."

Trying to lighten the mood, he added, "I promise we'll plan more trips. Just think of all the places we can explore - like that little diner you love." With understanding in his eyes, he grinned, "And you can finally try that blueberry pie."

I took a deep breath, struggling to contain my swirling emotions. Frank's presence had provided a sense of security that I hadn't even realized I had been missing. When he walked away, a pang of loss settled over me, the reality of his departure creeping in. "Just promise you'll take care of yourself," I said, my voice barely above a whisper.

"Of course," Frank replied. With one last lingering look, he was gone.

"It's going to feel different without you," I called after him, even though I knew he was already halfway down the stairs.

"Hey!" he shouted back, turning at the last moment. "You've

got my number. Text me whenever you need a laugh—or just to vent."

I nodded, even though he couldn't see me. "I will."

He added, "Remember, distance doesn't change anything between us," reassuringly smiling.

"Yeah, but it still feels like a big gap. Don't get too comfortable without me!" I laughed. The sound of his footsteps faded away, and I realized just how much I valued our friendship.

While I prefer solitude, Frank's friendship was a meaningful connection beyond my family. Each day, I got up and faced the world. There was a constant battle between staying functional and succumbing to the depression, anger, guilt, and hopelessness I carried. "Hey," I murmured, shaking my head to clear the dark thoughts. "Just keep moving forward," I'd say to myself. Every action and every step felt mechanical and calculated; I was merely following a program to keep going. The pressure to maintain this façade of normalcy was immense. "It's okay to feel bad sometimes," I told myself. "You're allowed to struggle." But the choice was stark: either continue to fight and fulfill my responsibilities or allow myself to fall into the darkness that threatened my life.

I sighed, regretting that I hadn't realized how close I was at that time to finding my brother. "Maybe if I'd just kept looking," I whispered, frustration creeping into my voice. "What if he's out there waiting for me?"

I closed my eyes momentarily, picturing Frank's encouraging smile and belief that I could overcome anything. "I can't let the past pain hold me back," I said aloud, the desire building within me. I took a deep breath. "I need to keep pushing," I vowed.

"For Caleb."

CHAPTER 18

Christopher

I had recently learned that a man named Peter, matching Sister Kathleen's description, was in police custody. Immediately, I called the detective in Florida. "While you have Peter there, could you ask him a specific question? Ask if he remembers a boy with distinctive blue eyes who might have stood out amongst the other boys. It's an important detail."

He assured me he would, "Sure, Christopher. I'll ask Peter and get back to you," the detective replied.

When the detective relayed Peter's response, I felt sick. "Christopher, it is the detective in Florida calling you back," the voice said, "I spoke to Peter. I will play you the recording of his response to your question."

The words swirled around in my mind as the tape played, "The boy stood out among the others; his blue eyes, a color I had never witnessed, remained wide even when he was scared. And he was smart, far beyond his age. Despite our attempts to silence him, the boy fought hard against us—caring for the other boys and trying to seek help when necessary. The boy was defiant, and his punishments were severe, depriving him of necessities for an extended period. I remember his eyes were the color of the sky." My concern for Caleb's fate surged within me, intertwining with the urgency of my mission.

I called Mike and Frank. "Hold on, Christopher, I'm putting you on speakerphone so we can all hear you," Frank said.

"Okay," I replied. "I called the detective in Florida, and Peter said he remembered a boy matching Caleb's description - with blue eyes, defiant behavior, and an unusually caring and intelligent demeanor."

Finally, Mike spoke solemnly, "Thank you for updating us, Christopher. I appreciate it, even though I don't want to hear negative news. At least we have some leads now," he said.

"I agree," I said, feeling the gravity of our conversation. "Alright, talk to you soon. Goodbye." As I hung up the phone, Peter's chilling account of the boy's ordeal replayed in my mind.

I listened closely to Pam's interview with the detectives. At first, she appeared eager to dissociate herself from the East Coast kidnappings, fervently denying any involvement. "I am hungry and would talk—maybe if you got me a snack."

The detective responded with disbelief, "You're putting your life and the lives of others on the line for a mere snack?" Unfazed, the detective pressed, "Fine, what do you want?"

Hunger drove Pam to respond, "Anything you have, but I'm hungry. Without food, I won't talk." Once she had her snack, Pam said, "Well, my brother Felix—no, I mean my brother Pete. Yeah, Pete was the mastermind. He was the smart one."

The detective interrupted, "That doesn't sound right."

Pam hesitated, "Well, I don't remember who the mastermind was."

"Can you tell us where Felix lives?" The detective pressed, "I need to know. Where does Felix live?"

Pam replied, "I don't know. I don't speak to him anymore. I have no interest or comment on this." The detective recognized Pam's lack of legal savvy and couldn't help but laugh at her remark about playing the role of the lawyer.

He said, "What if I offer you immunity for revealing Felix's location, along with a lifetime supply of food from the Piggly Wiggly?"

To his surprise, Pam responded, "Okay, I agree. My brother Felix lives in San Jose, California, and I have no doubt you'll find him there. I also have a sister, Misty, who was involved in the kidnappings."

Felix's unsettling appearance, his towering frame, greasy hair, scarred brow, and disturbing tattoos—including a swastika and teardrop—matched my preconceived image of a serial killer. I watched his interview, an icy chill of fear ran down my spine, and a profound sense of dread overcame me, knowing this dangerous individual had evaded capture for two decades.

My phone's ring shattered the tense silence. Dread already gripping me, I answered. "Hi, this is Christopher."

A detective from Massachusetts spoke with a pressing concern, "I have crucial information about the East Coast kidnappings case. There's a boy named Max Hamlin, who was seven years old at the time he went missing; we believe he was a part of the East Coast kidnappings," he said.

"Go on," I urged.

The detective continued gravely, "An eyewitness, a young girl, described seeing a large woman at the scene of Max's abduction." It was horrifying to imagine someone committing such a crime. But the worst was yet to come.

"We have also recently discovered bones nearby, belonging to another missing child—Jeffrey Scott. He was five years old when he vanished from his backyard," he shared.

"I can't even believe this," I said. "I have been researching that case for as long as I can remember," I told him.

"I know," the caller replied. "I'm hoping this information helps us put these scum bags away for life," he said.

"I agree. Thank you for getting in touch with me," I said, my mind racing with the implications of this news. Each additional detail felt like another nail in the coffin of innocence. How many more children were out there, lost to this tragedy? After I hung up, I sat in silence, considering each boy and the challenges they had endured.

CHAPTER 19

Mike

Christopher called as Frank and I were about to leave for the night, and Cara was within earshot. "Frank, Christopher is on the phone. Can you please shut the door? What's up?" I said.

Christopher's voice came through, apologetic. "Hey, guys, I am sorry to keep calling, but there's another boy named Oliver Benson from Georgia." I sighed.

"There's an overwhelming list of missing boys," I said.

"I know," Christopher replied. "An eyewitness described a homeless-looking individual grabbing a young boy. We're not sure it's connected, but it was around the same time frame and along the East Coast kidnappings," he shared.

"I can't even believe all these revelations," I said.

"I know it's been tough," Christopher continued, "but I pray this leads us to Caleb," he said.

"Me too, Christopher," I replied.

"Same here," Frank said.

My connection to Diane made it challenging to approach this

case objectively. After years of silence, the sudden influx of new information angered me, and I wondered, "Why has this taken so long?" In just six months, the floodgates had opened, exposing potential perpetrators and the names of missing children—revelations that would typically have sparked my investigative drive and passion but instead left me drained.

I spoke to Christopher again the next day. "The results came in," he said, his voice heavy, "they revealed that the remains belonged to a six-month-old boy named Thomas Meyer, who had vanished from a park in Pennsylvania." I took a deep breath. "The description his mother gave of the perpetrators—a tall man and a shorter one, with one having a drooping eye—struck a chilling resemblance to the circumstances of Caleb's disappearance," he said.

"I am dumbstruck; so many people have been affected. It's too similar," I replied.

"We need to investigate this further."

I nodded, conviction settling over me. "We can't let this go. We have to find out everything we can."

Christopher's voice sounded tired as he spoke with concern. "Sorry to bother you again tonight, but the sheriff's department in North Carolina called. There are two similar child abduction cases from the same area, just a few days apart." I braced myself, dreading the news. "One involves an 8-year-old boy named Jayden Gore, who has autism. His caregivers reported that he was abducted from a local park so quickly that there is no description of the perpetrators." My heart sank. "Rescuers found Jayden alive four days after the kidnapping, battered with a broken leg, left in a ditch by the roadside."

I shook my head in disbelief. "In all my years, I've never seen this many children abducted in such a short time frame, resembling the same type of abduction. I am overwhelmed."

Christopher continued, "The other case is similar." I felt a chill.

"We can't let this continue. I appreciate you updating me, but we must act fast." The tension was building in my chest.

Christopher sent me the interviews. I closely watched Misty's face; I noticed her every move, looking for any signs of deception. My frustration simmered. "Look at her," I muttered under my breath. "How can she be so calm?"

Misty's responses were a jumbled mess of contradictions. "This is infuriating," I said, clenching my fists. "Her desperate attempts to cover her tracks made it worse." When the detective mentioned the boy with the captivating eyes, I noticed Misty was pale. "There it is," I said, leaning closer to the screen. "She's shaken. Why won't she just be honest?" I shook my head as she clammed up, refusing to cooperate without legal counsel. "Peter was right about one thing: they're all dumb. They think they can outsmart everyone."

I saw through Misty's deceit, viewing her as a manipulative liar willing to betray innocent children for her gain. "She thinks she can play us," I muttered, shaking my head.

Felix's interview is the one that got under my skin.

Detective: "The police department will record this interview. Can you tell me where you lived exactly twenty- two years ago?"

Felix: "Nowhere, really, I was living in a van on the East Coast."

Detective: "Great, that takes me to my next question. Did you own a white van around that time?"

Felix: "Yeah."

Detective: "Were your siblings, Pam, Misty, and Peter, ever in the van with you?"

Felix: "Don't remember, really, but I guess?"

Detective: "So, yes or no?"

Felix: "Yes."

Detective: "Do you know a police officer named John?"

Felix: "Yeah, I don't know where you're going with this; I am getting impatient."

Detective: "Thank you for your patience. Were any of your three siblings involved in the kidnapping of multiple young boys?"

Felix: "No idea, I don't speak to them."

Detective: "Were you ever involved in the abduction of young boys on the northeast coast?"

Felix: "I want an attorney present."

I called Christopher. "We have enough information to bring the case to the DA."

"We have to be sure. We can't risk it getting turned down, and we know the DA will take forever to respond. Hopefully, they'll accept it and open the case immediately."

Christopher responded, "Well, we have Sister Kathleen's testimony, and the discovery of the children's bones. The facts speak for themselves." I responded.

Despite my typically sharp detective instincts, I somehow overlooked that Caleb's whereabouts had been right in front of my face the entire time. I had all the answers right in my pocket; did my objectivity prevent me from seeing the truth?

CHAPTER 20

Diane

Mike stopped by early in the morning, "Diane, I have a special evening planned for you. We're skipping bingo tonight, and I want to take you to one of your favorite restaurants—Ruth's Chris Steakhouse," he said.

"Oh, what a rare treat! I've been craving their steak," I exclaimed. "You know I love those stuffed mushrooms and the roasted Brussels sprouts!" I told him.

"I know, me too! Just thinking about it makes my mouth water. Be ready; I'll come back tonight at six for you," he said.

"Okay!" I replied, excited.

Driving to the restaurant, I was engrossed in a text conversation with Anna about James's school day and lost track of our surroundings.

Mike pulled over on the Liberty Bridge, "Hey, Diane, pull away from your phone for a moment. Look at the colors in the sky."

I glanced up, captivated by the view. "It is stunning. Thank you for stopping to let me see it," I told him.

"Let's get out," he said.

I hesitated, my stomach growling. "Oh, I'm starving. I don't want to get out," I said.

"Just get out for a few minutes," Mike insisted. Lost in my thoughts, I didn't notice Mike dropping to one knee. I was absorbed in the moment and almost missed him patiently waiting for my attention. The magenta lights danced across his face as he smiled up at me, his eyes filled with kindness. "Will you marry me?" he asked, his voice steady.

I don't know how I said it, but it was a quick "Yes!" A smile spread across my face as I realized what had happened.

At that moment, everything felt perfect. The unexpected question left me speechless, my eyes locked on the dazzling five-carat diamond in the gold ring.

"Diane, you deserve to be happy," Mike said. "This won't take away from your love for Caleb. You deserve happiness, and I love you. I want to spend my life with you." His words filled me, lifting and minimizing my self-loathing. Tears of joy filled my eyes; I felt the depth of his feelings and saw the future we could build together.

I ventured out early the following day, heading to the duck pond. Tears flowed as I walked, mourning the life Caleb never got to experience. I gazed across the pond, my breath caught—there he was, the elusive man dressed casually with a serene aura about him. His presence brought an unexpected calm, as though he were there just for me. Visiting the duck pond, hoping to glimpse the man whose eyes seemed to hold the heavens, became a cherished ritual that lifted my spirits more than I could have ever imagined.

Yet, returning home, an uneasy feeling lingered. "Girls, what's wrong?" I asked, but neither Anna nor Cara responded. "Anna, Cara, talk to me," I pressed.

Cara said, "Nothing, Mom. Just leave me alone," rolling her

eyes dismissively. An air of turmoil seemed to surround them.

I asked Mike and Ted, "Have you noticed anything off with Anna and Cara?"

"Honestly, I've seen nothing unusual," Ted replied.

Even Mike shook his head, saying, "Yeah, everything seems normal to me." The air of secrecy fueled my growing apprehensions. I withdrew from the world, finding strength in the company of my grandchildren. My interactions with Mike became strained as I fought with my conflicting emotions.

I prepared breakfast that morning; I absentmindedly turned on the television—a habit I rarely indulged in. Humming while watching the birds at my feeder, the mention of "East Coast kidnappings" suddenly jolted me. Instantly, I understood the source of Anna and Cara's distress. I had to steady myself, utilizing the coping strategies my therapist, Erica, had recently taught me. With a silent prayer for courage, I turned off the television and steeled myself to face the challenges ahead. Refusing to let despair consume me, I knew that feeling sorry for myself wouldn't bring Caleb back. I would uncover the truth about his disappearance before my time on Earth ran out, clinging to knowing he was still out there.

I am unsure of what got into me that evening; something came over my mind—a force beyond my control. I grabbed a bag, jumped in my car, and drove north, back toward Milford Falls, where everything began. While driving, my phone pinged with a new text: Anna. "Mom, where are you? You need to come home." I sighed.

Cara's message popped immediately: "Mom, we checked your location. We know you're heading to New York."

Then Anna chimed in again. "Mom, if I don't hear back from you, I'm driving to New York."

Frustrated, I pulled over and quickly typed a response. "Thank you for your concern. I'm okay. Please just let me have some space."

Anna replied almost immediately: "Fine, Mom. twenty-four hours, or I'm heading to New York."

"Whatever, Mom," Cara added, her typical sarcasm bleeding through the screen.

I knew it was just a matter of time before Mike's name flashed on my screen. I sent his call to voicemail, and his worried text was as follows: "I spoke to Anna and Cara, please be careful."

I pulled into the stone driveway of the Milford Falls home; I felt like my reality had shifted. I parked in the driveway of the old blue house beside the double doors I always entered. When I tried the doors, they were locked. Confused, I yelled, "Anna, Cara, why are the doors locked?" Then I remembered the old windows around the back that never shut adequately, and I let myself in through the open space.

When I entered the home, I sensed something was off. The smells were unfamiliar, and the place felt different; I refused to accept a change. Sprinting up the steps, I rushed to Caleb's room to find the room was a different shade of blue. Alarmed, I cried, "Who painted my son's room?" Then, I noticed Caleb's belongings were missing; I yelled, "Where are all of Caleb's things? Someone has taken them all!" Panicked, I yelled out, "Anna? Cara? Phil? Caleb? Is anybody home? Where is everybody?"

The room was spinning, and I didn't know what was happening. I ran to Caleb's closet and opened the door. Even though everything looked different, I glanced up to the top right corner and saw the familiar scribble Caleb had gotten in trouble for—"Caleb was here." Relieved, I thought, "This is my home." Nothing looked familiar, so I started going through the child's belongings. "Whose stuff is this?" I threw myself onto the cool floor, closed my eyes, and waited for a family member to return home.

A strange woman standing in my son's room jolted me from

my dreamlike state. She said, "Excuse me. Can I help you?" The woman looked at me. "I'm sorry, this is my home. I'm going to have to ask you to leave. My son is downstairs, and you're going to frighten him. I'm going to have to call the cops," she said.

I replied, "Go ahead and call them. They all know me. They'll tell you this is my house," I told her.

"Ma'am, I'm sorry, and I don't want to have to call the police. Please tell me who you are," she asked.

My phone rang. I refused to answer, so she did. "Hello," she said. After a brief conversation, the woman continued, "Okay, my name is Lisa. Yes, I live here. Okay, Anna, I'll wait for you to call back. Thank you for letting me know. Yes, no problem."

"Diane, I need you to stay calm," Lisa replied. "A man named Frank is coming to get you," she said.

"I know, Frank!" I shot back. "Of course, I know Frank!"

She said, "Anna said he is a family friend and a detective working on your son's case. He's going to drive you back to South Carolina."

I yelled back, "I'm not going back to South Carolina! This is my home, and this is where my son lives! If you don't believe me, look in the closet. His name is in there!"

Lisa remained patient, sitting across from me. "Diane, I'm so sorry. I'm so sorry for everything you've gone through and continue to endure. Although I can never fully grasp what you have experienced, my son and I lost his dad and my husband this past year. I know it's not the same, but I understand the grief of losing a loved one. I must check on my son; I will be back soon. Please stay calm."

I could hear the woman speaking softly to her son downstairs, her voice laced with distress. Something wasn't right. My mind raced, torn between reacting and staying put —it felt as though a demon had taken control of my thoughts. I wasn't leaving without my son. I heard Lisa's voice downstairs. "Hi, Frank! Thank you for coming," she said.

"It's nice to meet you," Frank replied.

"She's upstairs. Let me show you where," Lisa replied.

"Thank you, Lisa. I'm sorry about this," Frank said, his voice steady.

"No problem," Lisa responded gently, "I can't imagine how scared she must feel right now."

Frank's tone was filled with patience as he said, "This has been an incredibly trying time for the family. Thank you for your concern."

When I saw Frank, it was a relief—as if the floodgates of twenty years had opened, and I unleashed my pent-up emotions into his arms.

"Diane, I know you're struggling," he said gently, "but we must return to South Carolina, and Lisa needs us to leave her home. This home now belongs to her."

I sniffled through my tears. "I know, Frank, I know. But I just want my son. I just want my son."

"I understand, Diane," he said, his voice steady. "We're working hard to get you the answers you need." "But I need you to know—it's been years, and nothing has changed. Everything stays the same." I felt a wave of frustration. "I can't promise you answers," he continued, "but I've never been the one working on your case before, and I am committed to finding Caleb. Christopher, the detective in South Carolina, and Mike are also working hard to find him. We'll do whatever we can to bring your son home." I nodded, feeling a mix of hope and despair. "And here's your choice," he said. "You can drive back with me to South Carolina, or you can drive with your daughters. What do you pick?"

I laughed, a sound that felt strange, given the situation. "Oh, Frank, please don't make me drive with them!" Frank and I drove back to South Carolina in silence. Eventually, I broke the quiet. "Frank, thank you for coming for me," I told him.

"Diane, I would do it again," he replied steadily, his voice reassuring.

I realized that day that Lisa, her son, and Frank had been my guardian angels. I could have been in serious trouble if the circumstances had been different, but Lisa had shown me unexpected kindness. Lisa's compassion and understanding helped me keep my composure during the ordeal involving my son. When the reality of the situation hit me, I felt like a complete fool. What had I been thinking, rushing back to a life that had ceased to exist over two decades ago? I didn't belong there. The only trace of my life there was a faint etching of "Caleb was here" in the closet, but that didn't mean he was still there.

CHAPTER 21

Anna

I poured my soul into preparing for James's upcoming sixth birthday, putting everything I had, emotionally and physically, into making it a great day. Yet, beneath the upheaval, a worry lingered like a shadow, constantly reminding me that Caleb was six years old when we last saw him. Before the sun had risen, I slipped out of bed and tiptoed downstairs; the quiet of the early morning was refreshing. I needed that moment of solitude to ground myself, so I ventured into the crisp morning air and attended a yoga class downtown. Each stretch and pose helped melt away my tension, leaving me feeling refreshed and renewed.

When I entered the house, I found my family just stirring. "Hello, boys! Happy birthday to my special boy, James! How does it feel to be six?"

James ran to me, throwing his arms around me. "Thank you, thank you, Mommy! It feels great to be six!"

"I'm so proud of you!" I replied, swelling with pride. Samuel squealed with delight, almost as if it were his birthday too. I felt so happy for my family. "James, are you ready to open your presents?" I asked, knowing it was a silly question.

He excitedly tore through the wrapping. "A bike! A red bike! My favorite color!" he exclaimed.

"Yes, your grandma made sure it was red," I said.

"Look at this, Daddy! I got a matching helmet with fiery red and orange flames!" James squealed.

"I'm going to play with all these new toys too!" Samuel chimed in.

"Don't touch them!" James protested.

"Well, James, we can share. We have a lot of fun things planned for your birthday party today," I reminded him.

"I can't wait!" he exclaimed, giddy with laughter.

Sierra arrived early to help with the preparations. "I'm here! It's me, Sierra!" she called out.

"Oh wow, thanks for coming early! There's so much work to do, and I'm a little overwhelmed," I replied.

"Don't worry; we're going to make it great! What do you think of the cake?" she asked.

"I love it, Sierra! You're a saint—thank you so much!"

"The house looks fantastic! Look at your yard; it's beautiful! And I love that you have the big blue number six balloon outside," she pointed. I could hear the boys' laughter in the background. It is going to be such a great day! It wasn't long before the boys were outside, playing together as Sierra and I worked on the final touches for the party. James's birthday party was coming together as expected.

My home buzzed with activity, laughter, and chatter filled the air. Soft music played in the kitchen as my family worked together to ensure that James's day was perfect. "Hey, Mike, Frank, come out and have a beer with me while I cook these burgers!" Ted called from the grill.

Cara propped herself up in the kitchen, listening in. "So,

what's new with you and Mike, Mom? Any gossip?"

Mom, still glowing from her recent engagement, smiled. "I just got this gorgeous new ring!" she said.

"I'm so happy for you, Mom," I said, beaming at her.

"Thank you, Anna, that means the world to me!" she replied, her rapture infectious.

Cara chimed in, "I'm thrilled for you too! Mom, you finally look content."

I smiled when I noticed my mom's choice of serving tray. "Well, Mom, you're breaking tradition! You've got Grammy's old serving tray out. It's so authentic," I said.

"I'm honoring your beautiful child—James's 6th birthday. What's more important than that?" We both laughed, and I felt a lightness in the air. The tray was an old vintage piece with faded stenciling, once belonging to my grandmother. In a family where the past often seemed left behind, I saw my mom honoring our family.

I turned to my mom, "Look at the cake Sierra made for James! Isn't it great?"

"You worked hard and did a fantastic job; you should go into the cake business," my mom said.

"Sierra, it is just perfect!" I added, feeling proud.

Cara said, "I can't even imagine making something like that. I'd make such a mess of everything, including myself!" she laughed.

"I love the dragon!" I continued. "He wanted a happy dragon, and I love how you made it. Thank you for writing "Happy 6th Birthday, James" on it. It looks like you put so much time and attention into it."

Sierra smiled. "Anytime! Anything for a good friend and my little buddy James. I'm just happy to be here."

Despite the spaciousness of my kitchen, it suddenly felt cramped and stifling as Ted, Mom, Mike, Cara, Frank, and I moved around, each absorbed in our tasks. The background music had been a gentle companion to our conversations, but it was quickly interrupted by the sharp, intrusive voice of the radio announcer: "They have arrested five suspects in connection to the East Coast kidnappings."

The room fell silent instantly. The only sound was my mom's sharp gasp as she dropped my grandmother's serving tray, its crash reverberating through the house. As it hit the floor, shattering into countless pieces, I felt like the last of my childhood memories had splintered. Each tiny shard of the tray seemed to represent fragments of my past, now scattered and irreparably broken. I quickly pulled myself together.

I carried James' birthday cake to the backyard; Ted excitedly said, "James, it's time to sing Happy Birthday!" James beamed with a smile. The group gathered together and joyfully sang.

"Alright, James, now it's time to blow out your candles," I said. Delighted, he took a deep breath and extinguished all six flames. "Don't forget to make a wish, but keep it to yourself," I added with a wink.

Smiling, James shouted, "My wish is for Caleb to come home."

CHAPTER 22

Mike

Frank and I met Christopher in his dimly lit, familiar office that evening. We settled into the meeting, and our responsibilities felt like a burden. "I'm not sure where to begin," I admitted.

"Why don't we start with the affidavits?" Christopher suggested.

"Frank, you can piece the evidence together, and we can go back and forth to see if we've missed anything," I said.

"That's a good idea. We have a lot to cover, and I hope we don't overlook anything. Tonight is going to be a long night."

"Well, it will be worth it," Christopher said firmly. "I'm committed to bringing Caleb home. We have no choice. We can't face these families without answers about their children."

We poured over documents, scrutinizing every detail and piecing together the puzzles of evidence. Each step brought us closer to our goal of bringing justice to the victims. Despite the hour and exhaustion, a shared purpose drove us to bring closure to the families affected by these heinous crimes. While my weary body yearned for rest, my mind raced with the tough decisions and revelations looming ahead. Yet, even in the night's darkness, a glimmer of hope flickered.

I knew I had to return to Anna and Ted's house, where the family waited for Frank and me to explain the arrests. The living room was quiet when we arrived. James and Samuel were already asleep. Cara interrupted, "What do you mean five people were arrested? When is the trial? How did you find out about the trial? Why didn't you tell us before?"

"We're doing everything we can, I promise," I replied. "We still can't discuss specific details, as protecting Caleb and the other victims is essential."

"The latest reports indicate there are five suspects in the case and the details that mirror Caleb's abduction," Frank continued.

I scanned the room, noting the mix of concern and fear on their face, and continued, "I'm not at liberty to disclose the children's names or any specifics about their cases due to the ongoing investigation. All the victims were minors at the time. The trial will be closed to the public, and the court will present recordings as evidence, including some involving Sister Kathleen."

Given the privacy of the case and the constraints, it was the most we could share, though the gravity of the situation was undeniable. Eager to alleviate their suffering, I offered the few details I had. Their silent pleas ignited a fierce purpose, fueling my renewed vigor to push forward and confront any challenges in the quest for answers about Caleb.

In hindsight, I regret overlooking the numerous clear signs directing me to Caleb's location.

CHAPTER 23

Christopher - The Trial

When I arrived in New York for the East Coast kidnapping trial, a wave of nervousness washed over me, gripping me from my legs to my chest. Each step toward the courthouse felt like I was inching closer to the edge, and I couldn't shake the sensation that I was the one on trial. The prosecution began their questioning with John, the retired detective, who responded with an unnerving confidence as if he had rehearsed his words. "I had nothing to do with the East Coast kidnappings or anything connected to Felix, Peter, Misty, or Pam," he claimed. "I was a good detective; I worked hard in my city."

John consistently deflected blame throughout the interrogation, "I was an innocent bystander." Yet, his admission of knowing about the kidnappings made it glaringly apparent to the jury that he was hiding the truth. The lies creased his face, betraying his façade. The prosecution skillfully leveraged John's earlier statements against him.

They asked probing questions, such as "Where were you at

the time of the crimes?" and "Can you explain why one of your colleagues gave a report to your supervisor that went unnoticed?" The prosecution also presented evidence suggesting illegal activities related to adoptions and asked John, "Can you explain the document?" Furthermore, the trial laid out evidence tying John to specific locations linked to the crimes.

The courtroom fell silent as John's colleague, Detective Ford, testified, "John's supervisor had received suspicious information regarding an adoption center named Fresh Start. I always thought it was strange that it didn't get investigated further." The relentless examination left no doubt about John's involvement. The courtroom's thick tension lingered as we awaited the trial's next steps, but I couldn't help feeling a grim satisfaction that at least one piece of the intricate puzzle now rested in the hands of justice.

When Misty took the stand, her testimony felt crucial. The prosecution asked, "Have you ever worked for Child Protective Services (CPS)?"

She replied, "Yes."

They followed up, "Why were you fired from CPS?"

Misty responded, "I left CPS."

The prosecution then produced a report and asked Misty to read it. "I have a hard time seeing," she said. The prosecutor offered to get her glasses, but Misty simply stated, "Just read it for me."

The report stated, "Misty's career at CPS was short-lived, plagued by complaints about her incompetence and lack of dedication. Misty had allowed confident parents, primarily men, to cloud her judgment and 'charm' her, leading to her termination due to a lack of respect for the children under her care."

Faced with the damning report, Misty invoked her Fifth Amendment right, stating, "I take the Fifth!"

The lawyer pressed on, condemning Misty's actions. "Your reckless decisions endangered the children by returning them to an unstable environment despite the valid concerns of the nurturing parent. Your misleading assurances to the judge about the children's desires to be with their dad enabled the abusive parent to retain full custody, leading to your termination." The litigation continued, "I have a letter I would like you to read aloud."

Misty responded, "Read it for me," leading me to question her literacy skills.

> *To Whom It May Concern,*
>
> *Unlike when I was a child, I now have the freedom to voice my opinions openly. In addition to advocating for myself, I also represent my siblings. While I work as a pediatric surgeon, my brother is a pediatric anesthesiologist, and my sister fights crime to protect minors. Based on our shared history, I have strong convictions regarding Misty's past involvement with our family.*
>
> *Misty, a site inspector, used her visits to our home as opportunities to engage in an inappropriate personal relationship with my father. While there, she would sit and chat with him, often sharing meals while my siblings and I went hungry. Misty never once acknowledged or interacted with us. During court proceedings, Misty returned us to our father's home, where she made claims that our mother was a danger to us.*
>
> *My mother is everything to us—caring, calm, loving, and playful. She devoted her life to her children and continues to do so. As adults, we choose her; we never speak to our father, who shows no interest in our lives. Over the years, I have struggled with anxiety due to Misty's misrepresentation of my family. My law guardian, whom I'll refer to as B.C., was also involved in illegal activities by coercing medical professionals along with the help of CPS worker Misty. Misty labeled my mother as an unfit parent,*

even though she was the person who cared.

*Despite her efforts, my mother faced constant dismis-
sal from new CPS workers, who would simply say, "You
have a claim against you." They tried to ruin our lives, but
we've all become resilient despite their actions. My mother is
the strongest person I know, and I believe people like Misty
corrupt our system.*

Sincerely,
Sarah Clarke

The prosecution asked, "Would you like to respond?"

Misty firmly replied, "As I said, I'm pleading the Fifth."

The lawyer questioned, "You don't even want to defend
yourself?"

The courtroom fell silent as Pam took the stand. Clad in ill-
fitting prison attire that revealed her protruding belly and breasts,
she was a visual distraction. The jurors shifted uncomfortably in
their seats as they adjusted the witness stand to accommodate her
size. Ordinarily, I try not to judge based on appearance, but in this
case, Pam's unkempt demeanor and apparent disregard for the
gravity of the situation were hard to overlook.

The young and eager prosecutor faced considerable difficulty
extracting truthful answers from Pam. "Can you please explain
your connection to Felix, Misty, Peter, and John?" he began.

Pam responded flatly, "I have no connection to them."

The prosecutor asked, "Are you willing to answer these questions truthfully today?"

"I take the Fifth," she replied curtly.

Sensing an opportunity, the prosecutor paused and said,
"What if I had lunch ordered here for you?" The defense
immediately objected, but the judge overruled it. "Well, I guess,"
Pam said, her demeanor shifting as she began to open up. The
details she provided suggested a surprising familiarity with the

kidnappings.

Eager to sway the prosecutor, Pam leaned in and began flirtatiously trying to charm him, creating an increasingly tense and awkward atmosphere. However, when the lawyer attempted to redirect the conversation back to the case, Pam abruptly veered off-topic, wistfully reminiscing about an upcoming lunch she was anticipating. Struggling to maintain focus, the prosecuting attorney needed help to regain control of the discussion. The defense attorney repeatedly interjected with objections, claiming the content required to be more relevant. Ultimately, the prosecution conceded, stating, "I have no further questions, your honor."

The atmosphere shifted as Peter took the stand, a stark contrast to the cocky defendants who had preceded him. When the prosecutor asked, "Peter, can you explain your relationship with the victims?"

Peter looked down, fidgeting with his hands. "I... I don't know them well anymore," he stammered, his voice barely above a whisper.

The lead council pressed, "Yet you were present during critical moments. Why should we believe you weren't involved?"

Peter's responses were hesitant, fraught with worry. "I swear, I wasn't part of any plan," he said, his eyes darting around the courtroom. "I just did what Felix told me to do."

A sorrowful expression crossed Peter's face, and his visible fear painted a portrait of someone overcome by forces far more significant than himself. "Are you afraid of someone?" the trial attorney asked, narrowing his gaze.

Peter nodded, his voice shaking. "Yes... Felix." In contrast to Felix's nature and dark deeds, the fragile Peter emerged as the most tragic figure among the defendants.

When Felix took the stand, a nagging dread gripped me. He approached with a chilling, almost mechanical calmness - a familiar quality in his eyes as if he embodied an unsettling combination of past suspects. His demeanor was devoid of emotion, cold and calculating like a serial killer's. When asked to testify, he simply stated, "I plead the Fifth." Felix's refusal to acknowledge the severity of his actions and evasion of the questions was infuriating. I couldn't help but imagine the terror the boys must have felt in his presence, and a wave of sorrow washed over me.

The courtroom simmered as Felix's refusals underscored his lack of remorse. As the prosecution concluded their interrogation, Felix's unmoving demeanor - a stark display of his inability to empathize - showed little regard for his victims' suffering. His invocation of the Fifth Amendment seemed less a legal strategy than a testament to his psychopathic nature. Sitting there unmoved and detached, he reinforced the notion of a man capable of unspeakable horrors without emotion.

CHAPTER 24

The Closing Argument

"Thank you all for your time. First and foremost, let us not forget the victims of the tragedy and their families:

Jack O'Neil: murdered.

Thomas Meyer: murdered.

Caleb Hart: whereabouts unknown.

Samuel Lewis: whereabouts unknown.

Jayden Gore: kidnapped with a severe disability, found dehydrated and with a broken leg in a ditch, alive.

Joseph Murphy: kidnapped, found on the side of the road with multiple broken bones, dehydration, and starvation, alive.

Max Hamlin: murdered.

Jeffrey Scott: murdered."

The counsel continued, "These heinous crimes have left families devastated, their children's deaths causing unimaginable anguish. Let's not overlook the immense tragedy or suffering of those left behind. The void created by their children's absence is a stark reminder of the horrendous nature of these acts. Our solemn duty is to seek justice for these innocent victims and hold the perpetrators fully accountable for their reprehensible actions."

The attorney then motioned the court to play the recordings from Anna and Cara, Caleb's sisters, and Anna's husband, Ted. As the people in the courtroom listened intently, the sisters' anguished sobs resonated through the room, underscoring the gravity of their terror. The jurors' eyes glistened with tears as they struggled to hold back their emotions.

Sister Kathleen's unmistakable voice on the tapes provided harrowing testimony about the abductions. Then we heard Ted cry out, "Sister Kathleen! Please." His voice broke with raw anguish. A hush fell over the room as everyone heard Sister Kathleen's breath falter. Panic rising in his voice, Ted shouted, "Someone help! Sister Kathleen is not breathing! Help, someone!" When the proceedings finally ended, no dry eye remained in the room.

The prosecutor stood tall and addressed the jury with conviction. "Ladies and gentlemen, let's discuss Misty's troubled past," he began. "CPS discharged Misty due to negligence, and her need for male attention raises serious concerns about her integrity and ability to protect vulnerable children." He paused for effect, allowing the gravity of his words to sink in. "The children under her care were left traumatized and unable to advocate for themselves."

A murmur swept through the courtroom as he continued, "Now, let's examine the evidence." Gesturing to a display board, he stated, "We have testimonies implicating Misty, Peter, Pam, and Felix in the kidnappings. Their accounts match the details of the abductions alarmingly similar." The prosecutor's voice grew more forceful. "The evidence is damning. It implicates those in positions of authority who may have been complicit in the abuse of these children. Tragically, the victims remain silenced, and we must demand urgent action to address these grave concerns."

The words hung in the air as the jury exchanged uneasy glances, the reality of the situation settling over them like a heavy shroud.

The prosecuting attorney solemnly addressed the jury, outlining the charges against the five defendants. "As you deliberate the evidence, I urge you to consider the overwhelming proof beyond reasonable doubt. The defendants' actions displayed a blatant disregard for the precious lives of these innocent children. With all the facts in mind, I request you hold all five fully accountable for their nine charges. Your decision today will bring the victims' families closure and deliver the justice they deserve."

The prosecution then closed his statement, "I rest my case."

CHAPTER 25

Christopher

While the jury deliberated, I clung to faint optimism, praying for a swift resolution to end the agonizing wait. To escape the intense stress, I sought refuge with Jimmy. While the distraction offered some relief, the weight of the trial never truly left me. By the third day of deliberations, my distress reached a breaking point. Unable to bear the mounting suspense any longer, I couldn't resist the urge and drove straight to Westerfield, hoping to catch Frank at work.

"Hi, my name is Christopher. Is Frank here today?"

She replied, "Oh no, Frank's in South Carolina doing some research." I turned to leave, and the phone rang. I overheard the secretary mention that a man named Christopher had just been there. "Wait, Christopher, don't go anywhere!" she yelled. "I have something for you. Frank told me to give you the important envelope. It contains the DNA results for Caleb. He wants you to hold onto it and return it to South Carolina after the trial. Do not open it, and please don't share the details with anyone," she said.

"Absolutely," I replied eagerly, taking the envelope. "I'll bring it back with me right away."

I retrieved Caleb's file from my briefcase and flipped through the pages until I found his childhood address. A sense of unease washed over me as I navigated the winding roads towards Milford Falls. My mind remained fixated on Caleb and the other children, consumed by their suffering. Passing by Caleb's old neighborhood, I felt a pang of gratitude for the happy childhood I had experienced, in stark contrast to the loss Caleb had faced.

The old blue house evoked a sense of nostalgia. Appearing nearly a century old, it stood alone, shrouded in the fading light of dusk. The weathered walls seemed to whisper secrets, and a palpable sadness seeped from its creaking doors and worn frames. The chipped windowpanes lent it a haunting quality as if the sorrows of years past still clung to every surface.

The house had once been a haven of happiness and serenity, a garden bursting with vibrant flowers brimming with love and joy. But now, it is a silent testament to loss and shattered dreams. As I gazed upon it, a deep regret stirred within me. I imagined the carefree childhood that had never come to be for Caleb, the dreams of Anna and Cara left in tatters. A mother betrayed and broken by cruel fate, a family torn apart by the devastating loss of a beloved husband and father. Where laughter and play had once filled its halls, the house now stood as a hollow shell of its former self.

I passed by the backyard and noticed a young boy playing. Our eyes met briefly, and I hesitated, not wanting to startle him. When I turned to leave, I heard him call out, "Have a nice day, sir!" I smiled, but a pang of wistfulness struck me. "Sir?" I thought. "How old have I become?" I saw myself in that carefree, innocent young boy for a moment. I wanted to rush over and warn him, "Don't talk to strangers, ever!" After years in my vocation, those deep-rooted fears were hard to shake. The world felt more dangerous now, and I wished the boy could see it through my tired eyes.

I wandered the quiet village streets and tried to imagine the daily lives of Diane and Caleb and the tragedy that had befallen their family. Seeking a mental reprieve, I stumbled upon a local diner, its old stainless-steel exterior evoking the feel of a vintage boxcar.

A friendly server named Ray approached. "Welcome to the Milford Falls Diner! Can I help you?" he asked with a warm smile.

"Yes, I'll have the pancakes, please. Do you remember a boy named Caleb who lived here about twenty years ago?"

Ray's expression shifted, and he nodded solemnly. "Of course, I remember Caleb. I was in my early twenties when he disappeared. I searched for days and nights, hoping to find that poor child." He gestured to the booth where I sat. "His family used to sit right here. After his father passed away, they rarely came in. Diane, Anna, and Cara were quiet when they did, but Caleb filled the diner with his infectious chatter."

"What happened after Caleb vanished?"

Ray sighed, his gaze drifting. "After Caleb went missing, you'd see his mother, Diane, sitting there, lost in thought. Cara and Anna would come in with friends, but it was never the same. I've heard rumors he went missing at the park on the hill. Is that true?" he asked.

"I'm not sure about the park and Caleb's disappearance," I replied.

"Anyway, what brings you here today? What's your name?"

"Oh, I'm Christopher, visiting from South Carolina. I'm researching Caleb's case," I explained.

"I wish you luck finding what you're looking for. I hope you have an enjoyable visit in Milford Falls," Ray said.

"It was nice to meet you, Ray."

I approached the park, and the diner faded behind me, replaced by the soothing sounds of chirping birds and rustling leaves. Steps led me to a clearing where bubbling creeks flowed over rocks, and children's laughter filled the air. Milford Falls felt like a quintessential small town, and something about its charm and familiarity tugged at my heart—perhaps a longing for the simpler life I had missed growing up in bustling Atlanta. I scanned the park; everything appeared normal. A few kids ran around as their mothers chatted nearby. I detected no cries for help or anything out of the ordinary. It was just a park—nothing to suggest the tragedy that had unfolded here decades ago.

I headed over to the small church across from the park, and a flash of movement caught my eye across the parking lot. Two boys were peeking out from behind a tree, engaged in a game of hide-and-seek. The sight stirred a wave of unsettling thoughts, and I couldn't help but imagine Caleb, terrified, meeting his captors in the park. "Christopher, stop!" I scolded myself. In hindsight, my instincts were right; I would soon learn that Caleb had been playing in that park when his abduction happened.

I stepped into the dimly lit church and spotted a figure standing at the altar. Before I could make out any details, the person disappeared. A voice echoed, "Christopher, you can do this; I have given you the strength to endure." The words lingered, offering an unexpected sense of comfort and relief.

"Who are you? Why are you telling me this?" I asked, my voice shaky.

I pleaded, "How do you know my name?" But there was no response.

I couldn't tell if it was my imagination or if I had encountered someone, but an inexplicable lightness washed over me.

Suddenly, my phone rang, breaking the stillness. "Christopher, we have a verdict. Get back here as soon as you can," the prosecutor said.

Without hesitation, I responded, "I'm on my way!"

***

"We, the jury, find Felix Hyde, Peter Hyde, Misty Hyde, Pam Hyde-Sewerstein, and John Augustus guilty of first-degree murder, kidnapping, false imprisonment, child abuse and neglect, first-degree assault and battery of a minor, concealment of a human corpse, abuse of a corpse, abetting, and falsifying physical evidence regarding all matters associated with the minors: Jack O'Neil, Thomas Meyer, Caleb Hart, Samuel Martin, Jayden Gore, Joseph Murphy, Max Hamlin, and Jeffrey Scott."

Armed with the DNA results, I immediately called Mike. "Mike, I have the DNA evidence from Frank's case, and the verdict is in. I need you to hear the verdict before it hits the news or anyone else finds out. I'm heading back to Greenville today, and I need you to call me as soon as possible." I left a frantic voicemail, my mind racing to ensure Mike was informed of the verdict before Caleb's family heard it elsewhere.

After landing in Greenville, I felt a sinking sensation in my stomach. Mike still had yet to respond to my repeated attempts to reach him. "Call me back, Mike! I've texted you a million times and left countless messages. Where are you? I'm heading to your house now! We must talk in person before Diane hears it on the news!" The gnawing tension was a reminder of the high stakes. Resolved not to waste more time, I drove straight to Mike's home. I couldn't bear the thought of Caleb's family learning the verdict from anyone but Mike.

CHAPTER 26

Caleb

My life felt like a storybook. I was surrounded by shimmering blue skies, lush green meadows, and winding rivers everywhere. Freshwater pools encircled the cities, and the people radiated happiness. There was no shame, no fear, no lack. Emmanuel was always there, sometimes even before I realized I needed Him, responding to my unspoken thoughts.

I sat by a large, weathered rock, admiring its grooved surface shaped by wind, rain, and countless hands over time. As I sat in the stillness, lost in contemplation, Emmanuel approached. He smiled warmly, his calming presence filling the space around me.

"Caleb, I've been searching for you. What brings you here?" Emmanuel asked, looking up at me.

I glanced up at the towering rock and then back at him. "I saw this big rock and tried to climb it, but I kept slipping off," I explained, perplexed.

Emmanuel's smile deepened, and his eyes twinkled. "This rock is significant to me," he said, his expression softening as he looked at the weathered stone.

Puzzled, I furrowed my brow. "A rock? Why?"

Emmanuel paused, his voice calm and full of meaning. "I named this rock Ebenezer. It's not just a physical stone—a symbol for my people, a testament to hope, resilience, and the assurance that I am always present."

I sat in contemplative silence, the weight of his words sinking in. Once just a simple stone, the rock now felt like something much deeper—a living testament to Emmanuel's promise.

Emmanuel looked at me with compassion. "Caleb, would you mind helping me with something?"

I was puzzled but quickly replied, "Not at all; I'm happy to help." Emmanuel's face lit up with a warm smile.

My thoughts swirled as we made our way back to The Kingdom. Upon reaching it, Emmanuel called for Jack, Carcarra, and Tercelot. When they arrived, He turned to us, his expression serious yet gentle. "I have an important task for all of you in Tarsus."

Jack, barely able to contain his excitement, asked, "Tarsus? Where is that? What will we do there?"

Emmanuel looked at both of us. "I will guide you," He said. "But you better get moving now. I will see you when you return."

I hopped onto Tercelot, her feathers sleek and smooth beneath my fingers. As I settled onto her back, I could feel the firm strength of her muscles, perfectly built for flight. With a sudden burst of power, Tercelot's wings beat strong, lifting us higher and higher into the sky. The wind roared in my ears, its sound deafening yet exhilarating. The world below rapidly shrank, the familiar landscape becoming a patchwork of green fields and winding roads.

Once we landed, I noticed the sun hung low over the city of Tarsus, its light stretching across the narrow cobblestone streets. The air was alive with the scent of spices and the chatter of merchants peddling their wares—colorful textiles, exotic fruits, and pottery from distant lands.

I looked at Jack, a frown creasing my brow. "What do we do

now?" I asked, still trying to make sense of everything around us.

Jack shrugged, his expression unreadable. "I guess we talk to that man over there guarding the streets." He nodded toward a prominent figure inside the city gates—a Roman soldier with an imposing presence. His armor gleamed in the afternoon sun, and his gaze swept over the crowds, sharp and unblinking.

I hesitated, eyeing the soldier warily. "He looks kind of scary."

Jack spoke quietly, his voice tight. "Yeah, he does. But if we're going to get any information around here, we'll have to face him sooner or later."

I took a deep breath, trying to calm my nerves. "We have no choice," I muttered, approaching the soldier. Jack's eyes flickered toward the guard again, then back to me. "Just stay calm. We don't know how he'll react to us, but if we look confident, we might be able to get him to talk."

"Excuse us, sir," Jack began, his voice respectful. "We're looking for someone—someone important. Can you help us?"

The soldier's lips twitched, but he didn't respond immediately. Instead, he studied us both for a moment, sizing us up like we were nothing more than an inconvenience to his post. Then, finally, he spoke, his voice low and gravelly. "Go find Saul." He said with no direction as to where to look.

We stood there, uncertain, the man's eyes pressing down on us. The streets of Tarsus seemed to grow quieter around us as he stared, unblinking, his armor gleaming in the sunlight.

After hours of searching the town, we finally found Saul. I cowered slightly, lowered my head, and shifted nervously on my feet. He looked down at us, his eyes narrowing as though measuring every word we spoke. "My name is Saul. What are your names? And who sends you?"

Jack didn't hesitate. He stepped forward, his voice steady despite the tension. "I'm Jack, and this is Caleb. Our friend Emmanuel sent us."

Saul crossed his arms and looked us over again as if trying to make sense of us. "I have no idea who that is," he said flatly. "Well, you seem harmless. I am on my way to Damascus to persecute those who claim to be followers of a false prophet. They are spreading lies—lies that threaten the very foundation of our faith."

I looked up at Saul, my heart pounding. His words were so stern, and the anger in his eyes made my stomach twist. I couldn't quite grasp everything he was saying, but something about his speaking made it feel like we were standing on the edge of something dangerous.

"W-what does all of that mean?" I stammered, my voice trembling a little. I wasn't sure why I asked—I was just trying to understand. But Saul's face twisted with frustration, his jaw tightening as if the question had irritated him even more than he already was.

He exhaled sharply, almost as if he were holding in his temper. "I am not babysitting the two of you," he snapped, his voice cold and impatient. "If you want to follow me, then come. But don't speak to me unless it's necessary. I have a headache."

I glanced at Jack, and we understood what the other was thinking without saying a word.

In unison, we spoke, "We will stay out of your way, sir."

Saul didn't acknowledge us directly but gave a curt nod, his jaw still clenched. His steps were quick and purposeful as he marched ahead, leading the way through the narrow streets of Tarsus.

My feet throbbed every step, and my body ached from the long journey. Saul had barely spoken to us, and his presence was as cold as his stare. I couldn't understand why we were following him, especially after the way he had treated us.

I looked ahead and saw Emmanuel standing before us. Jack and I glanced at each other, and without a second thought, we ran toward him, eager for relief from our situation.

When we reached Emmanuel, I couldn't help but spill my thoughts. "What are you doing here? And why are we here? This man is mean and scary," I blurted, catching my breath.

Before Emmanuel could speak, a scream pierced the air—it

was Saul. I whipped my head around, startled. "Caleb, Jack! Do you see the bright light? I'm blinded by it!" Saul yelled, his voice strained and filled with panic.

I paused for a second, then shrugged, a little confused. "I can see just fine," I said, glancing at Jack, who nodded in agreement.

"Yup, me too," Jack added. "Must just be you, Saul."

We both exchanged looks, and something about the moment felt... strange. It wasn't just Saul's panic but the whole scene. He was standing there, his hands on his face as if trying to shield his eyes from something only he could see.

Emmanuel remained still, watching Saul quietly as if he knew what was happening. I didn't comprehend it all, but the unease in my chest was growing. What had happened to Saul? And why did it feel like the journey had just shifted in a way none of us could have predicted?

"What's happening to him?" I whispered to Emmanuel, unable to keep the question in any longer.

Emmanuel's smile faded slightly, but his focus never left Saul. "He's seeing the light. Saul's life, once full of violence and persecution, will be transformed into compassion and truth."

Perplexed, I asked Emmanuel, "But why Saul? He's a horrible person." Emmanuel looked at both Jack and me with kindness in His eyes. "To show people that My grace is beyond any wrongdoing."

I ran towards Saul, who asked, "Who called my name? Help me get up. I need to get out of here—I can't see."

I told Jack, "Help me lift him; he's heavy."

Jack and I stayed with Saul for what felt like an eternity— three long and agonizing days. Saul refused to eat or drink, and with each passing hour, he grew more agitated and restless. I could sense his frustration, but there was nothing we could do.

Finally, I saw a figure approaching us in the distance. As the man drew closer, I felt a glimmer of hope. He smiled kindly and greeted us, "Hi, I am Ananias. What is going on here?"

Jack and I quickly explained everything—from the time we

landed in Tarsus to the strange encounter on the road and, finally, to Saul's sudden blindness. We told Ananias everything, hoping he might have some answers.

Overhearing our conversation, Saul suddenly said in a strained voice, "Are you the man I dreamt of?"

Ananias smiled gently, his eyes filled with quiet confidence. "I believe I am. I will touch your eyes, and your sight will be restored. And your name will no longer be Saul; you will be called Paul."

I looked at Jack, and we exchanged stunned glances. I thought to myself, there's no way this will work. Without warning, Ananias stepped forward and touched Saul's eyes. I was both nervous and fascinated, and my stomach twisted with uncertainty.

Then, something strange began to happen. Things started to fall out of Saul's eyes—tiny, dark scales began to fall away. The sight was both eerie and unsettling.

Jack was the first to speak, his voice filled with disbelief. "Look at Saul's eyes! They're... disgusting!"

I couldn't bring myself to look directly at him. The sight was too much for me to handle. I turned away, clutching my stomach, feeling the bile rise in my throat as I tried to compose myself. The sound of what was happening was enough to make me feel sick.

But there was a strange silence as the last scales fell away. For a moment, it felt like time stood still. I dared to glance back at Saul, who was now blinking rapidly, his eyes wide with astonishment.

He gasped, "I... I can see!" His voice shook with a mixture of awe and fear. "I can see!"

I couldn't help but feel a wave of relief wash over me. Despite all the confusion and fear, Saul's sight had been restored. And with it, something else seemed to change in him—a subtle shift that I couldn't quite understand, but I knew it was profound.

I slapped Paul on the back. "I like you better as Paul than Saul. I'm glad you can see again."

"Yeah, thanks, kid." His voice was rough but grateful.

I immediately knew our time in Tarsus was coming to an end. Something inside me somehow hoped we'd see what became of

Paul in the future.

As we returned to our hawks, Jack finally broke the silence. "Did we just witness another blind man see?" he asked, still in awe.

"I guess we did, Jack," I replied, shaking my head. "Emmanuel is full of surprises."

The wind felt different on the way back—like something was ending, yet something new was about to begin. It was a quiet shift, almost like the air released a long, silent breath. As we soared toward The Kingdom on the backs of Tercelot and Carcarra, I could feel it—like the journey was winding down, but there was still more ahead. When we finally landed, I collapsed, both mentally and physically exhausted from my time in Tarsus.

Emmanuel sat beside me, his presence reassuring. Speaking softly, almost as if sharing a secret, he said, "I have no doubt you will go on to do great things, Caleb. You will help my friend Jacob restore his relationship with his family, watch my good friend David rise to kingship, and accomplish many other brave feats. But perhaps my favorite moment will be when you, Jack, Carcarra, Tercelot, and all her children—yes, she will have many—come together to fight the darkness that threatens to take over their planet. It will be a story people will fear for thousands of years. And there will be many blessings given to those who believe."

A warm smile spread across his face as he spoke those words, and I closed my eyes. A deep peace washed over me; Emmanuel needed me, and I knew He had big plans for me yet to come.

CHAPTER 27

Diane – The Wedding

"Mom, we're going to plan the wedding, and it needs to be special, not just small and simple. You deserve something elaborate!" Cara said.

I smiled and replied, "If you feel passionate about it and have the time, go for it!" Anna and Cara's infectious excitement was palpable, like two giddy teenagers full of laughter.

"Of course, we have to make James and Samuel ring bearers!" they exclaimed, and I didn't even question that.

"Mom, you have to walk down the aisle. Cara and I will make sure this day is unforgettable for you," Anna insisted.

Cara quickly agreed. "Yes, what if we create a rose walkway to the altar?" she asked.

"That's a great idea," I replied.

"Maybe we could get some blue hydrangeas to match the color of your eyes," Anna added.

"You should have been a wedding planner," Cara teased.

Anna simply smiled and replied, "There's so much more I'm

good at!"

The girls' radiance made the entire process even more meaningful. They dove into planning as if it were their wedding, and their happiness was contagious. They chose soft pink attire for themselves; each would carry smaller bouquets of white hydrangeas. Mike and Ted set up chairs on the lush green lawn, perfectly positioned for the best view of the wedding. Surrounding the chairs were the blooming flowers Mike and I had nurtured together.

The intimate family ceremony would include Mike, Anna, Ted, James, Samuel, Cara, and Frank. Cara, beaming with pride, approached me. "Anna and I have finalized the menu!" she announced. "The buffet will feature an array of delectable options: brick oven pizza, savory chicken and waffles, crispy chicken nuggets, and fries for James and Samuel, a flavorful barbecue, succulent lobster, and an assortment of breakfast dishes. It's going to be amazing!" she exclaimed.

"Thank you, Cara, it sounds impressive. You are so helpful, and I love you; don't forget that."

Anna chimed in with a grin. "And let's not forget the desserts! I ordered fluffy doughnuts, classic milk and cookies, cake pops, and ice cream sundaes," she excitedly continued. "And at the center of the dessert table will be a grand multi-layered ivory cake adorned with delicate blue edible hydrangeas and intricate blue fondant ribbons."

"Anna, you have gone out of your way. I love you. Thank you both! Everything sounds perfect. I can't wait to spend the day with my family!" I responded, feeling the love radiating from my daughters.

They spoke in unison, "We can't wait either, Mom!" The thrill of the celebration filled the air, and I felt so thankful to share my moment with them.

Anna beamed, announcing, "I made reservations! We're going to have a bridal luncheon!" Before the big day arrived, Anna and

Cara had organized a special lunch for the three of us at Limoncello, a charming Italian eatery in downtown Greenville. They had reserved a table on the patio, offering picturesque views of a four-tiered water fountain adorned with delicate flowers. The soothing sounds of the trickling water created a serene backdrop, perfect for our conversation.

Anna and Cara happily chatted back and forth when Cara said, "Mom, on your wedding day, you will need to wear something old, something new, and something blue."

I replied, "Oh, I almost forgot about that. I already know what my something old will be—my necklace with the green gem from Caleb."

Anna didn't like that idea. "Mom, you can't wear that for something old; that's hideous," she said.

"You have to take that off on your wedding day," Cara added.

"No!" I said firmly. "I am wearing my necklace as something old, and you two can decide on something new and blue."

Anna and Cara exclaimed, "Mom! You can't wear that!"

"After lunch, I need to try on my dress for my final fitting. Would you guys like to come?"

Cara's eyes lit up. "We wouldn't miss it! Of course," she exclaimed.

"Really? You're both coming?" I asked, excitement rising.

"Absolutely!" Anna replied, grabbing her bag. "I wouldn't miss it for the world!" I stood before the mirror at the dress shop, and a swirl of unexpected emotions flooded me. The dress was simple yet elegant, white with pearls along the back, exuding Southern charm.

"Mom, you look like the person I remember before Caleb went missing." Cara smiled.

"You look stunning, just perfect!" Anna chimed in agreement.

Feeling a swell of emotion, I replied, "I'm sorry I was a terrible mother to you both for so long, but know I love you both deeply."

Cara laughed, "Well, I wasn't the easiest child," she admitted.

"You still aren't!" Anna added playfully. Anna couldn't resist, "And that ugly green necklace doesn't match the dress!"

I shook my head with a smile. "Will you both stop with the necklace? The necklace will bring your brother home one day—I'm never taking it off."

They both laughed. "Okay, Mom," Anna said. At that moment, I felt the love and support of my daughters.

Anna and Cara worked their magic the night before the ceremony, turning Mike's home into a fairytale wonderland. When I saw the transformation, I could hardly believe my eyes. "Oh, girls, everything is beautiful! You're both so talented and thoughtful. Thank you so much!"

Satisfaction shone in their eyes as they smiled. "That is where you and Mike are going to exchange your vows. Doesn't it look amazing?" Cara asked.

"Yes!" I replied, feeling excited for the journey ahead. The majestic arch was covered in cascading white roses and was breathtaking, making the entire scene feel like something out of a magical realm.

Anna and Cara meticulously dressed the tables with crisp white linens and elegant, towering floral arrangements. Twinkling white lights draped gracefully around the trees, casting a gentle, romantic glow across the backyard. A path of vivid scarlet rose petals stretched toward the altar on the dock, each step inviting a sense of enchantment and awe. I listened to my family, and I couldn't help but chuckle. "Anna, no! James and Samuel should be over here," Cara argued, adding, "They'd probably do better where they can see the lake."

Anna firmly replied, "No, they're my children; I know where they'll behave!"

Cara persisted, "James and Samuel will just run off and not

WHERE ARE YOU, *Caleb?*

take it seriously, anyway."

The family gathering was filled with lively conversation and laughter, creating a joyful, relaxed mood. Anna made everyone, including James and Samuel, rehearse their roles for the upcoming day. "I'm hungry! I don't want to practice anymore; I know my job," James protested. Samuel simply mimicked his brother, moaning in agreement.

"One more time, James, until everyone has it perfect," Anna insisted.

"I am not doing it again," James replied. And with that, our rehearsal was thankfully over.

After dinner, we enjoyed some casual conversation. Listening to James tell jokes was the highlight of my day. "Knock, knock!" James said with a grin.

"Who's there?" Frank replied.

"Orange," James answered.

"Orange, who?" Frank asked.

With a laugh, James responded, "Orange, are you going to let me in?" Laughter erupted around the table. The innocent humor of my grandsons never fails to lift my spirits.

On the morning of my wedding, I found strength in my usual walk to the duck pond, a brief moment of calm amid the chaos. Sitting by the peaceful waters, I prayed for another encounter with the man who had offered me such kindness, hoping for clarity before committing to Mike. Though the man didn't appear again, I heard his gentle voice, "My power is unlimited and mighty enough to heal all your wounds, Diane, no matter when or how they occurred in your life. Diane, your pain is not beyond my tremendous power. I am the Great Physician, capable of reaching into your past and healing your soul," the voice said.

"Are you there?" I called out, feeling a mix of longing and desire. "Please come back; I want to talk to you. I'm getting married today. I need your help. Are you there? Who are you?"

The air felt charged with His presence, though I couldn't see Him. I clung to the belief that He was with me, guiding me through such a momentous day. I started walking home and suddenly had an "aha moment." I realized that every interaction and message from this man was a profound manifestation of something far greater than I could understand. The pieces fell into place, and I could see He had been steering me through my life all along.

Overcome with emotion, I knelt at the pond's edge, tears streaming down my face. In a trembling voice filled with gratitude, I cried to heaven, "Thank you, thank you, thank you for my family! Thank you for showing me mercy and blessing me. I will not ask where Caleb is; I only pray that you keep my beloved son protected wherever he may be."

As I continued home, I heard Him say, "Diane, forgive yourself."

The house buzzed with last-minute preparations for the day ahead. I had envisioned a simple, understated look, but Anna and Cara had other plans. "Mom, the hairstylist is here! We've been waiting for you!" Cara exclaimed.

"And you have to get your makeup done too!" Anna added, her eyes shining with enthusiasm.

"Oh, I was just planning on doing something simple, like every day," I replied hesitantly.

"Mom, you can't do that! You always look a little ragged. Today is a day for you to shine!" Cara insisted.

Seeing their hard work and determination, I finally relented. "Alright, hair and makeup it is," I conceded. They smiled brightly.

I slipped into my dress, and the soft fabric soothed my skin. "I'm going to zip up your dress now," Anna said.

Cara added, "And I am going to put on your veil!" When I turned and saw my reflection, I gasped. The woman staring back was unrecognizable—a vibrant version of myself that had been absent for more than two decades.

Cara's eyes welled with tears as she exclaimed, "Mom, you look perfect!" My ocean-blue eyes sparkled with a newfound radiance, and my skin glowed with a youthful, worry-free sheen. I felt transformed, ready to embrace the adventure that awaited.

The caterers bustled in the kitchen, arranging every detail of the reception while the rest of the guests prepared for the ceremony. Just as I was about to walk down the aisle, I saw James tug at Cara's hand with a look of urgency, "I need to use the bathroom right now!" he insisted.

"Quickly, James, we have to hurry back! Grandma's waiting to walk down the aisle to marry Mike!" Cara called out.

"I know!" he replied, his eyes wide. "Today is Grandma's wedding day!"

Feeling hurried and not in the mood for games, Cara snapped, "Stop getting your nice suit wet and stop splashing water on me!"

Heading back to the ceremony, Cara spotted a strikingly tall, handsome man. Something was intriguing about his presence. "Can I help you?" Cara asked.

Breaking into a friendly smile, he replied, "I'm here to see Mike." His voice was smooth and confident.

"Mike's at the altar, eagerly awaiting his bride," Cara said, glancing at the white envelope in his hand. "And look at that— you've even got a wedding gift for them!"

Christopher nodded, his expression a mix of eagerness and optimism. "Yeah, I hope so," he said.

Christopher looked flustered in his khaki shorts and crisp white shirt. "I'm sorry for the intrusion. Please have Mike call me," he said.

"Well, you're here now; you might as well stay!" Cara said. "Come on, come sit in the back."

Christopher hesitated. "I don't think that's a good idea. I'm not dressed for a wedding," he said.

"That's okay!" Cara insisted.

After a moment, Christopher relented. "Okay, I'll sit in the back row."

As they walked, he glanced at Cara. "Have I seen you somewhere before?" Cara shrugged.

"No, I don't think so," she replied. "You do look familiar, though. Come on, let's sit down before the wedding starts!" she urged.

The music's soft, melodic tune floated through the air, signaling the start of the ceremony. I waited at the back of the yard, consumed by expectation and sorrow for Caleb. Rose petals scattered along the path ahead, almost symbolic as they led me to a new chapter with Mike. Yet, even as I prepared to take those steps, my thoughts drifted back to Caleb. I tried to focus on the moment, but one relentless question distracted me: "Where are you, Caleb?" I murmured.

I slowly made my way to the altar. My heartbeat quickened and pounded in my ears. The delicate hydrangea bouquet trembled in my hands, but I steadied myself with each determined step toward Mike. With each pace forward, the world around me faded into the background until I could see Mike standing before me, his eyes shimmering with love.

"You look beautiful!" Mike said.

"Thank you, Mike. You have to say those things," I replied, half-joking.

"No, Diane. You're stunning," he insisted, his eyes filled with sincerity.

The ceremony proceeded, and Mike and I incorporated the timeless scripture: "Love is patient and kind; love does not envy or boast; it is not arrogant or rude. It does not insist on its way, is not resentful; it does not rejoice at wrongdoing but rejoices with the truth. Love bears all things…"

Yet, as the ceremony continued, an unexpected wave of emotions washed over me. I turned away from the altar; I felt the eyes of everyone on me, their expressions a mix of fear and shock. With each step I took backward along the rose-strewn walkway, a silence enveloped me, a quiet storm of uncertainty and raw emotion. I knelt on the ground and started to crawl. Once a symbol of elegance and fancy, my dress was now stained rose petal red.

The scene erupted as Anna's voice rose. "Please, Mom, not today! Please, no!" she pleaded.

Ted responded, unsure, "I don't know what to do."

Anna cried out, "She's embarrassing herself! We need to stop her!" Her distress was palpable. Mike's face mirrored the concern, but he remained frozen. He tried to move towards me but was held back by Frank's firm grip.

"Stop," Frank commanded firmly, his tone leaving no room for argument. Mike looked at him, shaking his head in confusion, struggling to discern the situation. Frank added gently, "Let her go."

Crawling with raw emotion, my once pristine veil now lay torn and soiled. The astonished guests stared, their silence deafening as they tracked my every move. The anguish across my family's faces mirrored the inner turmoil within me. Frozen in place, Christopher clutched a white envelope, his blank and unblinking gaze struggling to process the surreal scene before him.

I crawled forward with unsteady, agonizing movements, my body suspended in disbelief. Reaching the stranger at my wedding, I saw dread in his face as tears streamed uncontrollably down my dirt-stained cheeks, my heart pounding. He struggled to break free; I clung to his legs and dug my nails into his tanned skin, leaving scratch marks.

Christopher's eyes frantically scanned the backyard, desperately seeking a way out as my emotional tirade bore down on him. With a trembling voice, the young man apologized, "I'm so sorry, Diane. I never meant to ruin your wedding or disrupt your family. Please, don't let me spoil your day. I'm leaving right away." I saw his sadness as he looked down at me motionless. He tried to stand and face Frank while waving an envelope, but I gripped him tightly, refusing to let go.

Christopher looked down; his eyes fixed upon something unexpected: my necklace with the green gem. He asked, "Where did you get that necklace with the green gem?"

I overheard Cara yell out, "Mike, stop her!"

Christopher said, "I remember giving that necklace to my mother when I was a young boy. I know it is the same one, I stared at that gem for hours before giving it to her." At that moment, Christopher seemed transported to a realm of forgotten memories.

The green gem appeared to serve as a portal, unleashing a flood of vivid memories in Christopher's mind. His voice grew distant as if recalling a dream. "I see myself as a child," he exclaimed, "with my mom, sisters, and a puppy in the park. I remember the white van, Felix the Cat, Stink Eye, Jack, and my adopted brother Jimmy, 'Sam.'" Christopher's voice trembled with emotion. "Emmanuel, Mother Mercy, reminding me never to forget the necklace!" He cried out, then continued amidst the swirling visions, "Mike, Gabe, Mr. King, Mo, Mr. Einstein, Minty, and Daniel. My dad! I see my dad!" As the gem shimmered brighter, he continued, "Tercelot, my faithful companion, with Thomas on his back—strong and healthy! And there is Carcarra, with Jack perched on his wing, smiling, sending me a salute."

At that moment, Christopher remembered who he was.

Bewildered, Mike attempted to separate me from Christopher but was stunned when I exclaimed, "Caleb, my son!"

ABOUT THE AUTHOR

Dr. Christa St. Germain is a devoted single mother living in Millbrook, New York. She leads a dual practice as a primary care physician specializing in family medicine and a chiropractor, with a deep passion for helping others achieve optimal health and well-being.

This is her debut book, a deeply personal work born from profound loss. Despite overwhelming challenges, Dr. St. Germain remained steadfast in supporting her children. Amid intense grief and self-reflection, this book emerged as a powerful journey of healing, resilience, and finding meaning in life's most significant hardships.

MORE FROM CHRISTA

The Kingdom

In the compelling follow-up to *Where Are You, Caleb?*, the lives of Diane and her family take unexpected turns that will keep you hooked. *The Kingdom* deepens the exploration of past and present, blending reality with fantasy as each family member faces life-changing challenges that push them to their limits.

Amid love, loss, and unbreakable bonds, a shocking revelation will shatter everything they thought they knew. When they believe they've overcome their greatest struggles, an unforeseen twist will leave readers questioning everything they once believed to be true. The unimaginable is about to unfold—setting the stage for a journey that will leave you eagerly anticipating what happens next.

www.ingramcontent.com/pod-product-compliance
Lightning Source LLC
Chambersburg PA
CBHW020638260626
47157CB00008B/2806